SNOW WHITE'S MIRROR

SHONNA SLAYTON

AMARETTO PRESS

PRINT ISBN: 978-0-9974499-7-6

EBOOK ISBN: 978-0-9974499-9-0

To Stacy and Lydia

PROLOGUE

*A*t last.

At the top of a winding staircase, she'd found it.

Disregarded by everyone but the aging queen. How could she ever forget the trouble it had caused her?

The mirror.

A fine coating of dust dulled its finish, and made it look deceptively old and harmless. Hesitantly, Queen Snow wiped the surface. She wanted a clear look at whatever, or whoever, was inside. The thought of meeting her adversary made her shiver, and she took a moment to compose herself.

She set her lantern on a nearby table and stood in front of the mirror, arms loose at her side. Taking a deep breath, she peered into the surface. Her reflection stared warily back, her cheeks flushed red from the climb, and her once black hair, now mostly gray, no longer a stark contrast to her fair skin. She breathed out with force. Time for answers. She began the poem:

> *"Mirror, mirror*
> *on the wall,*
> *Who's the fairest*

of them all?"

The glass rippled near the edge of the frame like it was melting. Slowly at first, then swiftly until the entire surface was a swirling, twirling mass of molten glass. Her reflection twisted until it was only a rush of colors that melded together and became a white mist. A silhouette appeared in the middle, growing increasingly visible as the mist cleared. At last, the figure turned to face the outside.

"Oh." Snow blinked in recognition. "It's you."

CHAPTER 1

Wilhelmina Bergmann lay in a patch of shade too close to a prickly pear cactus for her liking. Arms spread wide, she aired out her armpits in a decidedly unladylike fashion. Truth be told, this wasn't the only thing she'd done in the last twenty-four hours that would shock her friends back in Boston.

She closed her eyes against the bright sun, bemoaning for the hundredth time her black crepe shirtwaist and long skirt. But she was in deep mourning, and thanks to Queen Victoria, God rest her soul, this was what fashionable women wore when in mourning.

Her uncle splashed in the small creek not twenty yards from her. As he swirled his pan, the sound of rocks scraping on tin rose above the gurgle of water. She prayed he would find gold soon, so they could move on.

"Water feels great," Uncle Dale called. "Grab a tin and join me."

Billie opened one eye and squinted in his direction. Wet up to his knees, with his sleeves rolled up to his elbows, his exposed skin paled from the cold water. His prospector's hat, filthy thing that it was, and purchased from a man leaving the valley, shaded his face so she couldn't read his expression. His chevron mustache bobbed as he chewed tobacco, and his formerly clean-shaven chin sprouted the makings of a beard, marking the hours they'd been away from civilization.

Ah, Uncle Dale. He could talk a dying man into buying a vacation home.

She shouldn't have given in so easily. Had they stuck to the original plan of mailing her cousin the watch and contacting an attorney to handle any other business, they would have been home by now. She didn't understand his quick change of mind, but after spending a day holed up in Daddy's home office, he was adamant that they travel through Bisbee.

Billie had never even heard of the place, but Uncle had caught her at a weak moment, when her brain was so muddled she couldn't even make basic decisions like, did she want toast or oatmeal for breakfast? Her whole life had changed when she moved out to California, and now she was returning to her old life, minus her father's oversight.

Uncle said not to worry; he would take care of everything, and she could return to her school before the fall session started to resume her social life as it was before.

However, if she were honest with herself, she'd admit that she was scared to go home, worried that Holly and Jane and Suzanne had replaced her with someone else and wouldn't make room for her return.

A side trip put off the unknown. That's why she agreed to this fiasco. Uncle Dale told her it would be a lark, a fun detour, and when would she have a chance like this again? She could go back home with a pocketful of gold to show her friends instead of the red-rimmed eyes she was currently sporting.

There was no gold, but there was no telling him that. There also wasn't any point asking him to hurry up, regarding either the gold panning or settling Daddy's estate.

Her friends didn't even know she was coming home. There hadn't been time to send word, and Mother wouldn't think to tell them. What with all her doctor's appointments and specialists, Mother's life in Boston was full, if not pleasant.

"Found something. Ah, no. Never mind." Uncle dumped the contents back in the water and scooped up more mud.

Billie groaned. "How much longer?" *My life is wasting away.*

"Not much."

Daddy died a few days after the finishing touches went on the big house in California, and then Uncle, instead of Mother, was there at her side taking care of everything. The funeral arrangements, the estate, going through Daddy's unorganized mounds of paper in his office. Before Billie knew it, Daddy was in the ground, and she and her uncle were on a train back to Boston. Back to their old life.

With one detour.

She fanned her face. What would her friends think of her lying in the dirt? What would Branson Hughes think?

If she'd stayed in Boston, he might have declared himself by now. She'd spent months trying to assure him his interest was reciprocated, but he was so shy the progress was slow going. They'd finally had a *moment* when she was leaving. He'd seen her off at the train when she'd left with her dad for California and offered to carry her luggage. When she handed it to him, he held her gaze, and deliberately brushed his hand against hers. Deliberately. No young man was able to make her insides flip like Branson Hughes, the biggest catch in Boston.

And, had she stayed, she would be with her friends right now planning the next season of parties. She and her girls. This was to be their year. They were the ones to set the bar higher than any other class, to show them all how it was done. Just like her daddy taught her.

Tears welled in her eyes, but she blinked them back. She didn't expect to miss her father so much. He was never around when he was alive, but in the end, he had been trying. Boston was going through a smallpox epidemic, and he wanted her away from the illness.

Mother refused to leave her own doctors. She was not in favor of moving to the west coast, but Daddy hoped to change her mind with a pretty new house near his new mine. In the end, it wasn't Billie's or Mother's health that was in jeopardy, it was his. *Heart failure comes without warning.*

A fortuitous event, Uncle had said, that their train ride east would take them from California to Boston via Arizona. What better time to see her long-lost relation, a cousin to whom her father had bequeathed a watch. Billie could exchange news about the German side of her family.

But she'd had no idea how difficult Uncle's little side trip was going to be. Nor had she realized her long-lost cousin lived out in the middle of nowhere in Arizona Territory. No wonder it wasn't a state yet. Miles of nothing but scrub. It was frightening. Wild. She'd never fully relax until curled up in a cozy hotel bed in Bisbee.

She considered her high-top boots, not made for traipsing about the countryside, and certainly not made for crossing creeks. They were made for tea parties and strolling Boston Common. They were her favorite pair; she'd begged Daddy to get them for her even though his secretary advised that they were too mature for her sixteen years. White leather with twenty-two lace holes— two more than Sally Johnson's fancy boots—and a buckle detail near the base of the foot. Most striking, they had a black leather flower rising up from the heel. No one had ever seen that before. They were perfect.

At least, they used to be. Now they were brown with Arizona dirt and the binding near the right toe was pulling loose. She'd snapped the left set of laces last night when she was angry at Uncle for taking so long panning that they had to spend the night under the stars with the coyotes.

She was sure if Mother knew where Uncle was dragging her, she'd never stand for it. Gold Rush fever was over. Her uncle was late to the party, and no amount of panning was going to pay off for him.

Uncle Dale splashed out of the water. "Got a little dust," he said. "May as well head into town and sell it."

Billie sat up. "Now?"

"Sure. Town's less than an hour that-a-way." He jerked his head to the right.

Billie widened her eyes. "What are we waiting for?"

Restaurants. Hotels. Proper bathrooms.

She was already standing and slapping off the dried bits of scrub from her black skirt. She could practically feel the warm bathwater washing away the dust clinging to her legs. It would be the best thing this side of heaven. "You should've told me sooner."

"I scouted the trail out this morning while you were sleeping."

Billie gasped, surveying the rugged land. "You left me out here alone?"

Uncle dried his tin pan along his pants. "You were getting your beauty sleep. It wasn't like you were going to wander off."

"Coyotes? Bears? Bandits?" Billie waved her arms to emphasize her point. She could have been killed—or—or worse.

Uncle raised his eyebrows. "You seem perfectly fine to me. Besides, you're tougher than you think. I just proved it to you, and now you're the better for it." He turned his back and shoved the pan into a sack. "Let's go."

She clenched her jaw while carrying her own carpetbag. The rest of her belongings had been checked through to Boston. Her shirtwaists and shoes would be home before she was.

They'd taken the train as far as Tombstone where Uncle had complained that all the jostling was affecting his lumbago, and the stage would only make it worse. Besides, wouldn't it be an adventure if they did some hiking in the desert?

The thing was, when they got off the train in Tombstone he

went into a saloon to ask word about the local silver mines. He was gone long enough to gamble their money away. It was the only logical explanation for why they were walking instead of taking the stage as planned. In fact, Uncle had been acting strangely ever since leaving California.

She worried about what terrible secret he was keeping from her. Was she a pauper now that Father had died? Or worse, had her mother finally succumbed to her illness, too, and Uncle Dale was putting off telling her? And if so, did he plan on leaving her in Bisbee with this relative they'd come to see?

"Tomorrow we'll take the stage to the nearest town with a train, yes?" she reiterated. She was determined to keep her uncle focused on their tasks. "Headed for Boston?"

"Hm. We'll see."

"I need to get home to Mother. She's grieving alone." *And so am I.* She felt like she couldn't freely grieve until she got home to the place where she knew her dad best.

"I know what my sister is going through," Uncle said with an edge to his voice as they reached the top of the ridge. "That's why we're here." He spread his arms wide where the town lay nestled in the valley. "To secure your future."

CHAPTER 2

*B*illie didn't understand the connection between her future and this particular mining town, but sure enough, they had found the place hidden in the narrow valley.

With nowhere else to go, wood and adobe houses climbed the steep sides of the mountain. Rickety wooden stairs leaned against the slope forming a haphazard array linking the street levels. It looked exactly like the network of stopes inside the mountain. It was as if the mine had inverted itself, creating a reflection above mirroring the work below.

The smell of sulfur, the clang of distant machinery. Daddy would have loved this place.

"Town's bigger than I expected," Uncle Dale said. "Look at the size of that one mine. I'd love to get a look at the generators powering that thing. You know anything about magnetic flux?"

"No, but I know plenty about the importance of warm bread," Billie said. "So why don't we get a look inside the nearest restaurant?"

She followed her uncle down the road, mindful of her dainty boots. The business end of town ran along the floor of the valley, and Billie and her uncle walked on through town until they entered a narrow gulch. Here, the buildings were a mix of false-front wooden structures sandwiched between solid brick buildings. The brick indicated the town was beginning to put down roots.

Billie's heart leapt. It wasn't Boston, but there were people. And where there were people there were amenities. A hotel, a cafe, a blacksmith. The usual trappings of a mining town. Several respectable buildings where one could buy a meal or supplies or have one's laundry done. Also, several unrespectable buildings over which Billie had best not ruminate.

She scanned for women, for they were who she wanted to see. Men seemed able to put up with wilderness, but if there were enough women in town she could judge how luxurious the hotel might be.

Overwhelmingly, there were mostly men riding horses through the streets or clustered in small groups. A few children played marbles in the dirt beside a candy store. And there. *Yeehaw*—to quote a ranch hand they'd met on the way—a group of women dressed in clean, respectable gingham. Another woman walking on the wooden boardwalk dressed as a lady with fashionable bell skirt and puffed sleeves as modern as any Billie would wear. There was hope for this town yet.

As she continued to sum up the place, she noticed the train depot. She stared at it in disbelief, clenching the handle on her bag.

"Uncle, did you know the train comes right through this town? You needn't have worried about your lumbago." She kept her voice even, masking her irritation. "We didn't need to walk at all."

His gaze darted past the tracks. "Of course, there's a train. How else are they going to get the ore out?"

Her face warmed. "But you said we'd have to switch to the stage, and it would hurt your back."

"Not my exact words," he said. He turned her attention to the general store. "Why don't you go shopping? I bet you could find yourself a trinket in that there building. Maybe something for your mother."

Of course, there's a train. Where was her head? She was the daughter of a mining baron. She knew how it worked. Once a strong vein was found the company moved in and set up shop. They used mules at the beginning to pack out the ore, but if the mine proved itself, it didn't take long to lay rails and increase production. With the demand for copper rising thanks to Tesla's invention harnessing electricity for light, copper mines were as valuable as gold mines. Maybe more so.

Billie needed to quit daydreaming about returning to Boston and focus on what her uncle was up to. He said to buy something for her mother, so that meant she was still alive. That was one less worry.

"I'll just see to some business and come back for you," Uncle Dale said. "Then we'll go find your cousin Lou."

Billie listed her head. By his tone, he was too eager to get rid of her. *Fine Uncle. I'll learn your game.* "And then we are on a train to Boston."

He handed her several coins. "Off you go," he said, before sauntering up the packed-dirt main street.

Out of habit, she picked out the pennies and slipped them into a pocket within her reticule. She caught her bedraggled reflection in the window and tucked a stray hair under her bonnet. She sighed. *Hopeless. It's a good thing no one of importance could see her now.*

Then she stepped up on the boardwalk, pretending she was going to the store, but as soon as her uncle was a reasonable distance away, she followed him. The only business they had in this godforsaken place was to find her cousin. Business that involved *her* side of the family, not his. There was nothing he needed to do alone. Except maybe gamble their train money away.

But instead of heading into a saloon, he stopped in front of the assayer's office. Brushed off his pants. Looked up and down the street.

She pressed herself against the nearest wall.

The gold dust? If he was having his gold dust weighed, what did he care if she saw? She knew how much, or should she say how little, he'd collected on the way. Maybe he'd found more than he let on. Still, why would she care? Her father's estate held more than enough funds to support her. Or it did.

Billie continued on up the boardwalk, half-heartedly examining the tea display in the small window panes of another general store. Once her uncle disappeared inside the assayer's, she edged along the boardwalk, nodding politely to the folks she passed.

The assayer's windows were dirty, preventing the curious from getting a look at the gold being weighed. She wiped a corner with her fingers, but the dirt was also caked on the inside. She could only make out muddled shapes indicating cabinets, a table, and a blurred image of her uncle standing before the counter.

Now what?

A boy across the street stared at her with a disapproving look. He wore the same outfit all the men seemed to be wearing in this out-of-the-way place: butternut trousers, dirty plaid shirt, and that awful style of prospector's hat. He seemed more suited to a cowboy hat with his tan face and hard look. If he smiled, he might hope to be as handsome as Branson. This lad appeared a little older than she and obviously annoyed that she was trying to get a look inside the office. *What was it to him?*

Their eyes met, and his face shifted when he realized she caught him staring. He pulled his hat low over his face before slipping down an alley.

Billie laughed. Silly boys. They were the same no matter what city or town you were in. Curious about girls, but slightly scared of them. He was quite nice looking. Too bad she was only in town long enough to pass off the watch, politely spend time with the cousin, and, if she had to, spend a night in luxury at the hotel before catching the first train headed east.

Dismissing the incident, she turned her attention back to the dusty windows. She cupped her hands to block the light when the door banged open.

Uncle stormed out of the assay office fuming. "Too early," he muttered.

When he saw Billie, he forced a smile on his face. "Good, there you are." He said it like he'd been looking all over for her. "Let's head out to cousin Lou's place next. It's back around that there mountain."

Billie eyed said mountain. "The one where the road looks like it turns into a path? Are you sure that's the one?"

"Yup. Your dad's cousin never was one to live in town. From what I hear, cousin Lou is unusual. Doesn't get along with people."

"Couldn't we send a messenger up?" The hotel down the street looked new and therefore filled with modern conveniences. Cousin Lou's place, with barely a road leading to it, did not sound promising at all. Nor did Cousin Lou.

Uncle hopped off the boardwalk. "No time like the present."

Billie reluctantly followed. She was pleased to finish their business but was beyond tired of trekking through the dusty mountains.

When she stepped off the boardwalk, she landed on a rock and wrenched her ankle. She took a careful step, hoping she hadn't caused a sprain, but she stumbled. In dismay, she looked at her pretty little boots. She'd broken off the heel on the left foot. *Figures.* She should have worn her all-black mourning boots instead of letting her vanity get the best of her for her trip across country.

"That's it," she said, letting annoyance flood her voice. A girl could only take so much. "I'm buying myself a pair of western boots." It would be penance for her vanity to give up her kid boots. Besides, she'd be willing to buy the ugliest pair in the general store if it meant she could trek out of this town faster.

Uncle Dale bent down to examine the damage. "I could drive a nail in there for cheaper," he said. "Those boots are so pretty, why'd you want to wear anything else?"

"Two dollars should cover it," Billie said, not budging an inch. "It is my money."

"Country boots won't match your city clothes," he said. "I know how important it is for you ladies to coordinate." He waved his hand up and down indicating her boots all the way up to her wide-brimmed hat.

Billie set her lips into a line and crossed her arms.

Reluctantly, her uncle led the way to the store.

As expected, the general store had little in the way of goods to attract a woman. Filled with canned beans, flour, and hardware implements, she wouldn't be spending much time in here.

"What can I do for you today?" asked the shopkeeper. Dressed in a long white apron, he stood behind the glass counter near the candy jars. Lemon drops and licorice.

Uncle nodded at Billie. "She needs some sturdy shoes. Not these dainty heels the ladies like to wear to parties."

The man nodded and indicated they meet him at the back of the store. He came around the long counter with two pairs of boots, not even remotely pretty. Billie tried not to make a face as she picked out the only pair of shoes small enough to fit her, likely made for a boy. Brown leather boots lacking all style and sophistication.

While her uncle chatted with the shopkeeper about the workings of the local mine, Billie slipped off her white leathers and put on the work boots. What would Holly and Jane say? Suzanne, with her head in books all day, probably wouldn't mind, but the other two would refuse to be seen with her if she showed up in these clumpy boots. It didn't matter out here. For now, she would willingly bow to practicality over beauty.

Billie wiggled her toes and took a few tentative steps around the store. Her heels pounded hollow taps on the wooden planks. Not bad. They were sturdy, only rubbed her ankles a little. They would get her up the mountain.

"I'll take them." She plopped her old shoes on the glass counter while the shopkeeper rang up her new boots.

"That'll be three dollars, ninety-five."

"Four dollars? For these?" She bent over lifting her skirts to show the plainer-than-plain footwear. That was almost as much as she'd spent on her designer boots.

"If you don't want 'em, just say so," said the shopkeeper, making a move to go back around the counter.

"No, I'll take them." Billie dropped her skirt and stood tall. When they got back to civilization, the first thing she would do is buy a decent pair of kid leathers and toss these into the charity barrel. She nodded to her uncle to pay the man.

Even more reluctantly, Uncle Dale pulled out the bills. Billie was not surprised to note the bulge in his wallet was significantly smaller than it should have been. Maybe her hunch about the gambling was right.

Uncle Dale grinned when he saw her looking at his wallet, and he quickly stuffed it back into his pocket. "Let's go find that cousin of yours."

CHAPTER 3

*T*he hike up the far mountain led them through scratchy brush, and Billie was infinitely glad she'd changed into boys boots. She was also infinitely glad she'd convinced Uncle Dale to let her use the bathroom facilities at the new Copper Queen Hotel before setting out.

It had cost them a sit-down dinner of roast beef with mashed potatoes and gravy, which, after eating barely anything but pork and beans cooked on an open fire for the past two days, was the best meal she'd ever had.

China plates. Silverware. Cloth napkins.

She was in heaven.

It didn't even bother her when that same disapproving boy walked by the window and saw her wolfing down her potatoes like she hadn't eaten in a week. Although, she did slow down and daintily wipe the corners of her mouth to make a point to him before he walked on. That rude boy had nothing on Branson Hughes.

Besides, he was much too forward if he was trying to catch the eye of a strange girl twice in one day. Queen Victoria wasn't in the grave yet two years, and already the Victorian age was changing.

This may be the Wild West, but it didn't mean *she* would act out of turn.

———————

"IS IT MUCH FARTHER?" Billie asked, stopping on the steep slope to catch her breath.

Uncle Dale pulled a small paper out of his pocket and consulted it before squinting at the mountainside. "We're here."

Billie stared at a pile of weathered lumber leaning against the mountain. It looked like any one of the abandoned and blown-over prospecting shacks they'd passed on their way to town. Beside the lumber, a large pile of rocks and rubble spilled down the mountain like the waste seen near a mine.

"Here, where?" She spun around, searching for a house. Surely there was a house. A cabin. A shack?

To her amazement, Uncle walked over to the wood and yanked off several boards, somehow uncovering a door. Without knocking, he strode in.

After several minutes, he poked his head back outside. "Aren't you coming?"

"You're serious?" she said. "Cousin Lou couldn't possibly be in there." Billie laced her tone with skepticism.

"You're right. By the looks of the place Lou's been gone a long time."

All this way. All this time. For nothing. And Uncle didn't seem too surprised or upset by it.

"We may as well spend the night," he said, "Seeing as we're family. I'm sure he won't mind."

Billie gaped while he continued pulling away the pile of graying boards. *Here?* She didn't know what was worse—staying in this hovel or out in the open under the stars.

"Cousin Lou might not mind, but I do. The hotel in town is worthy of any I've ever visited. I'll be quite happy there. By myself, if you want to stay here." She looked back at the way they'd just come. Not much of a trail, but all she had to do was go downhill. Eventually she'd find the town, wouldn't she?

"It's not so bad," Uncle Dale said. He sneezed. "It's bigger than it looks, and a bit of shelter will keep the coyotes away."

Billie shivered. The coyotes were out last night. Their howling was the creepiest, most spine-tingling sound she'd ever heard. It kept her up most of the night, trying to determine if they were moving closer or farther away. Uncle Dale, on the other hand, could sleep anywhere, anytime.

He yanked at more boards to reveal a small square-paned window, and then worked his way around the building. Before he was finished chipping away, the pile of wood revealed itself into the rough shape of a shack built right into the side of the mountain.

Well enough made for a rugged outdoorsman, perhaps, but nothing near what she required. She kept her arms crossed, foot jutted out.

"Come now, it only needs a woman's touch. There's a broom at the back wall; why don't you have a go while I round up some firewood for our grub later?"

Grub. That about described Uncle's cooking ability.

Gingerly, Billie stepped into the building. Her eyes took a moment to adjust, and then she saw something surprising. The one-room home was indeed a lot bigger than expected. From outside, the building looked the size of a closet, but Lou must have built into the mountain itself. Likely this was both his home and his claim. It was surprisingly tidy, albeit dusty. Of course, the markings of a prospector's cabin were all over it. A pickax was secured to the wall, and empty buckets were placed near the door. The broom Billie needed leaned against the wall.

One corner was obviously supposed to be the kitchen with a large, shallow pan sitting on the counter as the sink, a step stool in front of it. Smooth wood cabinets matched the small table and one small chair. A low rocking chair was the only other place to sit. The size of the furnishings struck a chord in the back of her mind. Her father's side of the family was known for its dwarfism. She wondered if her cousin Lou was a dwarf.

Opposite the kitchen, a single bed with a thin mattress had been shoved up against the wall. It was surprisingly free from the dust that coated every other surface. *Hmm. Uncle can sleep there while I go back to the hotel.*

Above the bed was another window. Unlike the standard square panes, this window was one large oval, the light blocked by wooden planks that Uncle hadn't taken down yet. That was probably for the better. The more light that shone, the more dirt she'd spot.

A door at the back wall looked ominous, barred with an X of wood across it and a lock on the handle. Cousin Lou's mining claim?

No amount of a woman's touch could fix this.

She picked up the broom and started sweeping where Uncle had tracked in dust. At least her cousin had thought it worth the trouble to make a floor instead of leaving it dirt.

Uncle Dale came back in and started banging through the cabinets. "Nothing. Looks like Lou's been gone awhile, maybe even left for good." His voice sounded oddly satisfied.

"Then what are we doing here?" Billie stopped sweeping and leaned on the broom. "Let's go back to town and get on the next train to Boston. Mother'll be worried it's taking us so long."

Uncle looked like he was about to say something when his eyes widened ever so slightly.

"Wilhelmina, honey. I want you to freeze. Don't. Move." He slowly walked toward her, fingers outstretched, and his eyes on her shoulder. He'd used her proper name, so he wasn't joking with her.

Her heartbeat raced. "What is it?" Her voice rose in panic, and it took all her concentration not to run wildly out the door.

Rattlesnake? Black widow? She couldn't hear or feel anything. *Oh, what was wrong with this place? Why did people even live here?*

Uncle Dale slowly advanced, hand up, and flicked her shoulder.

She screamed and ran for safety. Outside, she wiggled and shook with the creepy-crawly feeling. She heard her uncle stomping, killing whatever it was. She also thought she heard laughter, as if someone was enjoying her distress. Glancing nervously around, she examined the hills for bandits. Meanwhile, her uncle came out, sucking his thumb.

"Dang thing got me," he said, spitting into the dirt.

"What was it?" Billie peered around him into the dark doorway. "Is it dead?"

"Yeah, it's dead all right. Scorpion."

She shivered again. "You need to see a doctor. Can you walk back into town?"

"I don't need a doctor. Unless I get a bad reaction it's not much worse than a bad bee sting."

"We should go anyway. Find a place to stay in town in case you react." She started walking back down the path, relieved she wouldn't have to stay in that hovel.

"Billie, no," he said in a soft voice. "Something I have to tell you. I haven't got the money to stay in a hotel or book the train."

She cocked her head, then turned slowly around. "What do you mean?" she said slowly. "The bank manager gave us money from my inheritance to get us back home. We had plenty."

He cleared his throat. "Yes. Well. Yes." He looked down at her boots, one of the last purchases they had made. With her money.

"Did you gamble it away?" She kept a steady tone, and with satisfaction she noted Uncle's eyes widen in surprise. She'd surprised herself with her boldness.

"Some," he admitted, "But that's not the issue. The money is tied up in a local endeavor. We'll have to wait it out. Stay in town a few days."

Billie's throat constricted. "But we're not in town. We're on the side of a mountain in a shack filled with scorpions."

"One less scorpion, mind you," he said with a grimace and held up his thumb.

"We can get more money. Talk to the bank manager." Of all her worries, money had never been one of them.

"Just give me a few days. Please. It's important. I want to prove to them that I can get the job done."

Billie had never seen her uncle so sincere. Maybe he was trying to make an honest go of things. But it would be so easy for her to go down to the bank herself, explain who she was, and get the manager to contact her father's people.

"What I'm doing is for your good. Yours and your mother's. I don't want to get either of your hopes up on this deal, so please trust me. Look. You just stay outside here while I clean out the place. All right?"

He ducked through the doorway and clattered around for a good twenty minutes. When Billie reluctantly ventured back into the shack, a miner's lamp had been lit, and tools that used to be up on the walls lay scattered around the floor near the locked door. *What was he up to?*

He followed her gaze to the tools. "I'm not breaking into Lou's mine. Just taking inventory. In case Cousin Lou has relinquished his claim. No point letting the family assets go to waste." He shoved the tools to the wall. "No more scorpions. I double-checked."

She nodded at the locked door. "Is that why you went to the assayer's office?"

He cleared his throat. "Don't you worry over these business matters. I'm handling it."

Billie frowned. While she thought they were making a quick detour on the way to Boston, it seemed, for Uncle, this was his stop. Somehow, she'd find out why.

That night, uncle camped outside, giving Billie the privacy of the shack all to herself. He probably welcomed the wall between them since she'd not held back her irritation with him.

Despite the privacy, she couldn't sleep. The bed roll was comfortable enough, but something was not right. Ever since returning from the awful outhouse they'd found out back, she'd felt a change in energy that made her restless. Like a thunderstorm was brewing, electrifying the air. They'd been warned it was the time of year when flooding became a problem.

She got up and curled herself into the rocking chair and began to whisper a song from her childhood, "Sleep, Baby, Sleep." Her father hadn't taught her many German words, but he did sing sometimes, and those lyrics she remembered:

> *Schlaf, Kindlein, schlaf.*
> *Der Vater hüt' die Schaf,*
> *Die Mutter schüttelt 's Bäumelein,*
> *Da fällt herab ein Träumelein.*
> *Schlaf, Kindlein, schlaf.*

Suddenly, the hair on the back of her neck stood up. Billie pressed her toe to the floor to stop rocking. She listened. Uncle was already snoring. Beyond the human sounds, some critter was scratching in the fallen leaves outside. She lit the lantern for courage and stepped through the door. A slight breeze blew, carrying the sweet scent of some desert bloom she didn't recognize. Nothing was amiss outside. The day creatures were settling in for their rest, and the night creatures were waking up. That's all it was.

She returned to the room but couldn't shake the feeling that she was being watched. It bothered her so much she walked around the four walls with the lantern making sure no one was hiding in the dark corners. Not finding anything, she curled back into bed and covered her head with the blanket. If she couldn't see them, they couldn't see her.

CHAPTER 4

$\mathcal{B}$illie's senses remained heightened all night. She'd barely fallen asleep before the sun's first blush lightened the sky, and a chirpy bird outside the window woke her.

Unbelievable. The sun wasn't even up yet. She dragged herself out of bed and quickly set the sheets to rights. Then she left the shack to get the first unpleasant task out of the way.

Cousin Lou's outhouse.

Tucked over a ridge, it was walls only, and barely standing. If she never saw another outhouse like that one, it would be too soon. Nothing about it was made for comfort, and there was barely enough privacy. Even though there were no close neighbors, she kept her gaze where the roof should be and listened intently for footsteps.

When she returned to the shack, her hastily made bed looked like someone had stood on it. Shooting an irritated look at Uncle Dale, who was opening a can in the kitchen, she smoothed out the sheet, tucking the corners in tightly this time.

He handed Billie a plate and stuck a fork in the can for himself.

"Thanks," she said automatically. *Ugh.* Canned beans, again. In the future, whenever Billie thought back to her time in Arizona she would think beans. Dust and beans. And sun. Dust, beans, and sun. That about summed up her trip thus far.

"Should've bought some provisions yesterday along with your boots," Uncle said. "Wasn't thinking long term."

Billie shook her head. During the night she'd formed her own long-term ideas. "I've been thinking about that, too. If you've got plans for this place, you can drop me off in Boston, then come back here and finish your business." She glanced at the mining equipment stored on the wall. "I'm sure nothing will change while you're gone. I'll wire Mother about the money, so the company won't know a thing has changed. No one will care if you gambl—"

Uncle dropped his fork in the empty can with a loud *clang*. "I can't let you do that. My sister is too ill to be bothered."

He didn't need to remind her of how sick her mom was. Billie had lived it.

The strange illness had left her mom with a limp, useless arm, mottled an ugly purple so that she wore long gloves to cover the discoloration. It bothered her mother so much that one day, she'd covered all the mirrors in the house so she wouldn't have to look at herself. She also suffered near constant headaches, and sometimes hallucinations. They'd exhausted all the experts in Boston, and still no answers. No cure.

"Send me on my own, then. It'd be half the cost, and since it's my second cross-country trip, I know what to do."

He shook his head. "Your mother would kill me if I put you on a train alone. Besides, she's not expecting us for several more weeks.

"Excuse me?" Billie was sure they'd sent word that they were on their way home.

"I told her we'd be sightseeing on the way home and not to expect you until school starts."

Unbelievable. "Any other plans I should know about?"

"Well, I could use your help."

Finally, he was going to let her in on what was going on. "How?"

"You see the look of the place. Cousin Lou is gone. We gotta go into town and find out what we can." He stood. "Will you chat up the women and find out if they know where he went?"

"Random women off the street? You want me to go up to them and ask if they know my cousin Lou?"

"Exactly. You never know what you'll find out from the locals. I'll be canvasing the men." He paused. "Just stay out of Brewery Gulch. Not a place for a lady."

"In other words, that's where you're going?"

He raised his eyebrows and headed out the door.

"I'll need some money," Billie said, following after him. She knew he wasn't completely broke. If he was going to Brewery Gulch, he'd be gambling with what little he had stashed.

"What for?" Uncle asked, warily. He stopped to wait for her.

Billie carefully closed the door to the shack. "For tea. How else am I to 'chat up' the women?" She planned to find a scenic location to park herself in. From there, she could talk to one or two women in order to fulfill the letter of Uncle's request, and then enjoy herself while he snooped around town.

If she was careful with the money, she might have enough left over for a magazine. She'd never had to be frugal with money before. When they made it back to Boston she'd ensure she had unfettered access to her bank account, so she'd not be in this position again. "You do have enough for us to buy food, right?"

He groaned but produced some bills. "At this rate, we *will* be forced to contact your bank to have more funds transferred."

Billie grinned. "I don't know what your reluctance is. You have my permission if you need it. Oh, and whatever amount you're thinking of transferring, double it." Billie tucked the money into her reticule.

In town, they parted ways. Uncle going off to work the underbelly of the town, while she concentrated on the genteel society. Someone from those different walks of life was bound to know Cousin Lou and where he had gone and, more importantly, if he was coming back.

Having enjoyed her meal so much at the hotel, Billie decided to start there. She climbed the steps, eager to get out of the warm sun. Her shoes clomped against the Italian tiles in the entryway, and she marveled again at how beautiful and modern the new hotel was. She had to convince Uncle Dale to let her stay here.

A waitress, a plain girl wearing a white shirtwaist and black gored skirt, directed her to a window seat. "Is this suitable?"

Billie smiled at her. "Yes, thank you. May I ask...my cousin Lou lives up on that mountain over there. Do you know him?"

The waitress raised an eyebrow. "Your cousin you say?"

"Yes, but his place looks abandoned. Is he coming back?"

The waitress suppressed a laugh. "You don't know your cousin very well, do you?"

"Uh..." Billie was shocked at the rudeness.

"Hey, Florence!" the waitress called across the room. "This gal's asking about her cousin Lou from up on Chihuahua Hill." She jerked her thumb in the general direction. "Wants to know where he's gone."

Florence smiled, shook her head, and went back to serving coffee.

Billie sensed they were making fun of her, but she didn't know why. She'd asked a perfectly normal question.

"Does this mean you know him?"

"May I take your order?" the waitress asked, suddenly turning professional.

"Tea and cakes for now," Billie said calmly, refusing to show the waitress how annoyed she was. *Why wouldn't the woman just tell her what she knew? Was he coming back or not?*

Billie had a notion that Cousin Lou might have a reputation. If so, Uncle Dale would have an easier time gathering information than she would. Perhaps Lou was a gambler and a ladies' man with a string of debts and broken hearts. Well, she wasn't about to pay for his bad habits, too.

When the food arrived, Billie took her time eating, smiling politely at the hotel guests to let them know she was friendly and in the mood for conversation. But no one took her cues. Seems the waitress got to them first, and they all stared at her in open curiosity. Eventually, she gave up trying to make friends. What did she care if Lou got the watch or not. If he wanted it, he could come and get it himself.

With her hopes of a pleasant day spent at tea gone, Billie rose from her table taking great care to keep her back straight, like there was a string pulling up from her head, the way they'd taught her at finishing school. She floated out of the room as if she had not a worry to her name. She was a queen, and these peasants could gossip all the louder once she left.

She was used to gossips back home, but they were the jealous sort, not the making-fun sort. Billie supposed she and her friends might have been the making-fun sort, and she didn't like how it felt to be on the receiving end.

Now where to go next? She followed the boardwalk to the center of town, noting the bakery, a newspaper, a quaint restaurant, and a shoe store. A pretty beaded shoe in the window caught her eye. She touched the glass. This was where she should have looked for boots; she'd been too impulsive in her earlier purchase.

She peeked at her sturdy brown footwear. No, she approved of her boots. They saved her feet during that steep climb up and down the mountain. Had she gone into this store, she would have bought a pair of shoes as useless as the ones she broke.

Clothes were her weakness. Her mother always told her to watch her vanity, but Billie couldn't understand why. If you had to dress your body, you might as well do so with style.

A horse and buggy passed behind her, the reflection sliding along the window. And behind them, there was that boy again.

Still watching her from a distance. In the mood she was in, she did what she would never do back in Boston. She turned and openly met his stare, arms crossed to convey her feelings. He acted like he owned this town, and that was irritating. He was rude, and she wanted him to know it.

He startled, pulled his hat low like the last time, then rounded the corner of the bank building.

Billie waited for another horse and wagon to pass before she followed after him to speak her mind.

CHAPTER 5

*B*y the time Billie had rounded the bank, the mystery boy was skirting another building to circle back to the main road. She increased her pace, determined to catch up, and only slightly worried that he was leading her into Brewery Gulch. Uncle Dale would have a fit to learn she stepped one foot down that street, never mind winding in and around the buildings following some strange boy.

Her new boots made her bold...or was it foolish? Whatever. She was irritated with her uncle and the people in this town. Also, her cousin for being gone.

And now she was trying to talk to a boy with no one to properly introduce them. Of course, it didn't hurt that he was handsome enough to remind her of Branson, but that wasn't why she wanted to talk to him. She wanted to know why he seemed to be following her. Or, in this instance, trying to hide from her.

When he dodged between two saloons, she ran up to the main thoroughfare and on to the next building. She stepped up on the boardwalk and waited. Sure enough, he rounded the corner, looking back over his shoulder.

"Ha." She jumped down in front of him, triumphant.

Surprised, he nearly walked into her, and then he spun around, ready to take off again.

"I can do this all day," she called out. There truly was nothing for her to do but wait for her uncle. No one was going to tell her about Cousin Lou. The women in this town weren't cooperative in the least.

He stopped. Turned. "What do you want from me?"

"What do *I* want from *you*?" She faltered, glancing around. Now she could see what was different about this side of town, and what her uncle didn't want her to see. A man was collapsed against a wall, passed out from the liquor he'd bought inside the saloons, while strains of "The Entertainer" by Scott Joplin pounded out joyfully on a player piano. Across the street, the two ladies who watched them with keen interest were not dressed modestly like the ladies back in Boston.

"I-I," she stuttered before squaring her shoulders. "I want to know why you keep staring at me."

Now it was his turn to look sheepish.

"I apologize," he said with a slight nod. "You're new, and I was curious is all."

Likely story. "Boomtowns are filled with new people. Why should I be any different?"

He quirked a smile, his confidence apparently returning, and leaned his shoulder against the building. "None of them are as pretty as you."

And did his blue eyes just twinkle?

She widened her own eyes in surprise, hoping her warm cheeks weren't signs of a blush coming on. Branson would never talk to her so openly. She quickly masked her face to one of indifference.

"If you're expecting me to swoon, you're mistaken."

He pushed himself off the wall. "Is that a Boston accent I hear?"

Her hometown roots were apparently too hard to hide. "Yes."

"Is Boston as nice as they say?"

She shrugged. "Of course." She hadn't really thought about it.

"I want to go there someday."

"Oh." She supposed she could see him fitting in with her crowd, if he got himself some new clothes. "Well, it's a lovely town." He really was quite handsome.

Meanwhile, the bawdy ladies across the street had come closer, pretending they were interested in the window display.

The boy saw them as well and abruptly started walking again. "You shouldn't be up here. I'm taking you back to your side of town."

Billie followed, with one last look at the ladies. Seeing them up closer, she was dismayed to see how young they were. Certainly, closer to her age than made her comfortable. How did they end up here? And what was their interest in this boy?

"Are you coming?" he called.

Tucking away her worry and jealousy, she caught up with him.

"So, who are you?" she asked.

"Name's Winn. Winn Harris."

He tipped his hat, and she caught a glimpse of his golden hair.

"Wilhelmina Bergmann," she said. "But you can call me Billie."

"Bergmann. From Bergmann Consolidated Mining?"

"Yes, that's the one. You've heard of it?" *Even here she couldn't escape the family name.*

"This here's a mining camp in case you didn't notice. Most of these folks have worked all around the world, even for your daddy, I bet. Is he here on business?"

They were nearing the assayer's office where they first saw each other.

"My dad passed away recently." She took a deep breath, hoping her voice would come out steady. "I'm here with my uncle, who is helping settle the estate. We had some business in town."

Winn frowned. "I'm sorry about your papa. I lost my mom

when I was little; takes some time to get used to it." He cleared his throat. "Your uncle's a lawyer?"

"A businessman."

"And what specifically is his business with the assayer?" He planted his feet in front of the dusty shop.

Billie put a hand on her hip. "Nosy, aren't you? I'd rather talk about why those *ladies*," she tilted her head in the direction of Brewery Gulch, "are so interested in you."

He looked like he was about to answer, but then changed his mind. "Let's just say they treat me like a brother." He started walking again. "They're probably more interested in you than me. Folks look out for each other in a place like this."

Winn was slippery with his answers, and she'd had enough of slippery with her uncle.

"No, seriously," he said. "We work in the same place. They're going to tease me awful fierce about you during my next shift."

Billie's face likely registered shock. "I take it you don't work in the mine."

"No, it's not the mine." He glanced her way. "And no, I'm not going to tell you about it. It's only a temporary job. I wouldn't be working there if I didn't have to."

"We always have choices, Mr. Harris." She lifted her chin.

He nudged a rock off the boardwalk. "Maybe you do. The path isn't always easy to see for the rest of us." He stopped. "Well, here we are Miss Bergmann. Your side of town. Shopping is that way." He pointed her down the street.

She would have been annoyed if his tone wasn't so sweet. Something about this boy made her want to know more about him. "D-do you know my cousin Lou who lives up on the mountain? We came here to find him, but his cabin is empty."

"Lou, eh? *He's* your cousin?"

Why does everyone repeat the question? "You know him?"

"What do you want to find Lou for?"

"Again, not your business. Is he gone for good?"

"No, Lou'll be back soon, I can guarantee." He stretched out the word guar—an—tee.

Hm. He knows something. "How soon is soon?"

"Let's just say Lou has several reasons to be back here."

Billie was about to question him further when she noticed Uncle Dale walking down the boardwalk toward them.

Winn noticed, too, and took a step away. He lifted his hat. "Do yourself a favor. Go on back to Boston before it's too late, city girl." He crossed the road, avoiding her uncle altogether.

Billie stared after him, wondering about the sudden change.

"That boy bothering you?" asked Uncle Dale, following her gaze.

"Not at all." She decided not to relate what Winn had told her. The sooner her uncle thought Lou was gone, the sooner they'd be on the train home.

Billie noted the confidence of Winn's gait as he strode away. She approved the look of his walk. Strong. Determined. She watched him until he cut between buildings and disappeared.

Uncle Dale grunted. "No more talking to boys when I'm not around. Your mother wouldn't approve."

She was about to argue when Uncle gave her a look too similar to her mother's that meant she was stepping too close to the line. She bit her lip.

"Any news?" Billie asked instead.

Uncle Dale frowned. "The men haven't been forthcoming. Seems Lou could cause us some trouble, yet. Do you know what he looks like? I know dwarfism runs in your family."

"I don't know. We've never met and no one has said anything. Does it matter?" Billie's words came out clipped. She was sensitive when talking about dwarfs because of Dad's stories about Snow White. The way he told it, you'd think the Bergmann family was descended from the dwarfs who sheltered the young girl. He thought the tales were funny to tell, but they made her a joke to her friends.

After he told one of the stories at her eighth birthday party, her friends started calling her Snow White to mock her. Only Holly, Jane, and Suzanne didn't. That was the start of their close-knit group.

"It might explain the reactions I've been getting," Uncle said. "When I ask about him, they respond with smiles. I don't understand."

"Me, too," Billie said with relief. So, it wasn't just her. "The women in this town couldn't tell me anything about Cousin Lou, either. I think he's long gone." She took a step toward the train depot, glancing up at the gathering thunderheads filling the sky. "Shall we inquire about the schedule to Boston?"

"Not yet."

Billie stopped.

"The men weren't forthcoming, but a woman at the Poisoned Apple Saloon had some interesting things to say."

"Such as?"

"All you need to know is that we're staying a few more days to see what turns up."

"If we're going to stay, please, let's wire in my money so we can stay at the hotel."

"Last night wasn't so bad. We'll pick up some groceries and wait at Lou's place. It's the only way to ensure we don't miss him."

It was hard to argue against that logic, but she didn't like it. One thing she did like, though... She glanced down the alley where Winn Harris had disappeared. Cousin Lou wasn't the only curiosity in this town.

illie stood at the window drying her long hair while water fell in sheets off the roof. The sky had split open seconds before they arrived back at the shack, dousing both of them from head to toe. Billie had never witnessed such a sudden and strong downpour of water. Rain pounded the roof while thunder echoed down the valley with a *boom* like dynamite.

"It's not going to wash us away, is it?" she asked.

"Don't worry. These storms are short-lived. Besides, the stove looks good." Uncle Dale wiped black soot off his hands. "We can cook in here from now on."

At least now they'd be able to have some decent food. Not hotel quality, mind you, but Billie knew how to cook a few things: potatoes, eggs, and stew, which was something other than beans. Uncle Dale claimed the campfire cooking, but she would insist the kitchen—such as it was—was hers. She couldn't be a worse cook.

"I suppose I can handle a day or two more." Billie hung the borrowed towel on a nail in the wall. She'd found a trunk under the bed filled with a variety of homey items and had already used them to spruce the place up.

Some of the things she found in the trunk looked like family heirlooms, such as the colorful rag rug she'd placed before the rocking chair, which itself was a beautifully carved item. The set of matching curtains also brought some needed cheer to the place.

These didn't seem like items a bachelor would own, though. Maybe cousin Lou was married. Perhaps his wife died tragically, and that's what made Lou crusty and bitter and feared by the townspeople. In a fit of despair, he packed everything away that reminded him of her and set off on a journey of grief.

And what did Winn mean by telling her to go home before it was too late? Did he mean before her cousin returned? Was he really that bad a character? While she imagined Cousin Lou's sad life, the rain stopped.

"Ah, perfect time to collect ore samples," Uncle Dale said, gathering his supplies. "Think Lou would mind if I used his pickax?"

"Probably. I'll get started on our supper," Billie said as she rifled through the sacks they had carried up. As soon as Uncle Dale left to collect samples for who-knew-why, the tiny hairs on the back of her neck rose. That feeling of being watched returned.

A quick survey confirmed no one else was there, so Billie shrugged it off as her unease at being all alone in a strange place. She sang her German lullaby as she peeled potatoes but froze when a voice joined hers.

The singing stopped when she stopped. She gripped the paring knife, her heart pounding.

"Hello?"

Billie did a sweep of the outside. Nothing but cactus and scrub. *Now I'm hearing things.*

"It's probably an echo," she said loudly. There was no echo back.

She stood by the locked door at the back of the shack and put her ear up against it. Silence.

This isn't a ghost town; it's a boomtown. Must be the wind.

Billie returned to preparing the vegetables, with her ears pricked for any unusual sound. City life was so different than this.

She was tasting the finished stew when a thump outside made her jump, and she looked up. Arms akimbo in the doorway stood a dwarf dressed in a red plaid shirt and dungarees. Several packs splayed out on the ground outside behind the woman.

"Care to explain why you've broken into my home, Goldilocks?" The woman's words carried a slight German accent.

So many thoughts flooded Billie's mind at once. She tried not to stare but couldn't help it. Not because she was meeting a dwarf for the first time, but more importantly, the dwarf was not a man.

The personage standing in the doorway claiming ownership to the shack had long black hair, highlighted with gray strands, plaited in two braids poking out of her prospector's hat. Her sharp eyes glared out from her sun-weathered face.

"Who are you?" Billie asked defensively. She glanced down at her own locks which were not blonde.

"I'm the owner of this here abode." The angry woman walked in and sniffed at the pot.

Her home? Billie stole a look around, her stomach sinking. They'd broken into someone else's home. She took a step back. "I'm sorry. I thought this was my cousin Lou's place."

The dwarf rolled her eyes. "You're standing on my mama's rug."

Billie looked down at her feet and noticed the dirt on the edges of her boots flaking off onto the rug. The rain had started when they were a hundred feet from the shack and quickly turned the mountain into a quagmire.

She took two steps until she was off the rug. "Sorry, ma'am," she said as she made for the door. "I didn't mean to intrude."

Where was Uncle Dale? They'd set up shop in some stranger's house.

The woman blocked Billie's exit. "Hold up there, girlie. I'm Lou. Born Louisa, but no one's called me that since my mama passed."

Both their gazes traveled back to the rug where the dirt from Billie's boots rested.

Billie cleared her throat. She'd often thrown people off with her use of a male name, too. She kind of liked it and thought Lou was the same way. If they had that in common, maybe Billie could find more common ground.

"I'm Wilhelmina Bergmann. There was no one here, and my uncle thought you wouldn't mind since we're family, and we'd traveled so far and my dad, Chester, died and left you a watch." As the words tumbled out of Billie, her voice began to rise and crack with emotion. She was so embarrassed to be caught like this. It wasn't proper at all to be staying in someone's house without an invitation. *Where was Uncle Dale?* She looked out the window and saw movement behind a creosote bush. She narrowed her eyes. *Coward.*

Lou pulled away from the doorway. "A watch, you say?"

"My uncle has it. He should be back soon." Billie didn't know why she was covering for him. She should call him out of his hiding place and expose him for the sneak he was. "We could have mailed the watch, but he wanted to make sure you got it. Seemed like a family heirloom."

"I'll be happy to receive it, then. My condolences on your dad passing. We never met, but I knew he was running Bergmann Consolidated for the family."

"Thank you." Billie searched for some way to make amends for barging in on her cousin like they did. "So, Cousin Lou. You can call me Billie, by the way," she boldly indicated Lou should sit at her own table. "How long have you lived here?"

Lou looked narrowly at Billie, still sizing her up. "I see you inherited the family forehead."

Startled, Billie rubbed her forehead wondering what Lou meant.

"High forehead. All the proud ones have it."

This is not going well. Billie sat in the rocking chair, hoping it wasn't another family heirloom. Applying all her social graces, she again indicated Lou should sit opposite her. Mrs. Foster from her finishing school would be proud to see her quick recovery.

Lou pulled the chair away from the table and sat heavily. "Been traveling a spell; it feels good to sit. I was looking forward to my quiet cabin." She shot Billie a pointed glare.

"May I offer you some tea?"

"My own tea? With boiled water from my own water barrel, using my kettle and my own cookstove and wood, too?" Lou frowned wryly. "How hospitable of you."

Billie ignored the dry tone and rose to make herself useful in the kitchen. Cousin Lou did look tired and maybe some tea would be just the thing. With satisfaction, Billie smiled when Lou took off her boots and sat back with her eyes closed. Everyone could use a little pampering. Even crusty old cousins suddenly put-upon.

Had the situation been reversed, Billie would have been overjoyed to come home to find someone had done all the hard work of setting up the home. She patted her hair, shuddering at the thought of all the cobwebs they'd cleared out. Lou should be thanking her for making the place a home instead of criticizing.

As long as there was tea, there was civility.

Billie chatted while she worked, rambling on about their trek across the desert and how happy she was to get to Lou's shack. She laid it on thick. "It was good you came when you did. I'm not sure how much longer we were going to stay here waiting for you."

She poured the tea and then turned around with a cup in each hand. "Here we go."

Cousin Lou's head rested against the back of the chair, mouth open. She let out a gentle snore.

Billie frowned, and set the cups on the table. After all her hard work, the least her cousin could do was stay awake. The tea would get cold.

"*Psst.*"

Billie glanced up. Uncle Dale had cracked open the door and was waving her outside, holding a finger to his lips.

Now he shows up.

She followed him, arms crossed. "What are you doing hiding out here? Did you know that's Cousin Lou? She's a woman!"

"How's her mood?" he asked, whispering.

"Irritated."

"They told me in town that Lou didn't much like visitors."

Billie gaped at him. "I gathered that. She called me Goldilocks. Basically, accused me of breaking in and taking over her house."

"Well, you did take over. I'm surprised she recognized the place the way you've redecorated."

Honestly.

"Besides, I thought he, I mean, *she* would be more amiable to find a young lady in the cabin, more so than a man looking like a lawyer."

Billie wanted to tell her uncle how he'd stopped looking like a lawyer back in Tombstone and was well on his way to looking like a rough-and-tumble miner himself. "Why don't you come in and meet her?" She tried to grab his arm, but he pulled away.

"Did you tell her about the watch?" He scratched his chin while trying to get a glimpse through the open door.

"Yes."

"And? Her reaction?"

Billie paused. She'd only mentioned the watch in her big long rambling explanation. Did Lou react? "I think she was interested. We should give it to her and get back to town today before it gets dark." Finally. They could be on a train bound for Boston first thing in the morning.

"Good. Good. I was hoping."

"What makes the watch special?"

"No idea. But I'm hoping to use it to make a trade." He turned Billie around. "Now, go back in there and warm her up some more. I'll be in shortly."

Billie stood her ground. "Warm her up? Did you *hear* her? Just come in with me."

"She's a woman who's lived alone her entire adult life. I don't think she'd take kindly to waking up from a nap to find a man in her home. Might scare her off. No, you go back in and wave through the window when it's time for me to make an entrance. I'll be waiting out here. Just don't take too long. I'm getting a leg cramp."

"Wouldn't want to inconvenience you," Billie said, hoping he noted the sarcasm in her voice. Meanwhile, she'd use the time alone with Lou to her own advantage.

She'd find out what Uncle was after.

CHAPTER 7

*C*ousin Lou was still out cold when Billie returned from talking with her uncle. If she felt embarrassed when Lou first walked in, she felt downright awkward now. The woman's mouth was open, and she was snoring as loudly as daddy used to.

There was no cleaning left to do.

The tea was getting cold.

She could sit and watch Lou sleep, but then when Lou woke up she'd find Billie staring at her. Seems like that wouldn't endear her to Lou.

She glanced at the mining journals on the shelf. Would it hurt her cousin to have *The Deliniator*, or a *Godey's* lying around? Given Lou's plaid shirt and dungarees, Billie surmised her cousin only shopped at the General Store where Billie'd gotten her brown boots. Did the woman even own a proper hat?

In desperation, Billie pulled out a mining book and turned to a random page.

The Law of Apex states that the vein closest to the surface, or the apex of the vein, takes precedent over claim boundaries. Therefore, if a vein traverses from one claim to another, the Law of Apex allows crossover mining.

Seriously? These were the kinds of books her father read all the time. If she read much more, she'd fall asleep, too. Billie laughed to herself. Daddy would have been thrilled if she'd taken an interest in the family business. With no sons to pass the company on to, and a daughter with no interest in mining or business, he'd been lax in grooming anyone to take his place. Who knew he'd die so young?

Billie straightened. Who *was* going to take over the business? She'd not given it any thought since Uncle Dale had stepped in and promised to make everything all right. And she'd let him. That was all before she'd realized how sneaky he was. Her gut told her he was not the one to let rise to the top. He'd secret everything away, giving Billie just enough to keep her from asking questions. That's what he'd done so far on this trip. She couldn't let him do that with the rest of her life.

Billie realized the room had gone quiet. She looked up from her reading to see Lou observing her.

"What did you say your name was, Goldilocks?" Lou looked tired. Resigned. Even though she'd just woken from a nap. Lou stood and closed the curtains over the oval window above the bed.

"Wilhelmina, but you can call me Billie."

Lou turned and nodded. "I like that. Good family name. A German name that means protector." She arched one eyebrow. "Sound like you?"

Billie shrugged. Her daddy always said she was strong-willed. But a protector? No.

"How did you find me?" Lou asked.

"My uncle, my mom's brother, tracked you down. He's taking care of things for the estate."

"He's the executor?"

Billie shook her head. "No, he's supposed to be escorting me back to Boston, where we're going to live. My mother's side of the family is all out that way." Billie smiled slightly. "You're the only one left here on my dad's side. The rest are in Germany."

"And where is this uncle of yours?"

Billie waved her hand nonchalantly. "He'll be back soon. Do you know anything about the watch my dad left you? Does it have sentimental value?"

"I don't know about any watch. Have you seen it, or is it your uncle's excuse to find me?"

What an odd question. "Yes, I've seen it."

Billie stood, beginning to feel uncomfortable. Maybe she didn't want to be alone with her cousin after all. She wandered to the window. Uncle was nowhere to be seen outside, but she knew enough to know he was there. Waiting. She gave a little wave, trying to be sly, but seeing Lou watch her out of the corner of her eye, Billie gave up any pretense. She gave a big wave. "There's my uncle now." She wondered if Lou was buying it. Billie wasn't used to acting so sneaky.

She withered under Cousin Lou's gaze and was relieved when Uncle stepped into the shack.

"Cousin Lou, at last." He came in with a big smile and held out his hand.

Lou didn't shake it. "I don't believe we are cousins."

"Right. Yes."

"I hear you have a watch for me?"

Uncle flinched but changed the subject. "Nice place you've got here."

Lou raised one eyebrow. "You've been enjoying it, have you?"

"It was long trip from California. I'm sorry about your cousin Chester's passing. Were you close?"

"We never met."

"Oh. Well, I'm sure you would have been close, had you met. With your interest in mining and all. Looks like you've got a nice little claim here."

Billie's gaze vaulted back and forth from uncle to cousin. He wasn't an unusually tall man, but he towered over Lou. Despite the disparity, Lou wasn't intimidated at all. Whatever Uncle wanted from her, he wasn't going to get it easily.

"You would know." Lou took a step closer to him. "Hear you've been to the assayer's asking about it. Plan to buy it out from under me, do you?"

Billie sucked in a breath. She knew that visit with the assayer had been suspicious. Uncle Dale wanted Lou's mine; that was the real reason they'd come. So, what was Billie here for? Use the girl-in-mourning to create sympathy? She subtly adjusted her position to be closer to Lou and crossed her arms. She shot darts with her gaze, challenging her uncle to justify his motives.

Uncle Dale splayed out his hands. "You've not been working the claim in six months. It's going to be declared abandoned tomorrow."

"Looks like I came home just in time, then." She pulled the ax off the wall, holding it with two hands. "Not selling."

"As you know, Chester Bergmann was a smart businessman." He acknowledged Billie with a sympathetic smile. "When I was organizing his desk, I noticed he had an interest in your mine. If it was his last intention to acquire your claim, I see it as my duty to fulfill that dying wish for him."

"And if he were as smart a businessman as you say, it would behoove me to hang on to my claim with everything in me, now wouldn't it?"

Billie was starting to like Cousin Lou. She liked the way the woman thought. She saw right through Uncle without even having to trek across the desert with him.

"Look, you know you don't have the means to develop the claim yourself or you would have done so already. I'm not the only one who is interested. It'll be me or Copper Queen Consolidated or someone else that takes it over. Wouldn't you rather keep it in the family?"

"You're not family."

"But I'm acting on behalf of Billie." He held his hands in her direction. "She's family, and by extension, that makes us family."

"Don't patronize me. Give me the watch and then leave my home."

"Would love to, but the watch is back in town."

Billie cocked her head. *When did he have time to find a place to store the watch?*

"Fine. I'll keep the girl here as collateral. Bring me the watch tomorrow. Then you can get the girl back."

Billie gasped.

"Don't worry, kid. I won't eat you."

Cousin Lou had misunderstood her reaction. It meant Uncle would probably go stay in the hotel with heated water, comfortable beds, and a dining room that served petits fours.

"Deal." He nodded at Lou. "See you tomorrow, Billie."

After he'd gone, Lou snorted. "Gave you up awful fast."

"You did promise not to eat me."

Lou winked. "Good one, kid. Now, help me bring in my bags."

Outside the door were several canvas bags that looked like they'd traveled miles on their own.

"Were you gone a long time?" Billie asked. She picked up the closest bag to her, and it was so heavy it was all she could do not to drag it across the threshold. "How did you get all these up here?"

"Got a friend with a mule train. He detoured up here for me. Didn't you hear us?"

Her face warmed. "I was daydreaming." About Lou—the male cousin's—tragic life.

"Doesn't surprise me. And I've been gone long enough to let your uncle think he could jump my claim."

Billie opened her mouth to defend her uncle, to say that wasn't his intent, but on the surface, it seemed it was. However, it was logical to keep the claim in the family if Lou didn't want it anymore or didn't have the funds to develop it. Billie dropped the heavy sack near the bed. There was no point picking a side until she knew more. And the sooner they settled the issue, the sooner she'd be back in Boston.

CHAPTER 8

*B*illie plunked down two plates of stew.

Lou surprised her with a quick German blessing of the food before digging in.

Billie recognized the blessing from her own grandmother. It was the first sign she and this prospecting woman were related. Billie poked at a potato and suppressed a sigh. She pictured Uncle Dale sitting down in the dining room to tablecloths, waiters, and fine china. Roast beef or veal. Her mouth watered.

"What do you know of our family?" Lou asked.

"A few stories. About my dad growing up, and how grandad brought him into the family mining business when he was about my age." Billie had spent plenty of time at her dad's office and was used to ignoring the mining talk going on around her. It hadn't interested her at all, past the idea that mining provided the lifestyle she enjoyed.

She swallowed, wondering how to be tactful. "I know that dwarfism runs in the family. I had a brother who died young, and they thought he would have been a dwarf had he lived."

And there were some other odd stories associated with the

dwarfs in the family that Billie was not about to reveal for fear of sounding like an idiot. As the story goes, two brothers were working a shaft with a collection of other dwarfs when a princess in need found her way to their secluded cabin. Something about a magic mirror, and Billie could only think that her family imbibed too much ale and mixed up their true story with that of the Snow White fairy tale.

Most of the family laughed it off, but a few were sticklers, insisting that every word was true. Her personal view was that the brothers had found a good vein, and they were trying to scare the rest of the people off to make sure they could mine in peace.

Lou nodded. "I've four siblings and I'm the only dwarf. There's several others in our German branch of the family, but I've only met Fremont. He's a bit of a black sheep who acts like a dark horse, if you know my meaning. Not a favorite among the aunts, but always seems to fall ahead, not behind."

Billie hadn't heard of any Fremont. Sounded like he wasn't someone she'd want to meet anyway. "And how did you end up here?"

"It was Fremont's idea. He set it all up through Bergmann Consolidated since he was still in Germany at the time. We were supposed to do some scouting for them. Fremont had a knack for spotting the look of ore in the rock based on the color of the rocks and the vegetation. But he never made it out until last year, so I was on my own. The mountain was pretty picked over, but I managed to buy this small claim for myself off a miner who'd given up. Wasn't big enough for the company to be interested in."

Despite carrying the conversation, Lou finished her meal and set about doing dishes. Billie had expected someone with Lou's reputation to be more tight-lipped. It might not be so hard after all to find out what was so special about the mine and the watch.

"And what about Fremont?"

"*Ach*, like I said, he eventually showed up. We didn't get on well, and one day he was just gone. Don't know what happened to him. Don't particularly care. He's been gone so long I should probably sell off the junk he left behind." She pointed to the locked door. Billie had thought it was Lou's claim behind that door, but maybe it was a storage closet.

"You've been working the claim a long time, you must have hit pay dirt?" The question was intrusive, but time was of the essence. If she could determine the value of the mine for Uncle Dale, they would know whether to press Lou or move on to Boston.

Lou raised one eyebrow as she studied Billie. "You are a Bergmann, aren't you? Have it in your blood? Does the metal call to you?"

Billie felt a chill go up her arms. "No, ma'am. Just making conversation. It's what my father would have done." Billie gulped down the last of her food.

"What other stories have you heard about the family? Got any good ones for me? Anything...odd?"

Snow White.

Billie maintained eye contact. "No, that's about it. You have any for me?"

Lou dried her hands. "Tell me about that uncle of yours. What's his game?"

The woman was too perceptive. After a slow draw in of breath, Billie admitted, "No clue. I thought we were here to give you the watch and then go home to Boston."

Lou narrowed her eyes. "You sure you seen this watch?"

"Once. He keeps it on him. Or at least he did till we got here." Saying so reminded her that her uncle was keeping a lot of things. Lou's watch. Billie's money. His own secrets.

Lou grunted and pointed at the sink where she'd left the soapy water for Billie.

While Billie washed her plate, she asked, "What do you think he is after?"

Instead of answering, Lou glanced outside. "It's almost sunset." She began preparing her miner's lamp. She poured a handful of carbide pellets into the bottom container, filled the top with water, and clicked the flow control four notches. After waiting for the gas to build up, she flicked the flint and the flame caught.

She used a key worn around her neck to open the door at the back of the room. A whoosh of cool air flooded the cabin with the smell of deep earth. The door really was the entrance to Lou's mine.

When Lou beckoned her to follow, Billie's heart began to race.

"You want to go in tonight?" She swallowed the lump forming in her throat.

"The inside of the mountain doesn't know what time it is. Let's go."

Billie quickly dried her hands and peered into the darkness after Lou. The small lantern cast a shadowy arc of light two feet in front.

Carbide lamps had always fascinated Billie. The fact that water dripping onto the pellets created a gas that, when lit, could produce a continuous flame brighter than a candle amazed her. Even more amazing was the thought that the copper the miners were pulling out of these hills would be used to light up the world. It was beyond her understanding. No matter how many times someone explained it to her, it still seemed like magic. What a wonder, this modern world was turning out to be. Next thing, she'd be riding in a motor car.

"You comin'?"

"In a second."

Billie steeled herself as the first wave of panic hit. She closed her eyes, let the darkness come. It was always like this going into a mine. Focus mind over body. Breathe.

Once the initial feelings of claustrophobia passed, she took a step and followed Lou into the mountain. The deep, rich smell of damp earth flooded Billie's senses. Rock. Dirt. Darkness. She braced herself against the wall, waiting for the second wave to wash over her.

She was brought back to her first visit to a mine when her father and several miners took her deep into the shaft before shutting off all their lights. Despite being held safe in her father's grip, she panicked. She'd never seen dark that dark before. Her scream echoed through the cavern, and the miner with the match instantly lit a candle wedged into the rock.

After the lanterns went back on she realized what she smelled wasn't darkness, but that unmistakable, oddly sweet smell of being inside a mountain. The miners exchanged bemused glances with her father, who seemed embarrassed that his only child was afraid in the mine. Billie had squirmed out of his arms, determined to finish the mine tour under her own power to show everyone she was not scared. But she was. She still was.

Complete absence of light was a terrifying thing. It felt like breathing in darkness that would eat her from the inside out.

"You all right?" Lou's gruff voice came from several feet away.

"In a minute." Billie continued taking deep breaths until the panic subsided. She pushed off the wall and followed the light. "I'm good." Her fingers trembled, so she clenched them tight.

Lou hesitated, then made a move to return to the shack.

Billie reached out to stop her. "No. I'm good. It happens every time I go into a mine. Once I'm through the opening I can breathe."

Lou grunted. "Bet your father loved that."

"He didn't take me into too many mines." Just enough to make sure she was able to work through the panic, and then he never invited her to see another. Which was fine by her. They all looked the same anyway.

Except for Cousin Lou's mine. It wasn't spacious like the company mines with their liberal use of dynamite to create stopes, open areas big enough to stand in. No, her methods were crude and not very effective. Billie wasn't sure how long she could keep her panic in check.

The two of them were soon bent over, rock pressing in on all sides, and Billie had to fight the urge to freeze, knowing if she stopped, she may never get out again. The weight of the rock overhead was especially hard to take. "How much farther?" Billie's voice sounded muffled.

Lou was now on her belly, pushing the light out in front of her. "Follow my feet. It's over this ridge." Lou's body blocked most of the light, which wavered with each push.

Billie did as told, hoping whatever she was about to see was worth it.

When Lou got out of the way, the lantern light shone fully in Billie's eyes and she blinked.

"Still doing okay? You'll be able to stand up here in this cavern." Lou held up the lantern, shining the light on the rocks.

Slowly, Billie took in the sight. This cave was different from any she'd ever seen before. Crystalline formations hung from the ceiling and rose up from the floor. Billie followed the arc of light from column to column as Lou spun around.

"A wonder, isn't it?" Lou said with pride. She shone the light close to the wall, revealing streaks of blue embedded in the rock.

"What is it?" Billie asked. She ran her fingers over the rough surface. It was so pretty.

"The formations are from the limestone and the blue mineral is turquoise. But the opportune fact is that it's not copper," Lou said. "That's all Copper Queen Consolidated wants. Oh, there is some—copper and gold—enough for me to live on. What I can get out on my own. The smelting's the problem. Darn expensive that is for my small operation, but I survive. Hard rock mining ain't for the faint of heart."

"If you had economies of scale—" The family company could help Lou out so much. She wouldn't have to live in her shack.

"Oh, listen to Little Miss Business."

Billie bristled at her tone. "I know how it works. You don't have enough ore in each load to cover the cost. You need to increase your production, and that's hard for you to do on your own." *So there. I know a thing or two.*

"The true value of my mine is in its beauty. That uncle of yours doesn't seem the type to want to preserve anything beautiful." Lou held the lantern between them so their faces were lit from below. "What do *you* think?"

Billie took another look around. She had to be honest. "I think they'll want to find out what's past all this. What's causing the formations to look so beautiful. You might have something more valuable behind the turquoise."

"Might. My methods are crude, but they give an idea of what's here, and I haven't found any vein worth following in this cavern. My main vein is in a shaft we passed back there. It produces enough for me but isn't enough for the corporation to even send a mucker out for. That turquoise is real pretty when polished up, but Consolidated tosses it in their slag heap. They don't want it."

"I don't know what Uncle Dale wants. Show him what you showed me to satisfy him, and we can move on."

Lou snorted. "Doesn't strike me as a reasonable man. More likely to stab me in the back when I'm not looking."

Billie felt oddly defensive. "I think you're wrong. He's not a criminal. He just thinks he can handle the business better than you can, and he wants to help."

"Even worse. Do you trust him?"

Billie paused. She did, but with caution. How could she explain that to this woman she'd just met? It was disloyal to speak against her uncle.

"*Ach, nee.* Your silence says it all. How's about you have a chat with your uncle first thing in the morning. You'll have to go to him, because he's just going to wait me out." She held the lantern high. "I'm trusting you to do the right thing. Get him to leave me that watch at the front desk of the Copper Queen Hotel, and then be on your way. The longer you stay, the more time he's got to figure out a way to get what he wants."

CHAPTER 9

While it was still dark, Billie woke to the inviting smell of coffee and flapjacks. Lou bustled in the kitchen area, not being subtle at all with the way she banged the pots around.

"What time is it?" Billie asked, her head still firmly nestled into her pillow. Lou had pulled out the extra bed roll from the supplies the other cousin had left behind in the mine. Billie was grateful he had left it behind when he skipped town.

"Look, Sleeping Beauty decided to join the rest of the world."

Billie rolled over and grunted.

"Get a move on. I need you out of here before sunrise."

What was it with Lou and the sun? Sunset. Sunrise. Why so precise?

Oh, to be back in Boston where she could sleep in like all her friends were doing. Nice, cozy feather quilts on cool mornings. Breakfast delivered on a tray with a silver vase and fresh cut flowers.

"Hey, no falling back asleep."

Billie startled. She opened her eyes and blinked away the last vestiges of her lace-decorated room in Boston. Her gaze landed

on the curtained window above the cot. "Five more minutes."
Billie buried her head farther into the pillow.

Thunk.

She found herself on the cold, hard floor. Lou was not messing
around.

After a quick breakfast, Billie was pushed out the door by a
very impatient cousin.

"I thought you wanted to exchange me for the watch?"

"Like I said, I don't trust him. You, on the other hand, haven't
been completely corrupted yet." She handed over Billie's bags.
"Do your best to get him out of town. Leave the watch at the
front desk at the hotel. You don't belong here, and I think you
know it."

Billie stumbled into the darkness with her carpetbag and
reticule. "Can't I even wait until sunrise?"

Lou pointed to the warm blush spreading over the
mountaintop. "You'll have full sun by the time you hit town. Best
to walk while it's still cool, anyway."

Billie yawned and gave an exaggerated stretch, hoping to play
on Lou's sympathies. Didn't work. She stumbled forward, glancing
back in case Lou wanted to give her a final reprieve.

"It's that way, darlin'." Lou pointed to the left of where Billie
was going.

Billie pretended that was the way she meant to go in the first
place and waved, hoping she wouldn't come to a fork in the trail
anytime soon. She should have been paying more attention when
they'd hiked the mountain, but she'd been too annoyed at her
uncle, never imagining they'd be separated.

Well, she'd pay attention now.

The sun was rising, and although still blocked by the
mountains, it cast a rosy glow on the sparse hillside. After hiking
awhile, Billie paused to take in the beauty of the moment. A noise
behind her made her jump, and she looked back, hoping it wasn't
a wild animal.

The dark form of a man stopped short and dodged behind a bush.

Her heart rate sped up. How long had he been following her, and what were his intentions? If she needed to scream, would Cousin Lou be able to hear her?

Billie picked up her pace, becoming reckless as she descended the mountain. Her boots skidded on the rocks, and several times she slipped. When she dared glance back again, the figure was still following her.

In desperation she looked for a weapon with which to defend herself. The hillsides were practically bare of any sticks or branches she could use to keep her pursuer at bay, but there were plenty of rocks. *Didn't anything grow here?* It was like she'd been dropped into the desert the Israelites wandered in for forty years.

Uncle Dale had told her the hills had been mined not only for the copper and gold but for the wood to make charcoal to heat the furnaces needed for smelting. It had left the mountains bare and unprotected. Floods were a worry this time of year with nothing to stop the mud from sliding down into town.

Suddenly, her legs went out from under her and she fell hard. She skidded several feet down the mountain on her backside, narrowly missing a cactus. Hands stinging and heart racing, she grabbed at a rock while she was down. At least now she was armed.

"You all right there?" the stranger called.

Billie glanced behind. He hurried after her, surfing the rocks like she'd seen a man do on the waves in the Pacific Ocean.

"I'm fine." She tried to scramble to her feet, hiding the rock behind her, ready to swing it hard if he wasn't friendly.

As he got closer, his face came into view and Billie's stomach leaped.

"Oh. It's you." *Winn.*

She froze, undecided whether to drop the rock or keep it ready. She barely knew the first thing about the boy from town.

"And you," he said, tipping his hat. He crossed his arms and looked down at her. "Need help, Miss Bergmann?"

"No." She struggled to get up, the little pebbles making it difficult.

"It'd be easier if you dropped that rock."

She glared at him. There he stood, his handsome face tilted to the sky and his rugged body braced against the tilt of the mountain.

"No gold in it, so no point in keeping it," he said.

"I know there's not gold in it." The daughter of a geologist, of course she knew.

He held out his hand and after a moment's reflection, she took it. But instead of pulling herself up, she yanked him off balance.

The look of surprise on his face was worth her boldness. She laughed, slapping her knee as he crashed down beside her.

He scowled. "What was that for?"

"Weren't you standing there thinking I was some city girl out of her league here in the mountains? Thought I'd knock out some of that smugness. Show you any of us can fall."

Winn got back on his feet, shaking his head. "Dames." He began to walk off.

Billie immediately regretted not taking his proffered hand the way it was meant. She pushed herself up. "Wait."

He knew the way to town, and at least he could keep her from taking the wrong path or getting attacked by wild animals.

He stopped walking.

Hmm. Maybe he was a little bit of a gentleman.

They descended in silence. Billie stole a glance, and he continued glaring straight ahead. Clearly, he didn't want her tagging along. He was probably trying to stay out of sight back there, so he didn't have to talk to her.

Traveling with her uncle had made her suspicious of everyone. She found herself constantly looking for ulterior motives.

"You must live out this way," she said, trying to draw him out.

"You could say that."

"Long walk in every day." She thought Lou's shack had to be the house farthest away from town, but Winn's must be even beyond that. She pictured another plain shack like Lou's but filled with a family. What different worlds she and Winn lived in.

The closer they got to town, the more houses dotted the landscape. Doors began opening, and dark-haired children began pouring out calling out to one another in Spanish. Farther down, they came across a group of children playing on a flat area in the ground. They'd traced lines in the dirt and had pebbles placed in the squares.

Winn exhaled, balling his fists. "What are you doing, *mijo*? You know your mama hates Faro." Winn kicked the dirt to wipe clean their playing area. "And you, Billy-boy quit pretending about things you know nothing about."

"Hey!" a sandy-haired boy complained. "I was winning."

"You all go home or I'll tell your mothers what I caught you doing."

The kids scrambled up and scattered, several shouting angry words in Spanish as they ran away. He laughed.

"At least they listen to you," Billie said.

"Naw, they're just scared of what their mamas will do to them."

"See that boy there?" He pointed at the sandy-haired boy running down the hill in front of them. "He shares your name, Billy. He's always getting the others into trouble. I catch him doing stuff all the time."

She stole a glance at Winn. His jaw was set, determined, but his eyes were kind. He really cared about these kids. It bothered him that they were playing at gambling.

"You speak Spanish?"

"A little. You pick it up."

"Why don't you live here?" she asked, indicating the community. "It's closer to town."

"Sure is."

Okay. She wanted to get him talking, but he wasn't giving out much information. "Do you plan to work in the mine?"

"No. I pick up odd jobs when I'm not in school. Besides, someone like me could only work up to being a mucker, and I don't want to do that for the rest of my life anyway."

"Then be a miner."

He shook his head. "You've got to come from British roots to be a miner. My pop came here from Finland. He'll never be a miner."

"Oh. I see." But she didn't. Who knew the mining rules were so complex?

"Listen, it's not like we can't do the work, it's that the bosses won't hire us for it."

"I'll ask my dad to—" Billie stopped. Her dad wasn't running any mining operations anymore. "You don't strike me as a fellow who wants to go to school, either," she said, then immediately regretted it when his countenance turned sour.

"I don't know how a fellow is supposed to look. Wear a sweater and glasses?"

Billie couldn't help herself. With his athletic build, tanned skin, and well-worn clothes, he had a weathered appearance, like a boy who never stepped indoors if he could help it. Picturing Winn dressed all prim and proper like the fellows in Boston didn't work. She burst out laughing until he cracked a smile with her.

"I'm sorry," she said. "I didn't mean to sound like I was putting you down. It's that you don't look like the fellows I know back home. You don't act like them either, and so I keep saying the wrong things."

"Maybe I'm not like the fellows back home."

He certainly wasn't. Winn was wild like this country. As foreign to her as the cacti. Yet, there was something about him that drew her in. She sensed he was putting up a front. He pulled off a tough-guy, don't-care image, but he gave off an underlying current of goodness.

She recognized his front because it was what she did every day. She grew up playing a role. She had to dress and talk and act the way the daughter of a mining baron should.

By now they'd reached the town, which was just starting to wake up. Shops were still closed, but several miners were headed into the restaurants serving breakfast.

Winn tipped his hat. "Good day, Miss Bergmann. Enjoy your trip back to Boston."

She shrugged. "I'm sure I will, eventually."

He gave her a quizzical look before jerking his chin in the direction of the hotel. "After you leave the watch for Lou, you've no more reason to stay. I'm sure you've got friends and family who miss you."

"How do you know about the watch?" She'd not told anyone in town what business they had for Cousin Lou.

His gaze skittered down the road and back to her. "You told me yesterday."

She crossed her arms. "No, yesterday you told me to leave town before it was too late. Were you listening to me and Lou?" She searched her memory to try to remember when they'd talked about the watch. It wasn't this morning, so Winn had to have been listening last night. "Do you eavesdrop on folks often?"

He held up his hands. "Never on purpose. I've got enough of my own worries." He backed away. "Now, if you'll excuse me."

"What did you mean by 'too late,' anyway?" she called after him.

He didn't answer, just held his hand high above his head in a dismissive wave.

CHAPTER 10

*B*illie found her uncle enjoying a leisurely breakfast at the hotel. His eyebrows lifted in surprise when she walked up to his corner table.

"I thought you were being held for ransom." He downed the last of his coffee.

"Got out for good behavior." She sat across from him. "I thought we didn't have enough money to stay at the hotel."

Uncle Dale shot her a look. "I stayed up all night."

For the first time Billie noticed his bloodshot eyes. "Lou wants you to leave the watch at the front desk. Then we can go."

His face hardened. "I'm not leaving something like that with a clerk. If it went missing she'd have the law after us."

"She wouldn't. She doesn't know anything about the watch, and I don't think she cares that much about it."

"Ah." He held up a finger. "That's what she wants you to believe. Didn't you see the greed in her eyes when I mentioned it? No, there's something special about this watch, and it's not its ability to keep time. The thing's broken."

Billie hadn't noticed any change in Lou at the mention of the watch. Uncle Dale was just hoping there was, so he'd have an excuse to stay in town and investigate the mine.

The waitress refilled Uncle's coffee. She was the same woman who'd given Billie a hard time when she asked about her cousin Lou. The townspeople could have just told her that cousin Lou was a woman. No need to make fun of her for not keeping close family ties.

Billie waited with an icy glare until they were alone again.

"Lou's not mining much gold. Just enough for herself. She says there isn't a strong vein at all. What she has is a pretty cave with some turquoise. Nothing big enough for our company to take an interest in."

"Of course, she would say that."

Billie thought about telling him she'd seen the mine, but something held her back. "She's proud is all," she said. "You see how she lives."

Uncle Dale added sugar and a generous pour of cream. "If she would accept help she'd be a lot happier for it."

"For now, she just wants the watch. Have you got it?"

Uncle Dale glanced around before reaching into his inside jacket pocket. He pulled out a gold pocket watch and handed it to her.

German made. Antique. The face was pearlized and quite pretty. The hands were frozen at 11:59. She flipped it over and saw the name *Fremont* engraved on the back.

Billie fought to keep the surprise off her face. That was the name of the cousin who had come over from Germany and helped Lou set up her claim. The same one who took off and hadn't been heard from since. *Why would her father have Fremont's pocket watch?*

She looked up and smiled. "You're right. It's just a pocket watch that doesn't keep time."

Uncle took back the watch, running his finger along the seam. "I tried to pry it open, but it's sealed tight and my tools are too thick to wedge in there. I'll have to take it to a jeweler to pop the back off and take a look."

"You can't do that," Billie said, her voice rising. The couple next to them looked over, so she lowered to a whisper. "It's not your watch."

"Until I deliver it to Lou, technically, I'm in charge of it."

"She's not going to get talked out of her claim," Billie said, her voice getting louder again. Lou was right. Uncle was digging in his heels. At this rate, she'd never get home to Boston. Her friends would all forget about her, and her mother would continue to face her illness alone.

Uncle tossed his cloth napkin on the plate. "Come with me."

After paying for his meal, he led her outside, away from the building.

With a low voice, he said, "We're not leaving until that claim is brought under control of Bergmann Consolidated. Now, are you going to help or not?"

"Not," Billie said. "It's a tiny claim. Certainly not worth staying in town for when you are supposed to bring me to Boston." She kept her voice even, controlled, but let her eyes express her anger.

Uncle's face reflected an internal struggle. He seemed to be vacillating between confiding in her and keeping her in the dark. Did he trust her to help him, or was he afraid she'd expose his scheme? Finally, he grabbed her elbow and led her to the back of the hotel. He waited until the busboy finished dumping the scraps and went back inside.

"Listen carefully. It's. All. Real. Everything you've been told about your family is the truth."

Billie squinted against the sun. "What do you mean? What's real?"

Uncle glanced around. "I'm talking about the *stories*." He raised his eyebrows, giving her a knowing look.

"What stories?" Billie asked, getting defensive. The only

stories she could think of were the fairy-tale ones. Surely those weren't what Uncle Dale was talking about. Being on her mother's side of the family, he wouldn't know about them.

"The fairy tale is a cover up. It's real. The mine. The mirror." He looked earnest. "They didn't want anyone to know. They wanted to keep the mirror to themselves."

Billie laughed nervously. "What did they feed you at the hotel last night? I think something's affected your sense of reason."

He squeezed her arm, pressing his thumb into the tender flesh on the inside of her elbow and leaned in close.

"I'm not joking. Your father had the documents in his safe. Deeds. Maps. He was tracking the location of the mirror, and he traced it to right here. He figured it was hidden in Cousin Lou's mine."

Billie's stomach lurched.

Uncle let go of her arm and dug into his sack. He pulled out a sheaf of papers and shoved them at her.

"Lou probably doesn't even know the mirror's there. Look for yourself."

Billie quickly rifled through the documents. A lot of it she didn't understand, but she caught enough bits and pieces to figure out Uncle Dale's plan. Lou's claim had been idle for too long, so, it was about to be marked as abandoned.

"That's why you wanted to be here on a certain day. So you could step in and buy the claim."

"But with Lou back, she's likely to be working the claim today to keep her ownership."

Billie nodded. When she'd left, Lou had been pulling out her mining equipment. "I don't understand why it matters so much to you." *Since, if it were real, it belongs in my family anyway.*

"Think about it. A magic mirror. According to the fairy tale, the evil queen made magic potions. What if she learned how to do that from the mirror? The mirror might be the key to healing your mother. We could ask it for a cure."

Billie had been prepared to counter whatever silly thing her uncle might say, but she wasn't prepared for him to give a selfless reason that actually made sense. Her father had done everything he could to help her mother. Nothing worked.

Frowning, Billie studied the papers until she began to see why he was so convinced. Father had collected ancient documents describing a truth-telling mirror that would answer one question a day. Not a magic lamp granting wishes, but an honest answer. It could answer anything from where someone was, to how to make a poisoned apple.

The tales sounded like make believe until they were paired with maps and newspaper accounts of strange goings-on. There was enough evidence here to indicate the mirror was special. Especially the report from the town Lohrs am Main in Germany which referenced a talking mirror. By the description, though, the "talking" came from aphorisms carved onto the frame. Maybe not magical, but certainly valuable. If she remembered her history correctly, aphorisms started out as medical principles. It was possible there might be some wisdom carved into the frame to help her mom.

And what if it was true? What if the mirror was real, in whatever form it might take?

Her father should have told her. It wasn't right that Uncle Dale was the one tracking it down. He might say he was doing it for her mother, but if he were to find it first, you can bet Billie wouldn't even catch a glimpse before he'd secret it away for himself.

Not that she believed it was actually magical, but it might be a gold mirror, and there would be value in that. Enough to make it worth Uncle Dale's efforts to find it.

If the mirror was something her dad had been tracking down, there had to be a reason he wanted it, and a reason why he thought they should have it. She owed it to Dad to find it. She owed it to herself.

She straightened her spine. Looked her uncle in the eye. "I'll do it."

He grinned and punched the air. "That's my girl."

"But not for you. For Mom." Dad had tried everything to help: doctors, an herbalist, and even home-grown tea from the concerned old woman down the street. She could make one last—albeit odd—attempt to save her. "The mirror is my heritage, and if we find it, I get to decide what to do about it. Understood?"

Uncle nodded, hands up in the yield position. "Of course, of course. I was doing this for you all along."

Billie raised an eyebrow. Neither one of them believed that was the truth, but at least now Billie felt like she was on the same level as her uncle. He'd come clean, so she knew what she was up against. The trick would be to keep an eye on him so he stayed honest with her.

She thought of Lou, who knew every inch of that mine. If there were a gold or a magic mirror hidden inside, she would know, because she would have put it there.

CHAPTER 11

*U*ncle Dale refused to let Billie join him at the jewelry store, instead, sending her to wait across the street. Billie agreed, but stationed herself at the window outside a pharmacy in the hopes of learning something anyway.

Two girls about her age strolled toward her, stopping to examine the display of soap in the window.

"You related to that lady up the mountain?" asked the brunette in a gray walking outfit.

The chubby girl beside her looked skittish, like the first girl was making her stand there, but she would prefer to be anywhere else. Billie prepared herself for something unpleasant.

"Is she as crazy as they say?" continued the first.

"What do you mean?" Billie asked.

"They say she sits in her rocking chair all night talking to the walls."

Billie quirked her lips to show she didn't believe the girl.

"I'm serious. My brother saw it with his own eyes. Walked past her place when he was late coming home from hunting."

"Maybe she was singing to herself. Ever think of that?" Billie didn't know what this girl's brother had seen, but it didn't matter.

"Alone in her cabin with no neighbors to bother, she could have been talking to God, and here you are talking bad about her."

The second girl looked at her feet, exhibiting a hint of conscience.

The first girl shook her head emphatically. "It wasn't like she was singing or praying. He said she was carrying on a conversation with someone who wasn't there. Crazy as a loon. Best you watch yourself."

"It's true," piped up the skittish girl, gaining confidence. "Everyone in town knows it. Stay up there too long it'll affect you, too."

Billie took a step closer to the girl. "Maybe it already has. Maybe you'll catch it next." Impulsively, Billie touched the girl's arm.

The girl yelped and backed away. "Not funny."

Someone chuckled behind Billie. She turned to see Winn leaning against the building.

"Aren't you afraid you'll catch my crazy?" Billie would never act this outlandishly in Boston, but she couldn't seem to help herself.

He shook his head. "Nope."

The girls crossed the dirt street, casting envious looks behind them.

"Friends of yours?" Billie asked.

Winn shrugged and started to walk down the boardwalk.

To keep him there longer, she blurted out, "So I guess you do know my cousin Lou. I figured out the whole town was laughing at me because I didn't know my own cousin is a woman."

He slowed his step, allowing her to meet his stride, and the tips of her ears warmed as he gave her his full attention.

"Everyone knows who your cousin is. She stands out even if she doesn't want to."

"Do you think she's as mad as they're saying?"

Winn turned to the side to allow a group of women to pass. "No. She's the sanest person in this town."

"So, the town is crazy?"

"Something like that. Guess you're leaving today?"

Did she detect regret in his voice?

"No, not today."

He stopped walking. "Why not?"

"Why do you care so much?"

"I don't," he said nonchalantly. "Got my own problems." He glanced over her shoulder, and his face took on a guilty look. He abruptly changed directions. "Gotta go, city girl." He crossed the street and went in the direction of Brewery Gulch.

Billie stared after him. She would have followed, but she had to wait for Uncle Dale.

"Whatcha lookin' at girlie?"

Billie spun around. "Lou! You startled me."

Cousin Lou marched up to her carrying a small sack. She was covered in sweat and dust, like she'd been working hard all morning.

"Keep away from that boy. He's trouble." Lou pointed her finger near Billie's face. "Now, where's my watch? Did your uncle leave it at the hotel, or do I need to see him again?"

"He'll be here soon," Billie said, trying not to look at the jewelry store. "Why is Winn trouble?"

"Winn, is it?" She blew through her lips. "Doesn't matter, since you and that uncle of yours are leaving, aren't you?"

Billie shrugged, not wanting to answer.

"I gotta make a stop before your uncle gets here anyway." Lou held up her sack. "Prove to the assayer I'm back working my claim. He ain't going to give it away to anyone. Tell those lawyers it's time to back down and step off my property." She lumbered past Billie. "Maybe get myself a mangy dog," she called over her shoulder.

Once Lou disappeared from sight, Billie hightailed it over to the jewelry store. Henkel's at 11 Main Street. *Is your WATCH on time? If not, Henkel will fix it for you.* The advertisement wasn't terribly poetic, but to the point.

The bell dinged overhead as she walked in.

Uncle Dale stood at the counter with a finely dressed gentleman holding a magnifying glass. Mr. Henkel, she assumed. A variety of tools were splayed out on the counter before them, a velvet cloth laid out with the watch resting on top. The jeweler looked frustrated.

"Excuse me," Uncle said and then met Billie at the door.

She leaned in to whisper, "Lou is in town."

He looked back at the jeweler, who was scratching his head and frowning.

"Can you stall her? Take her to the hotel for lunch."

"I'll try. Can't you get the watch open?"

"Darndest thing. It won't budge."

"Maybe it's not supposed to open."

Uncle didn't look convinced. "They have to be able to open it to fix the gears. We're trying to find a secret spring lock now. These fancy timepieces have trigger spots on them."

"Well, don't take too long. I don't know how much conversation I can make with her. We don't exactly have a lot in common."

"You're family. Talk about family *stories*." He lifted an eyebrow before turning back to the jeweler. "I say, Henkel, if you can't do the job I'll take it up the street to that fellow under the post office. Keenhold. Saw his ad in the paper, too."

"Don't be hasty. I've almost got it."

Billie slipped out the door, relieved to see Lou up the street, facing away from the jeweler. Billie skirted around a wagon and crossed the road, trying to cover up where she'd come from.

"Cousin Lou," she called.

"There you are. Well?"

"My uncle said to meet him at the hotel. He'll have the watch with him."

"I'm not buying you two hooligans lunch."

Billie frowned. "I can buy lunch." Not that she had the money on her. She was relying on her uncle having some left over from his evening venture in the saloons, or from wiring in some from her mother. If he hadn't wired in the money yet, Billie would take care of it. "The food at the Copper Queen is quite good."

"I'm sure it won't kill me, and it's bound to be better than what you fed me last night."

Billie breathed out slowly to keep herself from sending another insult flying back. There was no need for rudeness. She never did claim to be a five-star chef, only better than Uncle's can of beans.

ONCE THEY WERE SEATED, Lou fussed with her napkin. "Don't like restaurants," she said. "I prefer to do my own cooking."

"I'm the opposite. Love restaurants. Wish I could eat in one every day. Although, at home we have a cook, so it's similar to eating out. I just don't get to choose whatever I want like you can when you order off a menu."

"Poor you."

"Tell me about your side of the family," Billie said, ignoring Lou's tone. "Any interesting characters or stories I should know about?"

"Know about your grandpa?"

Billie nodded. "A little."

"He was my uncle. I only met him once. He gave me a candy, so I liked him."

"I know he took over the family company when he was nineteen. His dad had died in a mining accident."

Lou nodded. "Brilliant man—but cocky and paranoid. Not a good combination. What else do you know about him or the family?"

Was this the time when Billie was supposed to ask outright if Snow White was real, and if the family harbored her in the woods and ultimately took possession of a magic mirror? *No.* Lou would think she was the crazy one.

Unless Lou believed it, too.

Billie decided to hedge, just in case.

"I've heard bits and pieces. Stories mainly," she said. "When I was a child they sounded like fairy tales." She laughed uncomfortably.

"I might have heard those same stories," Lou said, noncommittally.

They stared at each other.

"Not that they were true," Lou finally said.

"Of course."

"Several generations ago there was a rift in the family," Lou said. "They all lived back in Germany then, and overnight, Eberhardt Bergmann moved the base of the family operations to America and got into hard rock mining in Colorado. The only one who truly believed in him was his younger sister, my grandmother, whom he invited to immigrate to America when he got injured. He wanted her to take over the company. The old coot didn't trust anyone who wasn't family, and she was the only one still talking to him. That's how I ended up in America." She tapped her fingers on the table. "But my grandmother didn't care for the work and against Eberhardt's wishes turned the reigns over to another branch of the family. Then many years later, your daddy took over."

The waitress came to take their orders.

"Should we wait for my uncle?" Billie asked, but Lou was already ordering.

"I'll have mock turtle soup with water thins and green apple pie for dessert," said Lou. She handed the menu to the waitress.

For someone who didn't like eating in restaurants, she was awfully specific.

"Hamburger, please," Billie said. When they were alone again, Billie cleared her throat. "Like I said, my dad used to tell me stories that sounded like fairy tales."

"Mmm?"

"He had me convinced that our family had a magical treasure hidden deep in the forest in Germany." Billie paused to study Lou's reaction. Nothing.

"Sounds like he had an active imagination."

"He said something about a special mirror that was in the family. Do you know anything about that?"

Lou shrugged. "Some members are wealthier than others, more vain than others, so they have lots of mirrors. My aunt Hildegard had one in every room." Her pupils dilated ever so slightly.

Got her.

"Dad was very specific about this mirror because it had a legend surrounding it." Billie leaned forward so she could whisper. "Mirror, mirror, on the wall."

Lou blinked. "Next you'll wonder if any of the family owns a glass slipper. Don't you beat all?" She fussed with her napkin. "Don't know what you're talking about."

The food arrived, stealing away the moment. Billie leaned back. *Almost had her.*

Then Uncle Dale entered the dining room. He saw them and waved.

Billie waved back, but her attention was fully on Cousin Lou, who was examining her. Billie smiled and pretended she hadn't said anything shocking or revelatory. Let Lou stew a bit before Billie brought the mirror up again.

"My two favorite girls in Bisbee," said Uncle Dale opening his arms as if expecting a hug.

"Got my watch?" Lou said.

Uncle Dale patted his jacket pocket as he sat. "How's the

food?" He eyed Billie's hamburger and signaled for the waitress. "I'll have one of those."

"Isn't this nice?" he continued. "You two enjoying the family reunion? Billie hasn't met many of her German relatives. I was hoping you'd get well acquainted."

"We're acquainted," Lou said. "Told all the old stories. So, now can I have my watch and be on my way?"

"You get lonely up that mountain, Lou? Ever think about moving to someplace like Boston where you've got family to rely on?"

They both turned to look at him.

"You're not suggesting—" Billie said.

At the same time, Lou said, "I like living alone."

He held up his hands. "Hear me out. Lou, you could move with Billie to Boston. We'd set you up in the grand house there. There's plenty of room. You'd not have a care for the rest of your life. You're family. Billie and her mother would love to have you, wouldn't she, Billie?"

Uncle Dale knew that her mother couldn't handle much right now. Her illness made her irritable and tired. No, her mother would not love to keep company with a stranger, even if she was family.

"And I suppose," Lou said with ice in her voice, "that in exchange, you'll take care of my claim. Bet what took you so long is you went to the assayer's office and found out my claim is solid, and you've no sneaky way to pull it out from under me."

Lou stood abruptly. "My home is here. It may not look like much to you fancy people, but it suits my needs just fine. I'll take my watch now." She waited, fuming.

Uncle shrugged and made a show of taking her watch out of his pocket. He handed it to her with a smile. She nodded at each of them and then stormed out of the restaurant.

Billie couldn't believe that final exchange. "What did you do that for? Now she's angry."

He calmly pointed out the window. Lou had pulled out the watch and flipped it over to read the engraving on the back.

Billie knew what the name meant, but did Uncle? He never asked her if there was a Fremont in the family.

"I'm keeping her rattled. She's bound to make a mistake sooner or later."

"Or you're going to make a mistake. Did you get the watch open?"

He shook his head. "The jeweler tried everything. Maybe it is just a watch." He reached over and took a bite of the apple pie that Lou had left behind.

"Oh, that's good," he said and finished it off.

Uncle Dale acted overly nonchalant about the watch. It was possible he was able to get it open, and he wasn't telling her. How was she to know? Since no one was telling the complete story, how was she to figure out any of the truth?

CHAPTER 12

"Now what?" Billie asked as she strode along the boardwalk with her uncle. She was disappointed she'd never gotten the chance to circle back to the magic mirror story with Lou before Uncle Dale had joined them, but she still felt like she'd made progress. Lou had visibly reacted, though she tried not to.

"I confirm with the assayer. Make sure Lou retains ownership before making the next move."

"Which is?"

"Don't know yet." He smiled. "But I'm glad you're on board. Tricky business this is. I didn't know how much you knew, or if you'd be interested in pursuing the opportunity."

"You mean if I would believe that such a mirror existed. The jury's still out on that one. But if we find something that would help my mom, well, we're already here. It wouldn't hurt anything to look around."

As they passed the townspeople on the boardwalk, the folks stepped aside, giving them a wider berth than was meant out of politeness. A whisper here, a whisper there. No one would make eye contact with her.

For being strangers in the town, their presence was already well known. Uncle Dale didn't seem to notice, the way he had his eyes trained ahead, focused on the assayer's office.

While Billie had never shied away from attention before, this kind of attention was unnerving. The questions they'd been asking must have stirred up something in the town.

This time at the assayer's office, Uncle Dale didn't tell her to wait outside. He had nothing to hide now. Their boots clomped on the wooden floor announcing their arrival, but the assayer didn't look up. A heavily mustached man, he was focused on testing ore the miner at the counter had brought in.

Billie, used to seeing such equipment lying around her father's office, took stock of the place. He had the usual glass beakers and scales and a variety of metal tools.

Soon, notes were made, money was exchanged, and the prospector left the building.

The assayer looked up and frowned beneath his mustache. Without saying a word, he retrieved an envelope and slid it across the counter to Uncle. "Not this time, mate."

"Any other ideas?" Uncle asked. He picked up the envelope, casually letting some money spill out onto the counter.

Billie's eyes widened. Was Uncle Dale trying to bribe the assayer?

The assayer's eyes glanced down at the bills, but he didn't move to take them. Billie wondered how often the man had been approached by desperate miners trying to make their claims appear richer than they really were.

"I'm not a lawyer, but my brother is," the assayer said. "Jenkins, on Commerce Street. He may have some advice for you. My advice is to leave town." His voice was gruff. "Strange things happen up on that hill." He glanced at Billie and nodded. "Miss."

Once outside, Uncle marched toward Brewery Gulch.

"Commerce Street is that way, if I remember right," Billie

said, hustling after him. She was still unnerved by what the assayer had said about strange things happening on the hill.

"I'll make it there eventually. First, I've got to find out more information, now that we know who we're dealing with."

"Did you notice that everyone still acts funny when you talk about Cousin Lou or her claim?"

Uncle shrugged. "It's a small town. People are protective of their own. Plus, it's a growing mining town, and people always get suspicious when 'there's gold in them thar hills.'"

Billie knew that already, but she was sure there was more going on in this town. There was protective and paranoid, and then there was hostile and strange. Everyone acted normally until she mentioned her cousin, and then the looks and the whispers started. Except for Winn Harris, himself full of contradictions. He said he wanted her to leave, but he was the friendliest of all.

She was eager to get back to Boston and her regular life, but her curiosity was getting the best of her. There may or may not be a special mirror hidden in Cousin Lou's mine. But there was definitely a mystery to uncover in this town.

Billie followed her uncle until he stopped in front of the Fish Pond Saloon, where a drawing of a tiger was displayed in the front window.

"I'll get in on a game of Faro and get the guys talking. You best skedaddle."

"You better not lose all my money," Billie said. She couldn't help but note as soon as Uncle got their money back he was taking it gambling. Faro was a game of chance he liked to play. Here in the west, Faro boards seemed to be everywhere. Even Billie, who'd never set foot in a saloon, knew that a picture of a tiger in the window meant they were playing Faro inside. It was nicknamed "bucking the tiger" because so many used the popular pack of playing cards with a tiger on the front.

"I've got a system. Don't worry about me. You go do whatever it is women do."

She held out her hand. "I want half."

She'd seen he had enough money with him to cover their hotel bill for a few days. She would safeguard their funds and make sure they had a place to stay in town. She wasn't going back to that shack if she didn't have to.

He shook his head. "As your guardian, that would be irresponsible of me. I'm tasked with taking care of the finances, and take care of them I will."

A pretty woman walked by, and Uncle smiled and nodded. "Ma'am." He turned back to Billie. "Tell you what, I'll give you some pocket change." He deftly slipped her some bills.

Billie glanced at the amount before tucking them into her reticule. It was more than she expected out of pocket money, so she didn't make a fuss.

"Do you promise we'll stay at the hotel tonight?"

Uncle patted the pocket where he'd placed his wallet. "Yes. Go book the rooms."

"Then I'll need some more money." Again, she held out her hand. She'd learned persistence from her father. He never gave up on the things that were important to him.

Uncle Dale handed her the money, and she left before he could ask for it back. She made her way to the Copper Queen Hotel where they had stored their bags earlier. The lobby was small, with a high wood-beam ceiling and a polished-wood staircase leading up to the second floor.

"Two rooms, please," she said at the front counter. She'd never booked a room for herself before, and when the male clerk eyed her warily, she pulled out her reticule and showed him the money. "With a private bath in mine."

He nodded. She signed the book, and he gave her a key.

Feeling quite mature, she went up the stairs and followed the hallway to her room. She grinned when she stepped inside. The room was elegant enough with a pretty wrought-iron bed covered by a white bedspread and pillow. The window overlooked the

street, and it was open to allow a breeze to blow through. Not
that the occasional gusts were refreshing. Even the wind was hot.
They told her Bisbee was cool compared to other parts of the
territory, but she couldn't imagine what another ten degrees of
heat would feel like. She'd melt into the red rocks, never moving
again.

She quickly gathered the clothes in her bag—not enough
pieces for her liking. They were encased in dirt and sweat from
the trip, and she couldn't wait another moment to get them
laundered. She brought them down to the front desk to be sent
out to the laundry. Her current outfit also needed a wash, but at
least tomorrow she'd be able to slip into a fresh gown, which
would go a long way to making her feel human again.

In the bathroom, she ran the bath water, thankful for modern
conveniences. Whoever invented running hot water deserved a
medal. After washing off the dirt, she slipped into her light linen
chemise to lie on top of the bed and wait out the hot afternoon.

When she woke the room was dimly lit by the waning sun.
She reluctantly put her dusty shirtwaist and skirt back on and
went to find out if her uncle had arrived. She knocked on his
door, but there was no answer. Next, she wandered down to the
restaurant, happy to see the waitress from this morning was gone.
After an enjoyable meal, she retired to the ladies' parlor to see
what the women in town did at night.

Now this is nice. Green silk curtains framed the windows and
the plush green cushions looked inviting. Several ladies in stylish
evening wear played whist. Others read novels.

"Come here, dear," said a sweet voice behind Billie.

She pivoted to see a striking woman in a classic navy gown
trimmed in lace. Her piercing eyes looked astute as she sized
Billie up. The woman patted the empty place beside her on a
couch, and her ruby ring caught the light. "You look slightly
bewildered. New in town?"

Billie smiled. "I've been here a few days." She sat, pleased to have found a friendly face. The woman's hair was styled to perfection, and Billie tried not to be envious, but she'd seen that hairstyle in Godey's and try as she might, had not been able to replicate it so well. The woman shifted her skirt and a sliver of a shoe the color of a deep-red strawberry peeked out.

What new fashion was this? Something new from Paris she could buy to replace her white boots? She must work it into the conversation at the appropriate moment. She'd loved the idea of red shoes ever since she'd heard one of the family bedtime stories...although those red shoes were made of red-hot iron and led the evil queen to dance to her death.

"And what do you think of our little boomtown?" the woman asked.

The town unnerved her, but Billie maintained her polite smile. "It has more amenities than I expected." She glanced around the finely-decorated parlor.

"The advantages of a prosperous new town. We get the latest and greatest the world has to offer. Once the town gets past its adobe shack and wooden clapboard stage, that is." She nodded appraisingly at the drapes. "And this new hotel is one of the finest."

"I've stayed in many hotels both here and in Europe, and I agree." Billie tucked her feet in their boots as far under the couch as she could. "Are there any stores here that import fashions from overseas?"

The woman smiled understandingly. "I see you are in mourning. I'm sorry for your loss."

Billie acknowledged the sentiment with a nod.

"You must be tired of wearing black crepe, although the color suits you fine. There are several suitable stores, though I do have a personal supplier for my needs." She shifted again, revealing more of her beautiful shoe that glittered in the light.

The deep red, almost burgundy was just scandalous enough of a color for a shoe to shock Holly but make Suzanne and Jane green with envy. Of course, she wouldn't actually be able to wear red for several more months. First, she would switch from black to other deep tones.

"Of course." Billie waved her hand like she had her own personal supplier as well. Then she self-consciously patted her hair down. It had turned unruly during her nap and she'd only hastily repaired it before coming down for supper. Without anyone to dress up for she'd gotten lazy.

The woman's smile deepened. She laughed, a deep, throaty sound. "I happen to be the proprietress of the finest salon in town, Lacey's." Her chin lifted as she studied Billie's hair. "You should visit tomorrow. My girls will have you feeling like your old city-girl self in no time."

Sounded heavenly. "How did you know I was from the city?"

The woman raised her eyebrows. "You have an air about you. More refined than most of these young things here. They are more used to riding bareback than sidesaddle. You could teach them a thing or two."

Not about riding horses. Billie much preferred riding behind the horses while seated on a Landau or even a hansom cab. She'd never been on a bus, not even for a pleasure ride with her friends.

"Staying in town long?"

Billie started to shrug but stopped herself. Girls in her circles weren't to shrug. *Use your words.* "Yes, ma'am. A little longer."

"A troupe from San Diego is performing at the Opera House tomorrow night. They're supposed to be quite good. I have two extra tickets. Perhaps you would like them? My treat."

Billie couldn't count on her uncle going with her. Cousin Lou? Not likely. Maybe Winn wouldn't mind taking her, seeing as though she was new and needed an escort.

"Thank you. Yes, I'd love them. That's very kind of you."

"Excellent." The woman rose gracefully, leaving behind the

citrus smell of bergamot and lavender. "They'll be waiting for you at my shop tomorrow."

"I'm sorry, Ma'am. We never officially introduced ourselves. I'm Wilhelmina Bergmann."

"They call me the Matron. So nice to make your acquaintance at last."

CHAPTER 13

*I*n the morning, Billie met Uncle Dale for breakfast. His eyes were bloodshot, and he held his hand to his pale forehead.

"Have any money left?" she asked. No sense coming at him sideways. It was obvious he'd had a rough night.

He looked at her through slits in his eyelids. "Surprisingly, I do. I just had to stay up a little late into the night to catch up."

Billie took a sip of tea. "You know, you'd be further ahead if you avoided the Faro table altogether."

He made a face, then went back to rubbing his temples. "This came from your mother this morning." He slid a telegram across the table.

B-
NEW SYMPTOM. BE CAREFUL WITH LOU.
-M

Billie chewed her lip, studying the cryptic message. "What do you think she means?"

Uncle Dale shrugged. "Her new symptom could be anything."

"I meant about the 'be careful' part." Billie was used to her mother getting new symptoms. Each one worse than the last. It was why her illness had stumped all the doctors.

"Don't know. At least she didn't say to be careful with me." He laughed.

Billie frowned. *What was mother warning her about?* "And the cash?"

Uncle Dale looked over the rim of his coffee mug. "She doesn't mention money."

She lifted an eyebrow. "I know my mother. She always wires me money when I ask."

He surrendered an envelope.

Billie stood. "Thank you. Now, if you don't need me today, I've made a connection of my own. I've been invited to Lacey's Beauty Salon to have my hair done."

"Isn't that the place run by the Matron?"

She pushed in her chair. "I'm shocked that you've paid attention to the women's places in this town."

"I pay attention to everything."

"I met the Matron herself, last night. She was quite welcoming to me. A nice change from some of the other folks around here." However, Billie didn't want to appear too eager to ingratiate herself. She knew what a careful dance it was to enter certain circles of society.

Too bad Matron wasn't her cousin. They had a lot more in common than she and Lou did.

In fact, Billie suspected that if Matron had the mirror, it would be prominently displayed, not hidden in the depths of a mine. Billie would feel more comfortable asking about such a mirror since Matron seemed to immediately understand her.

Uncle Dale downed the rest of his coffee. "Matron is quite the entrepreneur. She also runs the Poisoned Apple Saloon where I ended up last night. Couldn't get anything out of those gamblers, but that woman, she seems to know what's what in this town.

Wouldn't be surprised if she becomes the most prominent woman in Bisbee one day. Good for you getting to know her." He winked. "Proud of you."

Billie was taken aback. A high-society woman who also owned a saloon? She chewed her lip. Was that possible? The very idea went against her upbringing. Men were allowed to own any business they wished, but women were to hold respectable properties. Perhaps her first impressions of Matron were wrong.

Uncle looked up, squinting against the daylight streaming through the window. "Thought you were leaving."

Billie blinked. "Right. I was. See you later."

Maybe she shouldn't take Matron up on her offer, seeing as though there was more to the woman than she realized. But on the other hand, she and her uncle wouldn't be staying in town for long. If anything at the beauty salon looked untoward, she'd leave right away.

Because, what she needed today was to reconnect to her old life. She needed a little pampering and relaxation. Having a decent bed to sleep in last night reminded her of the good life she was used to.

As long as she kept an eye on Uncle and caught up with his doings in the evening, she should be able to keep up with his plans. It wasn't like he could smuggle a wall mirror out of town without her knowing. Once found, he would never let it out of his keeping.

She ambled down the street looking for Lacey's Beauty Salon. Big wooden signs hung out over the streets vying for attention. With the electric light poles and wires crisscrossing everywhere, the streets were somewhat claustrophobia-inducing, though she'd take them any day over a dark mine.

Here it was. Lacey's Beauty Salon. Only one letter separated *saloon* from *salon*, but how very different businesses they were. The outside of the salon was modern-looking, with silk drapes framing the window and a display of wigs styled in the latest ways. It looked like a perfectly respectable establishment.

Before going inside, she looked in vain up the street for a familiar boy to be watching out for her, but there were only strangers amidst the bustle. Disappointed, she entered the salon and was hit by the inviting scent of expensive shampoos and other perfumes. Billie practically melted, leaving her cares at the door. *Oh, she had missed this.*

A young woman, only a few years older than Billie herself, broke away from a gathering of women at the hairstyling stations.

"You must be Miss Wilhelmina Bergmann." The beautician came forward with a wide smile. "Matron told us to expect you today. We're going to give you the royal treatment."

Billie eagerly followed the woman to a leather chair and sat. This was just the thing to keep her mind off her mother's unsettling telegram.

The young woman, Miss Brooks, kept up a steady stream of conversation while she applied a cooling concoction to Billie's face.

"This is a deep cleansing to take away the layers of dirt you've accumulated on your trip. Your face will positively radiate."

"Bless you. Is there any place on earth as dusty as Arizona Territory?"

Miss Brooks laughed. "I should hope not. What brings you to town?"

Billie relaxed further into the chair, thoroughly enjoying her treatment. "My uncle and I had something to deliver to my cousin."

"Must be something important to come all the way out here."

"Hmm," Billie was beginning to get sleepy with Miss Brooks massaging her temples. *So relaxing.*

"What was it?" Miss Brooks prodded. "That you brought out all this way?"

"A pocket watch."

"Wow, must be some watch. Wish someone would bring me a nice piece of jewelry. Although, I prefer the kinds with diamonds myself. This watch special or something?"

"Not that I can tell."

"Does it open or anything? Have a message engraved on it?"

Billie shrugged. "Just a watch."

The beautician stopped massaging. "So why are you still in town? Thinking of moving here?"

This lady sure asked a lot of questions. Billie opened her eyes. Miss Brooks stood over her with a steaming towel.

"Eyes closed. You're going to like this next part."

"No, we're not moving here. My uncle has business." Billie settled back, and when the hot towel was placed on her face she couldn't help but smile with pleasure. "So good," she said, barely moving her lips so as not to eat the towel.

"Told you. If I could afford it, I'd come in here every day for the works."

When the towel had cooled, Billie peeled it off and handed it back to Miss Brooks.

"Hair next?" Miss Brooks said, depositing the towel into a bin. "I'm thinking we curl it, pull it up with a poof in front, then drape it over your one shoulder, like this, in a twist. It would look amazing on you." She pulled out a newspaper clipping. "Here. I cut it out of the San Francisco paper. 'My Lady's winsome curl.' Ain't it dreamy? It's real classy, like you."

Miss Brooks set to work, deftly styling Billie's hair. As a final touch, she took out a jeweled comb and set it at Billie's crown. It would be a shame to put her hat back on and cover it up, but that summer sun was so bright.

"You are almost ready for your night out to the play," said Miss Brooks, taking one of Billie's hands in hers. "I'm rubbing beeswax into your nails. Not only are they going to shine after I buff them, but they'll smell so good you'll want to eat them—but don't."

They shared a laugh, and Billie began to relax again. The

young woman was just talkative and making conversation. No need to be paranoid.

"Who are you going to the play with? Your uncle?" She dusted some complexion powder on Billie's forehead. "We want you to radiate, not shine."

"My uncle's not much into dramas."

"Then who? You can't go alone."

Billie couldn't tell if Miss Brooks was hinting at an invite or not. "There's this boy I've seen around. Talks to me sometimes. I thought maybe he might like to go."

"Oh yeah? Who? Maybe I know him. Could tell you if he's worth your time."

Billie hesitated. What would it hurt? "Winn Harris."

"Winn! About this tall, blond, and handsome-as-the-day-is-long Winn?"

Billie's face warmed. "Maybe."

Miss Brooks glanced at the other beautician before shaking her head emphatically. "Girl, you know how to pick 'em. But I've never seen him around town at night. Several of the girls have tried to go out with him, but none have succeeded. He's one of the Finns and I hear the Finnish people are a bit standoffish. Good luck."

Billie's confidence faded. She'd thought with her freshly-styled look he'd be won over. Now she wasn't so sure. Maybe she shouldn't even ask him.

"Oh, honey, look at your sad face. Don't mind me. Maybe he's waiting for the right girl to come along. Could be you."

Miss Brooks led her to the front of the shop where Billie reached for her reticule. But Miss Brooks held up her hand.

"On the house. Matron was clear about that. And here are your tickets." She handed over a small envelope.

"Thank you. It was lovely." Billie left the salon feeling refreshed in body but rumpled in spirit. She was out of her element, was all. In Boston she knew what to wear, how to act.

There were rules to follow. Out West, it was different. And with her dad gone, she'd lost her mooring. Her emotions were getting the best of her. She needed a place to get out of the sun and collect her thoughts before deciding what to do about her extra ticket.

A small sign on the corner building across the street caught her eye. *Copper Queen Library*. Perfect. She'd see what the advice columns in the magazines had to say. If what Miss Brooks spoke about Winn Harris was true—and it did seem true to character that he'd snubbed all the girls in town—likely he would do the same to her.

What did Winn matter anyway? He was simply a distraction in an entirely boring town. It wasn't like they could have a future together. As soon as she and her uncle found the mirror, or Uncle Dale decided there was no further point looking for it, they'd be on the train to Boston without a glance back.

CHAPTER 14

*B*illie climbed the stairs of the corner library and skirted around the splotches of tobacco juice on the porch outside the entrance. The library was a bright, open room filled with glass-fronted bookshelves tucked into alcoves. The place was so new it didn't yet have that smell of old books.

Last night she'd heard two ladies in the parlor mention that James Douglas, representative from Phelps, Dodge & Company, had personally stocked the library to help raise the level of the town. There had been a bout of frontier justice carried out when a bar fight led to a lynching. Douglas thought literature was the answer and had sent a collection of hand-selected books. Those all burned in a fire, but, like most mining towns, the citizens were quick to rebuild. Billie was quite glad the town had matured before she arrived.

Her gaze swept the room, landing on a certain handsome-as-the-day-is-long boy choosing a book from the shelf, his hat tucked under his arm, his blond hair a bit mussed. As if feeling her gaze, his eyes met hers, and her face warmed.

She reacted despite the fact he couldn't have known she was talking about him at Lacey's, and he couldn't know her thoughts right now. Apparently, Winn did matter to her, which was why it bothered her so much that he wasn't behaving the way boys usually did around her. That is to say, most paid particular attention to her.

Out of politeness, nothing more, she went over to him, standing almost toe to toe so she could whisper. "Good morning, Mr. Harris. I'm surprised to see you here."

"Surprised that I read, Miss Bergmann?" He placed a finger in the book to mark his spot and closed it.

"Of course not. It's an expression."

What surprised her was that this was the first time she'd seen him without his hat on. His golden hair and blue eyes reminded her of the prairie grasses and clear blue sky she watched for miles on the train out west. Again, she mused how attractive he would look in a proper suit and tie, and with her on his arm, but she couldn't tell him what she was really thinking.

"I thought we'd already covered this. You assumed we were a backward town filled with uneducated, classless people, and," he indicated the library, "we're not."

His tone was teasing, but Billie couldn't help but correct him. "That's not what I said, and you know it."

"Did you know we're the largest city between St. Louis and San Francisco? Quite metropolitan if you ask me. And this here library is Arizona's first community library. Not bad for a town in the middle of nowhere, is it?"

"Okay, stop." She put her gloved hand on the top of his book. "I told you that wasn't what I was thinking."

He lifted her hand off the book, holding it for a heartbeat before releasing it. Her stomach fluttered at the touch and wondered if he felt anything.

"Then what is it you are thinking right now?"

With her adrenaline racing, she definitely couldn't tell him *that*. She clasped her hands together. "What are you reading?"

He held up the volume. "The latest." *The Hound of the*

Baskervilles: Another Adventure of Sherlock Holmes. "Just when we thought Holmes was dead, Conan Doyle writes another story for us."

Billie lifted her nose, and then, feeling self-conscious of her actions, proceeded to rub it. She wasn't hoity-toity, *she wasn't*. "Haven't read any them."

"You're joking. Everyone reads these."

"Not in Boston."

Billie didn't want him to know she preferred women's magazines over novels. Even if the Holmes adventures started out as serials, they weren't published in the ladies' magazines she read: *Godey's, Ladies Home Journal,* and *Harper's Bazaar.* Those were filled with housekeeping hints along with tales of great love and adventure. Not murder and mayhem. Tips she could use later in life, like how many tablecloths a well-stocked home should have.

"Well, watch out if someone steals your shoe."

Billie let out a burst of air. "What?"

"You might get haunted," he said in a mysterious voice and wiggling his free hand at her.

She stared, not knowing how to respond.

His countenance fell. "Never mind. You'd have to read the story."

"About haunted shoes? No, thanks."

"Look. It's not about haunted shoes, it's—" His voice trailed off as he appeared to notice her mock wide-eyed innocence. "You're teasing me."

She laughed and finally got an honest grin out of him. For her being the proper one, he was sure uptight most of the time.

"Before I met you I used think my powers of perception were pretty good," Winn said. "I once considered becoming a lawyer and used Holmes here to practice making observations."

"Really?" she splayed her hands out, inviting his comments about her.

He hesitated before crossing his arms. "All right. Mr. Holmes would say that by the way you are eyeing me sideways, there is something about me that you don't approve of, my worn clothes, perhaps. All that fluffy black lace on your dress indicates you are used to the finest things in life, and maybe you've never actually conversed with someone below your station, but for some reason you find me irresistible to talk to." He winked cheekily. "How'd I do?"

"Fluffy lace? My station?" He might have hit a little too close to home. "I have high standards, mind you, but I don't look down on people. I never have."

He shrugged as if she had just proved his point, and then went to the counter with his book and a lunch pail.

While he checked out she waited, thinking about what he'd said.

It would be disingenuous to pretend she didn't come from money when she did, or to pretend that it wasn't just as obvious that Winn didn't come from money. But that didn't mean in this out of the way place that they couldn't be friends. He was the only one in town who had made an effort with her—even if he was trying to get her to leave.

When he made for the exit, she followed him.

"In case you didn't notice," she said, "I'm wearing black crepe as a sign I'm in mourning. There is nothing frivolous about my clothing."

Although, she didn't mention that she had picked out the shirtwaist with the largest puffed sleeves and had asked the dressmaker to add one more layer of lace since she had found the original to be lacking. One could mourn and look good at the same time.

He didn't say anything but went through the door, and she followed—again—despite her pact with Holly, Suzanne, and Jane to never chase after a boy. She was alone in town and wanted to see a play. She couldn't go by herself.

"I have two tickets to the Opera House tonight, and it would be a shame to go alone."

She paused appropriately, giving him time to ask her out.

"I appreciate you trying to fit in, but this town isn't your kind of town. You really should go back to Boston."

"Oh really? Well, you know what? You didn't give me the opportunity to give you my own Sherlock Holmes' observations."

He kept walking down the street but raised his arms in a show of resignation. His lunch pail banged against his forearm.

She took his action as an invitation. "I've seen you skulk around town, so therefore, you are probably up to no good. You, you—" Billie hesitated when he looked at her. The eyes. His beautiful blue eyes were so sad, like a lost puppy. She'd never seen such a forlorn look, and she wondered if he even knew what signals he was sending out.

"What? Don't hold back on me now." He'd come to a bench and sat down, pulling out a bag of almonds from his pail.

"You're sad. In trouble." Billie squared her shoulders. "Maybe I can help you."

He let inhaled sharply. "I'm not a charity case."

She examined his so-called lunch. Almonds and a chunk of rye bread. "Never said you were, I just offered to help. Here's another observation. You're too prideful to accept help. You might think I'm privileged, but you're too prideful for your own good."

He scowled. "I'd accept help if it would do any good." He cracked an almond open with a small nutcracker.

"I'm very good at helping my friends. There was this one time when Suzanne was supposed to—"

"We're not friends."

"Only because you're so rude. If you don't want to be friends, why do you follow me around town?"

The irony of that statement wasn't lost on her.

"You don't know what you don't know."

"Enlighten me."

"Forget it."

"Try me."

"No one can help me." He stared straight at her, and her heart skipped a beat. She heard the words, but the meaning she understood was indeed a cry for help. How could he feel so helpless when he was still young, with his whole life in front of him?

She tipped her head. "Now there's a challenge I'd like to take." What help could she possibly offer him? She didn't know enough about him to know what his problems were. "I've got a lot of time on my hands until we go back to Boston. What could I do? Babysit a sibling so you have more time to get work? Set you up on a date with a girl you have a crush on?" She hoped it wasn't that last one, but she wanted to know if he had his sights set on a local girl already.

"Really? Do you really want to help?" His voice was stiff, filled with bitterness. "Could you sneak into the Poisoned Apple Saloon one night, and spy on the Matron? Tell me how she spends her nights?"

He threw the challenge down like he didn't think she would do it.

And he was right. She wasn't the kind of girl to go into a saloon in a mining town and spy on its owner. Especially alone and at night.

"W-why would you want to spy on her?" she stuttered. She pictured the elegant woman she had met and wondered what connection she had to Winn. He didn't know that she'd already met the Matron or was holding tickets from her in her reticule. She might be able to help him without going into the Poisoned Apple.

He laughed, a cold sound. "Never mind. Stupid idea." He offered her the bag of almonds. "Want one?"

She plunked beside him on the bench and accepted the nutcracker, wondering where she would put the shells. She'd never eaten outside like this before except for company and church picnics where things were set up properly. It made her feel like a young girl again. Unburdened. It made her want to help this boy.

"The Matron also owns Lacey's Beauty Salon. Maybe I can get information there. What do you need?"

"I'm sorry. I shouldn't have said anything. It's too dangerous. Stay away from her."

"Too late." Billie patted her hair. "I'm already a client."

"Let me guess. She found you first?"

What did it matter who found who first? Billie refused to confirm his suspicions, and instead pulled out another almond. When she cracked it open, she found it had a double meat. Grinning, she passed one to Winn. "Will you eat a philopena with me?"

He accepted. "Where I come from we call this an almond." He popped it in his mouth.

She laughed. "Sharing a philopena is a game of wits. A game that started in Germany, called *viel liebchen*. Since you've agreed, you are now bound. The next time we meet, whoever says "philopena" first, wins and gets to suggest a prize."

"Not much of a game of wits."

"You have to name your prize by way of a hint, not coming right out to ask what you want. You can be specific, by saying something like 'I prefer chocolate to candy.' Or more challenging by saying something such as 'I like things that are undervalued, overlooked, yet precious.'"

"Still not much of a game." He tossed his shells onto the dirt road.

"We could play as they do in Germany. They extend the play by trying to catch one another off guard...and it ends when one is tricked into accepting the gift. For example, if you invite me to get an ice cream with you, I'll refuse. If I ask you to the Opera House, you should refuse."

"I don't know. You wouldn't rather go back inside the library and play checkers?"

She looked up through her eyelashes. "I'm rather good at this game. Are you afraid you'll lose?"

"I'm rather good at games of chance myself."

"There is no chance involved in this game. It's skill and cunning. A test of our character and communication. We have to pay attention to each another and not be mindless in our interactions." Billie never could get Branson to play properly. He always let her win, but Billie had a feeling Winn would be a worthy opponent.

"Fine. Walk with me across the street, city girl?" He raised his eyebrows in challenge.

"Not on your life," she answered. She spun to go in the opposite direction, shooting a smile over her shoulder. "The game is afoot."

He grinned. "I thought you didn't read Sherlock Holmes."

CHAPTER 15

*U*ncle Dale caught up to Billie as she was about to re-enter the library. After talking with the enigmatic Winn, she really needed to search the advice columns. At home, she and Jane and Holly and Suzanne would have taken apart the conversation piece by piece, look by look. But out West she was on her own.

"There's my favorite niece."

Billie stopped with her hand on the door. "What is it you need?"

"A quick word." He led her to a quiet place on the street in full sun. "I want you to find out what Lou does with the watch. Does she keep it on her person? In a drawer? On the counter?"

Billie adjusted her hat to keep the sun off her face "I thought you wanted me to look for a mirror."

"Yes, but also the watch."

"Why not just ask to see her mine? Then you can see for yourself that it's just a mine like every other mine out there."

"You really think she'd lead me right to the mirror? If she doesn't know about its special qualities, maybe. But if she's hiding the mirror, she won't let me—us—near it. No, I need to go in by myself. If she suspects what we're looking for, she'll be gone faster than Jesse James can hop a train."

Would she? It was hard to know. As it stood right now, Lou claimed to know nothing about the mirror.

"Seems simpler just to ask her."

Uncle Dale took out a kerchief and wiped his brow. "We could. And she could leave with it. Can we risk that? Can your mother? This mirror is her last hope."

Billie groaned. Her uncle was so good at making her doubt motives. They didn't know Lou well enough yet to know how she would act.

Uncle raised his eyebrows questioningly.

"What? What is this look you're giving me?" Billie asked.

"We could save a whole lot of time and effort if you help me sneak into Lou's mine while she's gone. That way we can get an idea of what we're up against. She might not even know what she's sitting on. We could relieve her of such a weighty responsibility."

"Steal it from her?" Billie couldn't believe what her uncle was suggesting. "We can't do that. It's not honest." She thought back to walking in on her uncle that first day at Lou's when he had her tools spread out on the floor. He probably would have broken in right then if Billie hadn't been outside. She had to put a stop to this before it got out of hand.

"I've seen the mine," she said, "It's just a mine. There's no mirror hidden in there." She pressed down the memories of crawling through those dark, narrow tunnels. She shuddered.

Uncle's face registered shock. And something else. Admiration?

"When was this?" he asked.

Billie ignored the question. She'd held on to the secret for too long. "It's a small operation. She works the mine herself and makes enough to support her modest needs. As far as why she wants to keep the claim, it's filled with this beautiful turquoise that even Copper Queen Consolidated views as worthless. They toss theirs in with the slag."

"That's because it is worthless. What matters is the copper and the small amounts of gold and silver." He shook his head in disbelief. "See? She has no idea the value of her mine. If I were her, I'd sell it to Queen Consolidated and be out of here. But no, she likes her trinkets." He pinched his fingers together as if holding up a piece of imaginary jewelry.

Billie decided not to tell him anything more about the beautiful cave. He might appreciate its beauty for a moment, but not if it stood in the way of mining out the minerals.

When Billie didn't answer, he plowed on. "I'm going to get in there one way or another. I'd rather have your help, so no one gets hurt."

"You mean caught." Billie frowned. "You wouldn't physically hurt her, would you?"

"No. How could you think that?"

Billie raised her hands, palms up toward her uncle. How could she *not* think it?

"I meant hurt feelings," he said. "You know how family feuds can get started over the smallest misunderstandings. I'd rather keep this business with the mirror quiet so it doesn't spread any further than this out-of-the-way place."

It was one thing to ask Lou to sell, but quite another to sneak around her to get what they wanted. The plan didn't sit right with her.

"Lou doesn't know what's best for her," said Uncle Dale. "In the end, we can help her. You know that's true. What I need you to do is keep Lou busy."

"How?" Billie crossed her arms. She did want to help Lou out of that strange shack that made ghost sounds when the wind blew. And definitely, for sure, no one should live with an outhouse in this day and age.

"Buy her supper at the hotel. She seemed to enjoy her lunch

out. Get her used to decent meals and comfortable chairs, and maybe she'll agree to sell her place so she can get out of that falling-down shack."

"Oh, I've got something better than dinner," Billie said, thinking about the tickets. "But what are you going to do while I'm showing my cousin the finer things in life?"

"Poke around." He held up his hands. "That's it. See what she's got back in there. Look for a vault, or a dusty mirror covered in cobwebs. Wouldn't that be a find if I struck gold the first time in?"

"And if you find nothing, then would you be satisfied and we could leave?"

Her uncle was going to press on until he exhausted all possibilities, so if she helped hurry things along, it might actually be better for everyone.

"Sure, sure, but the only place it could be is back there. And when I find it, I'll polish it up like Aladdin's lamp and make a wish."

"Do you really think that's how the mirror works?" Billie said. There were so many things she'd wish for. One in particular. "You think we can wish for things like medicine for Mom?"

"The evil queen loved that mirror for a reason. Until we find it, it's all speculation, but I doubt that its only use is to tell who is the fairest in the land. What good would a mirror like that be?"

Uncle Dale had a point. The queen could look into any mirror to see how beautiful she was. A magic mirror that only pointed out beauty would either fuel jealousy or feed the ego, since only one person could be the fairest of all. Who'd want a mirror like that?

Billie had enough problems comparing herself to her friends. Holly had the beautiful shiny hair that poofed out brilliantly in the Gibson girl way. Jane's eyes were large and fawn-like; she looked as if she were wearing makeup from the moment she woke, but she wasn't. And Suzanne had the shapely figure that drew the boys' attention like no other.

Imagine a mirror that told you all the critical things you already knew about your appearance. Or, worse, pointed out what you had missed. A mirror like that should be destroyed because every day you would be held up to a standard you couldn't achieve.

"I still think the easiest way is to just ask her outright," Billie said. "If she denies it, I can tell her I don't believe she doesn't know anything about the mirror and ask her to show it to me."

Uncle's eyes about popped out of his head. "No, no. Don't even joke about playin' our best card. Tread delicately, like your expensive finishing school taught you. This has been a carefully guarded secret for years. There's no telling how many people have lost their lives by either protecting it or trying to get to it. Play the fool until you have reason to act differently."

Billie nodded. She'd continue to fool everyone around her until she figured who was after what and *why*.

CHAPTER 16

*B*illie was used to playing her role in society and with her friends. As the daughter of Chester Bergmann, mining magnate, she knew her part.

A Bergmann knew how to dress, what to say, and who to say it to. A Bergmann never rushed but maintained an air of confidence at all times. A Bergmann was a perfect example of a young lady.

Even her closest friends were fooled.

Billie knew what a Bergmann was all about, but she barely knew the first thing about who Wilhelmina was. She'd always felt the disconnect but brushed over it with all the parties and busyness at school. Being out West where no one had expectations of her, she didn't know quite how to act.

She paused on her trek up the mountain to Lou's shack to look down on the town of Bisbee.

Out here in this boomtown with its false fronts and barroom deals, not everything was as it seemed. The town gave her the freedom to experiment with being herself.

Winn gave her that freedom to be herself. He seemed to know exactly when she was about to act falsely, and he challenged her on it.

But now Uncle was asking her to play a role she wasn't sure she wanted to play. Or ought to play. They didn't know if the mirror was real, or if it was, that they could get the answers they needed to help Billie's mom. Still, if there was a chance, it was worth finding out.

A trickle of sweat dripped down her back. Ugh. The heat. Her shirtwaist and long skirt were not meant for this kind of activity. Her pretty, but cumbersome, outfit was meant to stroll down the boardwalk, sit in the parlor drinking tea, or attend a lecture. She glanced around to make sure she was alone before hefting her skirts up above her knees. Not exactly cool, but at least it allowed the air to circulate around her legs.

When Billie spotted the cabin, she saw Cousin Lou outside, sitting in the shade like she had been waiting for Billie to hoof it up the mountain.

"Let me guess. Your uncle sent you to find out about the watch."

Billie stopped and dropped her skirt back over her knees. "Nothing like that," she said. *It was much worse.*

"I've got an extra ticket to the play tonight and thought you might like to come. I'd rather not go by myself and seeing as you don't have a telephone up here, I had to walk all this way." Billie wiped the sweat off her brow, only slightly self-aware that the telephone comment was unnecessary. While the Copper Queen Hotel had plans to install a switchboard soon, her own home in Boston was not yet connected.

"Wouldn't happen to have any iced tea, would you?" Billie asked.

"Got tea, but it ain't iced." Lou pointed into the shack.

"Right." Billie went in and poured herself a glass. The curtains were closed, making the room dark, but she still surreptitiously looked around for the watch and the mirror. Neither were lying out in the open.

"You know you can buy ice in town," Billie said, blinking

against the bright light outside. "They make it over in Benson, and the ice seller packs it on his mules. I'm sure he could bring it up here for you." She joined Lou in the shade, looking for ants and scorpions before sitting down.

"I know it. I am the one who lives here, remember?"

"A wonderful modern convenience." Billie drank deeply of the tepid tea, and then made a face. "Would change your life."

Lou burst out laughing. She slapped her knee. "I don't know what to make of you, girl. Can't believe we're related."

Billie straightened her back. "Distantly." She wasn't partial to the idea of being related to Lou, either.

"Don't go all high and mighty on me," Lou said. "I'm not making fun. Just pointing out the differences. World would be a boring place if we were all the same, now wouldn't it?"

"Does that mean you'll go to the Opera House with me?"

Lou looked out over the distant mountains. "Never been. Don't see why I should go now."

"That's the very reason you should go. Ever been to a play? At all?"

Lou shook her head.

"I won't take no for an answer." Even if Billie didn't have ulterior motives, she had to get Lou to the play just so she could experience it. "You must come. If you don't like it, you can say no out of a place of knowing you don't like it instead of being afraid to go."

"Who said I was afraid?"

Billie took in Lou's silly school-girl braids, her miner's uniform, and her isolated existence. She supposed that Lou was afraid of a lot of things. Not coyotes and scorpions, but people.

"I'm guessing you haven't tried too many new things since you were little. You've grown up in body, but you've not had enough experiences."

"Shows what you know—nothing." Lou stood and disappeared inside the cabin.

Billie followed her, banging into the edge of the table in the darkness. "You should let some light in here." She made a move to open the curtain hiding the pretty oval window near the bed.

"Stop. Leave it. I like it dark in here."

Billie turned, and then deposited her glass in the sink. "Thank you for your hospitality. Guess I'll go by myself. Or try to talk a random boy into going with me."

Lou's eyebrow arched. "Which random boy? Careful about the men out this way. They're not used to a pretty city girl like you."

Billie, sensing an opportunity, replied, "I'll find the wildest one I can, just to see if I can tame him with a little culture."

Lou pursed her lips. "You would, wouldn't you?"

"No chaperone. No one to tell me not to."

"Fine. I'll go this one time. Get you off my back. When do we have to leave?"

Billie grinned. "As soon as we get you ready." She was more thrilled with the victory of introducing Lou to some culture than with accomplishing her mission to clear out the cabin for Uncle to snoop. Besides, she had an idea. "Do you have anything..." she was going to say 'nice to wear' but feared that would come out wrong. "Fancier for a night in town?"

Lou examined her clothes. "What's wrong with this? If it's good enough for the daytime crowd, it's good enough for the evening folks. They're the same people."

Billie bit her lip instead of commenting. She was pretty sure the daytime crowd would not be offended if Cousin Lou wore a different look now and then. "Have you got a mirror?" she asked, innocently, though feeling anything but.

"Nope."

"Are you sure? Maybe one you've forgotten about? One tucked away somewhere for safe keeping?" She looked around, wondering where Lou could hide a mirror.

"No, I don't have need of a mirror," Lou said, more annoyance creeping into her voice.

Billie let it go. It was possible Lou didn't know about the mirror. That cousin she'd said helped with the claim might know more about it. Lou did say he came from Germany. What if he took the mirror with him when he left?

CHAPTER 17

*B*illie didn't know what to expect from a play being performed in an out-of-the-way mining town. In Boston, she was used to the best touring groups, and the local talent was equally as good. But Bisbee was a growing town, and a prosperous one at that.

A decent line had formed outside the Opera House. Billie scanned the crowd and approved of how nicely folks dressed up for the occasion. The ladies wore their silk evening gowns, or their finest pigeon blouses and flared skirts, while the men donned waistcoats and ties and their tallest bowler hats. Beside her, Lou fidgeted. She'd changed out of her dirty dungarees into the only skirt she owned. But despite Billie's best efforts, Lou still wore a plaid shirt.

After the fourth person walked by giving them a pointed look, Billie whispered, "Do people always stare at you?"

Lou frowned. "They're not staring because of my stature, if that's what you're thinking." She gripped her skirt. "I knew I shouldn't have let you talk me into wearing this getup. Now they'll all expect me to dress proper when I come to town. Never gonna happen. This was a one-time deal."

Billie turned away and smiled. *Not if she had anything to say about it.*

Soon, they entered the Opera House. It was pleasingly stylish with its velvet curtains draped across the stage and the filigrees decorating the pillars. Evidence of the copper mine was all around in the electric lights illuminating the stage and the seating area. This was a thoroughly modern venue.

An usher led them to their seats, center, near the orchestra pit. Again, Billie was impressed. Matron hadn't skimped on the seats. She glanced at Lou to gauge her reaction. Did she realize how good these seats were? It might spoil her for any other location in the theater if she ever came again.

Lou grunted as she settled in and examined the interior. "Not bad looking in here," she said.

Again, Billie hid her smile. She didn't want to scare Lou off with too much encouragement.

"Father always said a mining town in its third stage was the best town to live in. The initial tent city with zero sanitation was necessary, but to be avoided. The second stage, according to him, was the first wave of the boomtown with buildings slapped together, false fronts pretending the town was more advanced than it really was." Billie nodded toward the lit stage. "And once a town has decided to stick around, solid brick buildings, proper sanitation, and now, electric lights, well, that is the best time to move into town. Everything is new and shiny and offers the latest conveniences. We can all feel as rich as Rockefeller."

"Rockefeller. The wealthiest man alive, but also the most unhappy."

"Never met him. Do you find fault with everyone?"

Lou started to answer, then stopped. Instead, she grunted. Then the lights dimmed and the orchestra made its opening note.

A ghost appeared onstage. Billie gasped. She'd seen Shakespeare and Dickens and Schiller, and while all were impressive, none had conjured up a ghost.

"How do they do that?" she whispered.

"A trick. It's a reflection," Lou said.

Billie tilted her head. "A reflection on what? I don't see anything."

"That's the beauty of it. The glass is right in front of us so we don't see it for what it is. It's called Pepper's Ghost."

"How do you know about Pepper's Ghost?" she whispered.

"I read."

"Shhh!" someone said behind Billie.

She and Lou stopped talking, but Billie didn't stop trying to figure out how the trick worked. At intermission, when the lights went up, she studied the stage.

"Still don't see it," she said as she followed Lou out to the lobby.

"That's the point. They don't want you to see it. You're supposed to enjoy the show the way it was meant."

"You come to one show, and now you're the expert?" Billie was teasing, but Lou grew silent when the front doors opened and Matron entered, jewels at her throat glittering. Spotting a couple, Matron waved and joined them near the punch table.

Billie heard her ask about the first act.

"There's the lady who gave us the tickets," Billie whispered. "Do you know her?"

Lou stiffened. "If I had known the tickets came from her I never would have agreed." She pivoted dramatically—for Cousin Lou—and went back inside the theater. If it had been one of Billie's friends to make that move, Billie would have called it a deliberate snub, but this was cousin Lou, the one who didn't care one whit what anyone thought of her.

Billie stood, torn between going after Lou and approaching Matron to thank her for her kindness.

Matron made the decision for her when she caught Billie's eye and waved her over. The woman then excused herself from the couple she was talking to and met her halfway.

"How wonderful for you to make it tonight. You look positively radiant. What did you think of my beauty salon?"

Billie smiled, thinking back to the scalp massage and deliciously aromatic hair treatment Miss Brooks had given her, not to mention the facial and manicure. "I was treated like a princess."

Something flickered across Matron's face. Had she misspoken?

Whatever the fleeting emotion, it was quickly captured into a smile. "I'm pleased. My girls are the very best at bringing the beauty out in even the most common girl." Matron reached up and tucked a loose strand of Billie's hair into the curl cascading over her shoulder.

Billie tried to mask her own confusion. Was Matron implying she was common?

"You should bring your cousin with you next time. I see you managed to get her out of her dungarees. That's a victory."

"I'd be glad to try," Billie said. "You wouldn't know it, but she has the most beautiful cheek bones if she'd stop scowling long enough for anyone to notice." Billie's voice faded off. She shouldn't be talking badly about Lou. Lou lived up in the mountains in a mining shack all by herself. She didn't care about hair salons and theaters, but she came anyway so they could spend time together. Lou was making an effort. No ulterior motives, unlike herself.

The lights in the lobby flickered, indicating intermission was over.

"I should get back to her," Billie said, conscience pricked. "We're having a marvelous time. Thank you for the tickets."

Billie felt the angry heat coming off Lou from three rows back. She shuffled her way through the seats until she reached her cousin who was staring straight ahead, jaw set.

"How do you know her?" Lou's voice came out hard and clipped. She was angrier than the day they met.

Funny, it was the same question Billie wanted to ask her. Or rather, why the anger? Matron had been nothing but kind and generous. Inviting Billie to the salon, giving her tickets to the show. She was heaps more friendly than anyone else had been in this town.

Lou shifted in her seat to get a better angle to glare at her. "I'll ask again. How do you know her?"

Fortunately, the lights dimmed, saving Billie from having to continue the conversation. For the remainder of the show, Lou fidgeted. She twisted in her seat. She sighed. She took out her handkerchief and wrapped it around her thumb, unwrapped it, and wrapped it again. She was so distracting that Billie couldn't concentrate on the play and ended up with her own stomach tumbling in worry over what Lou was going to say once it was all over.

She didn't have long to wait. As soon as the curtain fell, Lou was up and moving. While the rest of the crowd clapped to bring the actors back out on stage, Lou squeezed between the people and the chairs.

"Excuse me, excuse me," repeated Billie as she trailed after her cousin.

Hopefully, Uncle Dale was finished with his sleuthing because Lou was going to make it home in record time. Once they were outside the theater, Billie had to jog to catch up. Her cousin's hands were clenched at her side as she marched down the boardwalk with fast, sharp, clipped steps.

"What's wrong?" Billie asked. "I thought we were having a nice time."

"Girl, what is the weather like where you live?"

Billie blinked. "What do you mean?"

"Your head is stuck in the clouds. Come on back down to earth and pay attention to what's going on around you. You lack street smarts kid, and that *woman* back there will be the end of you if you let her get close."

Billie's temper kicked in. "You are prickly on purpose. You

think everyone laughs and talks about you because of the way you look. You're so busy judging them that you don't stop to think that you're the one doing the judging. Did it ever occur to you that you push people away? You live all by yourself, alone up on a mountain about as far away from town as you can get. You dress like a lumberjack and refuse to participate in town life. What are you afraid of?"

Lou paled and Billie gulped back the next words she was going to say. She'd said too much already. Lou pressed on ahead while Billie stopped in front of the library. Lou didn't turn around once.

The rage drained from Billie's mind, being replaced with regret. She didn't mean to hurt Lou. If the woman wanted to live by herself, why did it matter? If Billie was sensing any underlying loneliness, well that was Lou's business.

Billie turned to go back to the hotel when she saw Matron standing outside the theater, watching, an indecipherable look on her face.

CHAPTER 18

*I*n the morning, Billie couldn't wait to talk to Uncle Dale, but he was nowhere to be found. She concluded that he was either in his room, sleeping off a long night, or still at the Faro tables. With the mine open twenty-four hours, most of the town seemed to be open twenty-four hours as well. A fellow could win and lose his fortune several times over in one night.

Wonder if he found the mirror? Or if Lou caught him.

And more importantly, how was Lou's mood today?

Billie could go up the mountain and talk about what happened at the play last night, but instead, she spent the morning puttering about town, avoiding confrontation. Or at least she tried to.

Walking outside the drug store, Billie nodded hello at a woman, and the woman looked away, pressing up close to the wall as she passed. Farther down, another woman darted across the road when Billie came near.

What is going on?

Eventually, she wandered over to the bench where Winn took his lunch, hoping he'd walk past on his way through town. He might know of Lou's mood if he'd seen her that morning. There was no way for Billie to make it look like she wasn't waiting for him, so she didn't try, constantly looking up the mountain.

A cactus wren fluttered down to the dirt at the side of the street, digging about for seeds and insects. It was an industrious little thing, turning over leaves and poking the ground. Winn was late. If he were even going to walk by at all.

When a shadow fell over the bird, it took flight.

Billie looked up to see Winn.

"Philopena!" they both said at the same time. *Drat.*

Their smiles mirrored each another, and Billie was thrilled he was playing the game. It meant a certain level of interest, despite his odd insistence that she and her uncle would be better off leaving town.

"What do you do when there is a tie?" Winn asked.

Billie adjusted her hat so she could see Winn better. "Play the longer game. See whose wits outlast the other's."

"Easy. It's going to be me. I don't give up." He continued his walk through town.

Billie hopped off the bench and kept step with him. "But I am an expert at this game."

"Oh? Do you play it often in Boston?"

"Once or twice," she said, again thinking how deeply unsatisfying the game of wits had been with Branson. "It's not a game you can pick up any old time since you have to have the right circumstances. A double nut for starters."

"Speaking of right circumstances, has your uncle finished his business?"

"No." *Here we go again.* Just when she thought they'd been making progress.

"You should have gone when I told you to."

"Well, we're still here."

"And you made friends with the Matron."

"Acquaintances. Didn't you want me to find out what she did at night? Last night she attended the play at the Opera House."

He frowned. "I shouldn't have asked you. I was frustrated that day. You should stay away from her. Far away. Like Boston far away."

"It's hard to take you seriously if you won't tell me your reasons. If you dislike this town so much, why don't you go?"

By now they'd reached the corner where Winn always left her. That meant they were going to part ways on a sour note.

"You don't understand," he said. "*I* can't leave. *You* can. If I were you, I'd pack up and be gone before the sun goes down. The longer you're here the more you're at risk."

"At risk for what? This town doesn't seem lawless." It was a downright quiet town aside from the shouts of children playing a game of tag. "There's no smallpox epidemic here like back in Boston. What am I missing?"

"You wouldn't believe me if I told you, and your cousin would kill me if I did."

"Well I can't leave either. My uncle's not done with his dealings."

Winn held up his hands. "Your life. Your funeral."

Billie cocked her head. "Why do you talk like that? Better yet, why are you the only one who will talk to me? Some of the people here treat me like I'm diseased."

With the name Bergmann she was used to people going out of their way to be nice to her. It was an odd turnaround to have people scatter in her presence. Especially in a mining town. Even Winn had heard of her family name, so what was wrong with everyone else?

"They know something strange is happening up the mountain. You gotta get out. Stay away from your Cousin Lou's place before you're caught up in it, too."

"Caught up in what? Do you owe someone money? Does Lou?" If that was the problem, she could help.

"What will it take to convince you? I don't want you to stay and get hurt."

"If it's that dangerous, maybe you should leave, too."

His face turned hard, and he looked away. "I can't leave this town. Ever. And if you stay, it might trap you, too."

"Now, that's not melodramatic." Billie raised her eyebrows to show she thought he was exaggerating.

"I don't know how to explain it, but I get to the outskirts of town and develop such a sharp pain in my head, I'm literally forced to turn back for fear my skull will split open."

She scoffed. "That's the best you can do? If you're going to lie, at least tell me something plausible. I'm not an idiot."

He rubbed the back of his neck, watching the people walk around them, giving them both plenty of space.

Billie waited, wondering if he were coming up with a new lie, and if she should stay to listen to it.

Finally, he said, "In the spirit of the philopena, please don't take a walk with me." Before waiting for an answer, he shifted directions and hiked up a new street that led out of town and up the mountain.

Billie ran to catch up. "We're walking out? How far?" And all this to prove, what? She reached out to stop him. "I can't go without telling my uncle."

"We'll be back. Soon as I prove to you I'm not lying."

"Anyone can fake a headache. I do it all the time when I want to get out of gym class at school." She slapped her hand over her mouth. She'd never told anyone that before. She fought hard to keep her image just so.

"We don't have to do this," she continued. "I get it. You don't want to leave town, but you want me to." She stopped walking. "I won't bother you again. As soon as my uncle is done with his business we are on that train."

He turned around, his expression not what she expected. Instead of a smirk of victory, or an open look of relief, he looked mad.

He marched over to her and grabbed her by the hand. His grip was strong and his callouses rubbed against her soft skin. When he didn't let go, her stomach flip-flopped. His touch wasn't a fleeting moment like she'd shared with Branson. This was...this was...What? Conviction. He felt so strongly about convincing her he was telling the truth. Maybe he was. He really wanted her to believe in him.

"I don't have to prove anything to you, but if that's what it takes to get you to leave this place, I'll do it," Winn said.

Is he telling the truth? Is there something wrong with this town?

He kept a good pace, and Billie surprised herself that she was able to keep up despite the steep slope. If nothing else, she was becoming stronger out West. There was so much hiking.

They climbed one peak, turned, and climbed the next. Billie's lungs began to protest, but she kept pace because she didn't want him to stop holding her hand. With his preoccupation, she figured he had forgotten he was still holding on to her.

She tried to hide her labored breathing, noting that Winn was as silent as the geckos scurrying off the path. But he must have noticed her struggles, because he slowed down.

"How far do we have to go?" Billie asked. You could keep walking and walking and find yourself in Mexico.

He jerked his chin to the summit. "Right about there."

Billie scanned the red-rock mountain. Like the other hills, the brush had been cleared to feed the furnace in the smelter and was only now starting to come back as stubby bushes of creosote along with a few sycamore trees.

"I can get to the top, look out over freedom, but that's it." His voice grew quiet. "I come here a lot." He was still holding her hand, as though drawing on her for support.

If he was trying to convince her to leave, he was accomplishing the exact opposite. The feel of her hand in his was too comforting a sensation for her to give up anytime soon. She had to help him, whatever his problem was.

There had been nothing she could do for her mom or her dad,

but maybe she could help this boy who had captured her interest from the moment she'd stepped into town.

She silently studied his profile, noting his furrowed brow and a trickle of sweat sliding down his neck. His tanned face took on an ashen look that scared her.

"How do you feel right now?" she said.

"I'm feeling the tremors. It's a warning to let me know I'm getting near the edge."

Billie took check of her own reactions. She felt completely normal for hiking up a mountain in her still-unbroken boots. Winded and sweaty, but not stressed the way Winn was beginning to look. They were almost at the summit now, and he was visibly shaking.

"It's an oval, far as I can tell," he said with a slight wheeze. "I can walk this edge all around town, but no farther." He bent over as if catching his breath.

"The town is the center?" That's why he was warning her there was something wrong with the town.

He cleared his throat. "Uh. No. Your cousin's place is."

Billie gasped as a chill ran down her back. She remembered the feeling that first night she stayed at Lou's place. Like she was being watched. It wasn't the town that was off, it was Lou's shack. What if Lou wasn't what she seemed?

"Why do you think Lou's place is the epicenter?" She tried to keep her voice light, but it came out squeaky. The conversation was getting weirder by the minute, but as strange as it was, she believed Winn—about *something*. It was hard to tell exactly what was going on. He couldn't fake the reaction his body was having. Maybe he had hay fever? Severe hay fever.

"I've said too much already. I can't tell you anything more about Lou's place. Just know that this is real, and you need to leave while you still can."

Looking down on the town revealed nothing unusual. It looked like all the other mining towns Billie had seen. A mix of shacks and false front buildings and brick structures. Ramshackle and fancy all at the same time. Beyond the town, smoke and steam from the smelter rose steadily from the smokestacks. It was quite serene and so opposite to the anguish being played out on the mountaintop.

Winn turned and faced the other way. "I wish I could go out there."

Undulating hills stretched on as far as she could see. No signs of civilization save a miner's shack or two. "My uncle made me trek—" She happened to look at Winn and saw the strain on his face.

"How much pain are you in?"

"I can handle it. It reminds me of my limits." He dropped her hand. "Watch this." He took not five paces down the side of the hill before he collapsed.

CHAPTER 19

*W*inn dropped like a marionette whose strings had been cut.

Billie's heart plummeted, and she scrambled down beside him. Dirt and small rocks slid down with her.

"Winn!"

She put her cheek to his lips and felt his warm breath. *Praise be*. He was still breathing but was out cold. She cradled his head in her lap, smoothing the hair back from his forehead.

"Oh, Winn. I'm so sorry." When she pulled her hand away, there was a streak of blood from where he must have hit a sharp rock.

"Come back to me." She patted his cheeks, trying in vain to wake him.

Now what?

She looked helplessly around at the hardscrabble landscape before setting her resolve. If he can't be this far from the center, whatever that meant, then she'd have to drag him back past the invisible line.

His long blond eyelashes rested sweetly against the top of his cheeks. The tremors had stopped, and he looked pain-free. A sleeping boy whom she would have to manhandle up and over the mountain.

At least he was out and wouldn't be able to make fun of her attempts to move him. She summed up his body, taking special notice of his broad shoulders and hoped she'd be able to lift him. There was no advice for how to move a comatose boy in *Ladies' Home Journal*.

She adjusted position, taking care to keep his head supported. "Okay, we'll just use my skirt as a stretcher to pull you back." She patted his head. "I'm so glad you can't see this."

She reached forward and put her hands under his arms, and then dragged him toward her, digging her heels into the ground for leverage. He was heavier than she thought, and the progress was slow. She wasn't sure how far to bring him, so she kept inching back until he began to moan.

Moaning was a good sign. It meant he wasn't dead.

Billie kept his head cradled as she hovered over him. Some of her hair had fallen out of her bun and now framed her face as she studied him upside down, waiting, waiting, waiting, for him to wake.

The sun was high in the sky now. People had to be missing him at work. Wouldn't they come looking for him? She realized she didn't know where he worked. He said odd jobs, but what did that mean?

Finally, he blinked, a dazed look in his eye. For a moment he just looked up at her and she at him.

"Winn. Thank God. What would have happened if you were alone?"

He shrugged. "I don't know."

She laughed, so glad he was conscious, and that she didn't have to drag him all the way back to town like this.

He shifted his torso but remained in her modified stretcher. "Someone has always found me and brought me back to town. I've woken up in some strange places."

He started to get up, and Billie pushed his shoulders back down. "Make sure you've recovered first."

"They think I'm a drinker, but I'm not. Even my dad doesn't trust me. He tells me the water's the same on both sides of the boat."

"That's an odd expression to use in the desert."

"It's Finnish. He thinks I'm acting out because I'm not content with life here." He closed his eyes. "I don't have the best reputation in town."

"So I've heard." Lou certainly didn't have much good to say about him.

"Why didn't the rumors about me scare you away?"

"I, personally, haven't seen evidence of you being trouble. Except that you keep telling me to leave. That's not very nice." She leaned back on her hands.

He snorted. "It's the nicest thing I can do for you. At least promise me you'll stay away from Lou's place."

"She's my cousin. How can I stay away?"

"Lou's all right. It's her shack I want you to stay away from."

Even if strange things were going on at Lou's shack, that was the one thing she couldn't promise. Uncle Dale was convinced the mirror was hidden there and, given what Winn had told her about the place, Uncle might be right. *Something* unusual was going on.

"If you want me to stay away, tell me why exactly." Winn, not Lou, might be the key to uncovering Lou's secrets.

"I'm afraid if you stay, you'll stay forever. You'll become like me. Not able to leave. Ever."

Billie scoffed. She'd always had the freedom to travel. London, Paris, Rome. She'd been all over Europe. As long as the Bergmann business continued to thrive, she'd continue to enjoy her lifestyle.

"Did you consider that you've got a bad allergy or something? So many odd plants out this way, what if all this is just your body getting overwhelmed with pollen. Have you been to see the doctor?" A medical reason made much more sense than what Winn was proposing.

"Pollen." He sat up and scooted off her skirt to sit beside her. "That's the best you've got to explain what happens to me?"

"It makes complete sense." Billie warmed to the idea, happy to have a logical explanation for what she just witnessed. The doctors had wondered if her mother's illness was caused by a reaction to her environment, but still Mother had refused to come out to California, saying she knew it wasn't that.

"Once you are removed from the source," Billie explained, "your body doesn't feel like it's in crisis mode, so it recovers. I'll prove it to you."

He laughed. "What are you going to do? Swing me over your shoulder and pack me a mile down the other side of the mountain? Your mysterious plant could be growing for miles."

It did sound ridiculous, the way he said it. Of course, that wasn't what she had in mind. When she traveled, she liked to do so in style.

"You want me to leave town? Then in the spirit of our philopena game, don't leave with me. Right now." She stood and brushed the dirt from her skirt. "I'll go grab my luggage, and we won't catch the train out of here."

He leaned back on his elbows. "You're serious? You'll leave if I *don't* go with you on the train?"

"Sure will." Though her definition of leaving included coming back. She'd made a deal with her uncle to help find the mirror. If it had the inscriptions on it like she hoped, there might be an ancient remedy to heal her mother.

A side trip with Winn didn't have to stand in the way of that. As soon as she proved to him he actually could leave, maybe he would. Maybe by the time she was ready to go back to Boston he would consider coming with her. He would be fun to introduce to her crowd.

He looked hungrily off in the distance. "Deal. Next train out leaves at six o'clock."

"Oh. So soon?"

"Look who can't leave town now." He scoffed and lay back, hands over his eyes. "I warned you, city girl."

Irked, Billie huffed. "I didn't say I wasn't leaving. I only commented on how soon the train was. We best not dawdle. Can you stand?"

Once Winn had recovered from his spell, it took them no time at all to hike down the mountain. In town, Billie would have to do a quick search for Uncle Dale. They hadn't spoken since before the play. She tried to part ways at Howell Avenue, but Winn wouldn't leave.

"I don't need anything." He stayed at her elbow as if ready to protect her from the town. He even tried to follow her into the lobby. Here, Billie put her foot down. She couldn't continue the charade if he didn't give her time alone.

"Wait out here. It wouldn't look proper."

"Of course."

She was testing him about leaving town, and he called her bluff. Which one of them would live to regret it? If he was telling the truth, he could be in some serious danger leaving town on the train. But if his fainting was caused by some medical mystery, Billie might be able to help him figure it out.

Uncle wasn't in any of the public places in the hotel, and he didn't answer her knock at his room. She'd have to leave a note and hope that was sufficient.

What to write? Uncle Dale would not be pleased if he thought she was taking a lover's day trip to the next town. But she couldn't tell him her true intentions, either.

She would be vague, a trick she'd learned from him, and let him come to his own conclusions.

Dear Uncle,

Running an errand. I'll see you tomorrow. You can buy me breakfast, and we can discuss what we've each found out.

-Wilhelmina

She collected her empty carpetbag and then met Winn outside. His back was to her, and for a quiet moment she studied him. Her heart thumped against her rib cage. She'd run down the stairs, but that wasn't what made her heart race. It was Winn waiting for her. Not meeting up by chance, but purposefully waiting.

"Ready?" she asked.

When he reached for her carpetbag, she hugged it close and shook her head. "I can carry my own."

She couldn't risk him finding out the suitcase was empty the same way she couldn't risk Uncle finding all her belongings missing from her room. Billie tried not to think how many lies were piling up. Her mother would be mortified at what she was doing. Her father? Disappointed. But neither were here now trying to figure out this mystery. Her only guidance was from Uncle Dale, and he wasn't the bastion of truth-telling either.

At the ticket counter, Billie stood in front of Winn. "I proposed this adventure, so I'm paying," she said. Mostly, she didn't want to embarrass Winn if he didn't have the money, but also, she wanted to pick the destination. She needed to make sure they could have a round trip back to town that night. "We'll go in small hops to see how you're doing."

When she reached for the tickets she knocked her reticule off the counter. It landed with a conspicuous thump and Winn was quick to pick it up.

"Wow, that's heavy. You keep rocks in there?"

Billie snatched it back from him. "I've got a few pennies in the bottom, not that it's any of your business." She hoped she wasn't blushing.

A stout miner behind them started laughing.

"She's collecting 'em for her weddin' shoes, jus' like my wee bride. She was German, same as you, eh? That way the union starts off on the right foot." He winked. "Catch the meaning?"

Billie nodded. *Yes, I'm saving pennies for my wedding day, not that I wanted him to know.* "Tradition," she said proudly.

"Look out, boy," he said, clapping Winn on the back. "Once they start saving up, you know you're in trouble."

Billie closed her eyes and breathed out slowly. In a town as diverse as this there had to be a friendly Irishman who had married a German woman. She nodded politely and walked away, refusing to look to see what Winn's reaction was.

CHAPTER 20

*B*illie bounced on the thinly padded seats in the passenger train. They would do for the short run they were making. Winn insisted she take the window seat, so she could see the cacti before she left for good.

Luggage stowed, tickets collected, they were ready. Winn hadn't backed down from his charade and neither had she. And now they were leaving town together. Billie paled. She hadn't thought of it in those terms. She barely knew the first thing about him. She did a quick safety check. Public place. Lots of witnesses. If she wasn't careful, her stubbornness would get her in trouble.

"Whatever happens to me," Winn said, "you keep going until you get home. Don't look back."

"What are you talking about? If you faint, I'll collect the doctor at the next town. You'll be fine in no time. Just because the doctor in Bisbee can't help, doesn't mean we can't find the answer."

He wiped his hands on his pants and shifted in his seat. He licked his lips. "I'm not meant to leave. I'm not sure what's going to happen."

"Nothing, silly. You'll be wondering why you didn't take the train earlier."

Winn continued to squirm.

"Relax. Let the engineer do his job."

He could not relax. He kept swiveling his head, studying the people in the car, the people outside.

"Did you need to ask permission to leave from someone?" Billie didn't know who he'd be beholden to, but he was more skittish than she was. She was the one who had genuine reason to worry if her Uncle ever saw her on this train.

"I just want it over with," he said running his hands down his thighs.

The engine cranked up, releasing a burst of steam. The whistle blew, and they jerked forward. Winn lay his head against the back of the seat and closed his eyes. He let out a deep breath.

"Take your mind off it," Billie said. "Tell me about your growing-up years."

He cracked an eye open. "You think that will take my mind off the feeling of a thousand needles poking into my skull?"

Billie smiled. "It might."

She tried to keep up her bravado, but he was scaring her. She recognized he was as stubborn as she was, but the look in his eyes was not stubbornness or bravery. It was fear. How much was she asking of him?

"I hope whatever happens scares you into leaving. I don't know what else to do," Winn said.

"You could tell me what you're not telling me."

"No. I can't." A bead of sweat formed on his forehead.

Billie began to regret making Winn do this. It was his choice, but if it weren't for her, he wouldn't be going through this ordeal for the second time today.

What was happening to him didn't make any sense, though. Just like her mother's illness. Maybe that's why she cared so much. If she couldn't help her mother, maybe she could help Winn.

It was slow going out of the valley, but then the train began to pick up speed. "That's better," Billie said with false cheer. "You know, my mother has a strange illness that the doctors haven't been able to identify. They've all but given up, saying it's her nerves, but none of us believe that. We're still trying to help her. Someone out there will know what's wrong with her. How are you —?" Billie looked over at him.

Winn had fainted.

Incredible. There went Billie's pollen theory. What if his body reacted to the minerals in town? She'd never heard of an illness like this, but it was a possibility. It made more sense than Lou's shack being the center of some...what? Curse?

She felt his forehead. It was cold and clammy, but he was still breathing. She took hold of his hand. It, too, was cold and clammy. She encased his hands in her own, trying to warm him up. "Hang in there. I'll get you to a doctor as soon as the train stops, and we'll solve this."

Bang!

The train shuddered. Metal screeched. And the passenger car lurched, sending everyone flying about the car. Screams mixed with sounds of bodies and luggage colliding. Billie hit her head on the seat in front of her and crumpled to the floor. Winn, in his relaxed state had flown even farther down the aisle.

Seconds after the train stopped moving, confused and bedraggled passengers picked themselves up.

"Everyone okay?" the conductor asked.

Folks stuck their heads out the windows trying to see what happened. Two men managed to wrestle the door open, and they left to investigate.

Meanwhile, Billie got help from an older gentleman to lift Winn back to the seat, where they let him sprawl out.

"Hit his head." The man pointed to a spot of fresh blood on Winn's forehead. *Not again.* She shouldn't have baited him into getting on the train.

Billie examined the bloody spot on Winn's forehead. The area round the cut was already starting to swell and turn red and purple. "Anyone a doctor?" she asked.

She wasn't the only one calling for a doctor. Several passengers held their hurt arms or legs and sported bleeding scratches.

Her own head was sore, and she suspected she'd have a bruise or two to show for the sudden stop.

The men who left hopped back on the train. "Everyone out. This train isn't going anywhere. You can stay here, or you can take the mules back. We're lucky a half-empty mule train was passing by, and we're not far from town."

"What happened?" someone asked.

"Hit a wild camel," the man said. He laughed. "That's right. I said camel. Darndest thing. Engineer said the army brought 'em out during the civil war but turned them loose to run wild."

The passengers looked dumbfounded at one another. Arizona Territory really was the wild west.

"Let the injured ride," said the older gentleman. "Starting with this feller here. He still hasn't woke up."

Winn. He wasn't leaving town today after all.

With help from the older gentleman and another man, they strapped Winn to a mule.

"A sturdy fellow, isn't he?" said the gentleman as he struggled under Winn's weight.

"Tell me about it," she said.

The rest of the passengers also decided to march back into town. Billie opted to leave her luggage behind. It was empty anyway. They could ship it back once they'd cleared the rails and fixed the front engine. A *camel*.

Some things you had to see with your own eyes.

She joined the curious at the front of the train as the sun was setting. She saw tawny legs sticking out from the train, lying on the side of the rails. And there it was. The camel that stopped a train.

Winn couldn't have planned that even if he could think it up.

The camel was thin, not too healthy looking even if it hadn't been hit by a train. The musky smell of camel and blood turned Billie's stomach, and she looked away. That was all she wanted to see. No need to stare at the thing.

It would be completely dark by the time they got back to town, so lanterns were being passed around. Billie took one and lit it. She followed the length of the train to the end, where everyone was beginning to set out.

She found the mule where she thought she'd left Winn. The mule with the black and white striped blanket and soft eyes. But Winn wasn't there. She scanned the bundles on the backs of the other mules in the dimming light, but no frustratingly stubborn and handsome boys were to be found.

"Excuse me," she said to the mule driver. "Did that boy wake up? Where is he?"

"What boy?" asked the driver. "There's no one here."

"The one who hit his head. We strapped him to that mule over there." Surely, he noticed them strapping Winn to his mule.

"Don't know what you're talking about, but we need to pull out now." He turned around. "Let's go, folks."

Billie lifted her lantern and searched the crowd. She found the older gentleman who had been helping her. "Sir, sir! Can you help me find my friend? The boy who hit his head."

He looked blank.

"You said he was sturdy?" she suggested.

"Sorry, miss. You were the one who hit your head and must be confused. Next time, you shouldn't travel alone. At your age, it's best to have a chaperone with you." He brushed passed her to join the mule train.

She stared aghast as everyone started to leave. They were a bedraggled lot, carrying various amounts of luggage, following the mule train driver.

"Winn!" she called. She spun around. "Winn!" Her cries grew

more frantic. How could he disappear like that? And why did no one else remember him?

The mule train was nearing the corner, the lights bobbing farther and farther away. What was she to do? Stay here and search for Winn by herself in the dark? Get back on the train and wait for help? Neither option was appealing. What if Winn was in trouble? He could have woken up, untied himself, and stumbled over the edge of the dark mountain.

The engineer and several others had stayed with the train, working on removing the camel. They had stronger lamps than she had.

"Sir, sir, could you shine your light down there for me? I'm looking for my friend."

"Everyone left," he said, pointing at the disappearing points of light. "Better catch up."

"Please, let me look, and then I'll join them."

He sighed, showing his annoyance, but he accommodated her. "Ain't no one down there, miss. I counted all the passengers myself. Everyone is accounted for. Now off you go. Quit playing games. I've got to deal with this camel. Next time don't travel alone."

He counted wrong, then. Someone is missing. Why wouldn't anyone listen to her?

"Could you keep an eye out anyway? I'm sure he's not with the group."

"Fine. You better run."

The gap between her and the rest of the passengers was increasing. If she didn't leave now, she'd be on her own going back to town.

I'm sorry, Winn.

Billie ran to catch up with the others. She tried to convince herself not to worry. Winn was familiar with the territory. He was tough. If she could survive a night out under the stars, so could he. How far could he wander away anyway? In the morning she'd make a report with the sheriff, and they could send a team out to find him.

Winn, where are you?

CHAPTER 21

*T*he trainload of passengers stumbled into town before midnight. Feeling like she'd abandoned Winn to the wild, Billie had a hard time sleeping. She tossed and turned, waking up several times with worry.

At first blush of the day, she raced through her morning routine and dashed out the door before she saw her uncle. How would she even begin to explain yesterday? Furtively escaping town by train only to hit a camel, and then one of the passengers mysteriously disappears with the sun. They'd haul her off to the mental hospital and never let her leave.

The sheriff was just coming out of his office with a cup of coffee when she arrived.

"Sir, I'd like to report a missing person."

"Who is missing?"

"His name is Winn Harris." She realized that she still didn't know where he lived. "He was on the train with me yesterday when it hit the camel. He didn't come back with the rest of us. He hit his head pretty hard and wandered off. I can show you—"

Someone cleared his throat, and the sheriff stepped back to allow him to pass.

"Wilhelmina." Winn tipped his hat as he walked past.

Billie stopped mid-sentence. She leaned around the sheriff to see Winn turn down the alley. What? How did—?

"That the Winn who's missing?" asked the sheriff. He cocked his head. "Listen, miss. I'd stay away from Winn Harris if I were you. He's trouble. A kid that young and already the most popular Faro dealer in town? Not anyone I'd want my daughter involved with."

The sheriff raised his coffee in dismissal.

Billie's mouth went dry as she stared at the entrance to the alley.

How could he? He was back in town looking perfectly fine. And a *Faro dealer*? She shook her head. "Thank you, sir."

Was it all a trick? Was he that mean, to hide on her and make her think he was in trouble?

Disappointed. Heartbroken. He didn't seem the type to toy with a girl like that. He was so concerned about those little boys gambling, yet he was gambling himself.

She blinked the moisture out of her eyes and took a deep breath before marching down the alley. All the worry that she'd done the wrong thing and left him hurt and alone, and it was business as usual for him. Not even a bruise on his forehead. She'd get her answers, then never speak to him again. The sheriff was right. Winn Harris *was* trouble.

And he knew it. He was waiting for her at the side of the sheriff's office, heel kicked back against the wall.

Before he could give her some false story about what happened, she lit into him. "How dare you! I was so worried. Did you have to muffle your mouth, so I wouldn't hear your laughter as you hid and I called and called your name? Was that gentleman who helped me in on it? How many people did you pull in on the joke? Everyone pretended you were never there. Was it a bet? Were you feeding your gambling habit?"

"Finished?" He raised his left eyebrow.

"I was worried about you! I was actually starting to believe your story that some weird force was at work, but now I know it's just you. Bored? Is that what you are? Go play with some other girl's affections."

He adjusted his stance, as if realizing the change in her. "I didn't lie to you," he said.

"Then explain yourself."

He looked away. "I can't."

"You mean you won't." She started to leave, and he reached for her arm. She brushed it off. "Stay away from me."

"It's not what you think," he said.

Fuming, she marched back to the hotel to meet Uncle Dale for breakfast. Winn wanted her gone? Fine. She'd find the mirror and then she and her uncle would leave this town. Good riddance.

"WHAT'S WRONG?" Uncle Dale asked.

Billie looked up from her oatmeal. "Nothing." She'd been humiliated by a con man and then let it slip she had feelings for him. How could she have let her guard down?

"You've been building oatmeal mountains and then crushing them back down again while I've eaten my entire breakfast." He indicated his empty plate, egg yolk in pale yellow stripes where he'd swiped his toast to mop it up. "You said in your note you were running an errand. Didn't pan out?"

She shrugged.

"Did you hear the train to Douglas hit a camel last night?"

Billie dropped her spoon and it clattered against the side of the bowl.

"Fine." He held up his hands in resignation. "No small talk. Let's review where we are with the *item*."

Billie didn't care that much about the item right now. Gamblers were liars. They said what you wanted to hear to keep you drawn in, but it was never the whole truth. It was only a game of manipulation. Winn had maneuvered his way into her affections, for what reason, she'd never know because he'd never get close to her again.

Snap. Snap. Uncle snapped his fingers in front of Billie's face. "Did you hear anything I just said?"

"Sorry, what?"

"I didn't find the item, but I did find another locked door. Why would she have a second locked door in her mine?"

"I don't know."

"Sure, you do. There's something back there she doesn't want anyone to find."

"So, what do you want me to do? Invite her to another play? That didn't end well." Billie pictured her cousin stalking angrily off into the night. Billie still wasn't sure what made her so mad. Who cared that Matron gave them the tickets? Billie had only accepted tickets to a play, not agreed to rob the bank. Whatever the reason, Lou was overreacting.

"You don't know the half of what went on that night. Lou twisted her ankle coming back from the play," Uncle Dale said.

Oh, no. Coals heaped upon Billie's head. Lou had been so mad when she walked away that night she probably wasn't paying attention to the trail. Something else that was Billie's fault.

"I found the old gal on my way back to town. She was doing her best to hobble home, but it was a struggle for her. I didn't want her to know I was out that way, but I couldn't not help her."

"I should hope not."

"So, I came to her rescue. Helped her get settled. I'm sure she's suspicious over what I was doing on that trail that time of night. Nothing I can do about that now. You would think she'd be grateful I came along when I did."

Billie nodded. Of course, Lou was grateful.

"But now there's trouble. Since she's injured, she's camped out in that shack practically lying in front of her mine. There's no way

I'll get into her mine that way again. So, change of plan. Can you hold out on Boston a little longer? This one might take a while. And some money."

"Mine or yours?" Always more money.

"The company's. I just need you on board in case someone at the office questions our purchase."

Now he had her full attention. "What are *we* buying?"

He chuckled. "The claims beside Cousin Lou's. Hers wasn't the only one up for abandonment."

"And why would we do this?"

"There is more than one way to skin a cat. If Lou won't let us have her mine in a way that benefits the both of us, we might have a legal way onto the property that won't require her permission."

"I don't like the sound of this. What are you going to do?" Billie ate a bite of oatmeal. She was going to need some fortification.

"Nothing illegal. Did some scouting when we were up there and found some weathered cerussite. It looks like any other red rock, but it's heavier. When you find it inside the mountain it's a whitish or gray color. Finding oxidized cerussite tells me there could be silver below. I have a hope that there's a small vein on that property that crosses over into hers."

Billie nodded slowly. "The Law of Apex."

Uncle did a double take. "Where did you learn that?"

"And the vein can't just cross over, it has to be closer to the surface than hers. It has to start on our property and then travel into hers. I read it in one of Lou's books. I'm sure she knows about it, too."

Finding a crossing vein by accident was one thing, but purposefully going out and finding a vein so you could blast into your neighbor's mine? That was underhanded. Was she falling under the wrong influences? First Uncle Dale and then Winn. Mother always warned her to be careful of the company she kept.

Uncle shrugged. "Then she won't make a fuss when I find it. By the way, I sent a telegram to your mother hinting at what we were looking for. I just wanted to give her some hope."

"You told her we were looking for a magic mirror?"

"Of course not. Someone will read the telegram to her so that would never do. The fewer people who know about the mirror the better. I spoke in generalities, calling her Snow White. She'll understand, but others would read it as a term of endearment."

"I've never heard you call her Snow White."

He took a swig of coffee. "Never have, but I'm referencing your family stories. She'll catch on."

Billie shook her head. Why in the world would anyone make the inference that they were looking for a magic mirror to help save them. No matter. They'd take care of it and then be home in time for the fall session where her life could go back to some semblance of normal. "What do you need me to do?"

"Keep Lou occupied as best as you can. If she's busy she won't pay as much attention to what I'm doing."

"How am I to keep her occupied if she's injured? She won't be able to walk to town."

"No, that's why I offered for you to stay with her as nurse. She loved the idea."

Billie choked down her oatmeal. She wasn't sure Lou loved anything. Except her mama's rug.

"I can't stay in that shack." Even if what Winn said wasn't true, the place still unnerved her.

"Only until I find the vein. Once my plan is in motion, she won't be able to stop it."

CHAPTER 22

"Lou?" Billie called out when she got close to the miner's shack so as not to startle her cousin.

Up here, Lou must not get many visitors. Billie looked around. Make that no visitors. She thought about what Winn said about this place. There had to be a plausible explanation as to why he thought this was the epicenter of all his troubles. Unless that was all part of his con.

She knocked.

"Go away," Lou said. Her voice sounded more gruff than usual. "I told that fool uncle of yours I didn't need any help."

"I brought food. Baked goods fresh from the City Bakery."

Silence.

Billie took that as an invitation. She put on a smile and entered the cabin. The room was dim with all the curtains pulled shut. Why did Lou insist on living in the dark? It was depressing.

"You look good," Billie said.

Lou was sitting up on the bed, which had been moved away from the wall and close to the kitchen and front door. Or, from Uncle's perspective, blocking the door to Lou's mine. Her foot was propped up on a stack of quilts Billie hadn't seen before, and a bed tray had materialized. None of those items had been in the shack when Billie had conducted her housekeeping search. She wondered if Lou kept a secret stash somewhere, or if Uncle had brought her those things in an attempt to sweeten her up.

"I see someone has been taking care of you," Billie said. She deposited the bag of groceries on the counter and began to unload them. She'd been overzealous in her purchases, making for a difficult climb. Canned goods seemed to work best out here where the produce was scarce and, if you could get it, expensive. But gracious, cans were heavy to pack up a hill.

"That uncle of yours! Never been so manhandled in my life." Lou adjusted herself, grimacing when her foot moved. "That man is slicker than a snake in a rainstorm."

Billie rushed over. "Let me help you."

Lou brushed her off. "I'm good. And grateful for the food, but there's no need to stick around feeling sorry for me. I'm sure you've got plenty to keep you busy in town."

Instead of leaving, Billie pulled up the rocking chair so she could sit and have a visit. "I'm here for a few days just to make sure you don't re-injure yourself. I can read to you if you'd like." Billie thumbed through the books and magazines on the side table. Another piece of furniture Billie hadn't noticed before.

"The Hound of the Baskervilles? I heard this one is good." She picked it up. "Oh, it's a library copy. Must be popular. I saw Wi— someone else reading a copy."

"Not my first choice, but go ahead, if you feel like you must entertain me."

"You're the one who took it out of the library, but if you want me to read something else, I can." She reluctantly put it down. It would be nice to know what Winn was reading. It would be like a peek inside his head. Reading the same words that he had read. Sharing the same thoughts. It might help her figure him out. Not that she cared anymore.

She sorted through the other books. "I could read this report on modern drilling methods." *It would put both of us to sleep*.

"Read the novel. I should learn what the young people are reading nowadays. But mind you, skedaddle back to town before it gets dark."

"Great." Billie cleared her throat and then began. "Chapter one. Mr. Sherlock Holmes." She brought the book closer to her eyes. "May I open the curtains? I need more light to read," Billie said.

"Hurry up and get yourself settled, girl. At this rate, my ankle will be healed by the time you get to the second chapter."

Billie flung open the kitchen curtains, taking a moment to get herself a glass of water. When she went to open the curtains covering the second window, Lou stopped her.

"Leave those. It'll be too bright."

Billie sat back down. "I suppose I have enough light to read by." She was disappointed as that window was so much prettier than the plain old square window, but Lou always kept it curtained. Why hide all the beauty in one's life?

She began to read. "Mr. Sherlock Holmes, who was usually very late in the mornings, save upon those not infrequent occasions when he was up all night, was seated at the breakfast table."

Billie read throughout the afternoon, stopping for meals and to help Lou get to the privy and back. She read until Lou had fallen asleep. That report on modern mining methods had done the trick. Someone should turn it into a bedtime story for children. They'd be asleep in seconds.

Billie tiptoed to the second window and opened the curtains. It was almost sunset. She had better make a quick trip to the privy herself before it was dark. *Lou won't be too upset to wake up to see me still at her place, will she?* Not if the smell of fresh biscuits did the waking.

As Billie ran around back she was reminded of her vow to never use this outhouse again. Yet, here she was, back in the dilapidated building wondering if it was going to fall down around her. Death in an outhouse. A terrible way to go. Uncle Dale owed her so much after this. He had better take her side on any future decision she wanted to make.

Hearing Lou call out, she yelled back. "I'll be right there." She quickly fussed with her clothing, not wanting to spend a second more than she needed to out there with the Sears catalog. The Sears catalog for crying out loud!

When she returned, Lou was sleeping, but a vase with a cluster of deep pink, bell-shaped flowers had been left by her bedside. Billie swung around the room. "Hello? Is someone here?" She popped outside and scanned the hills for movement, but it was too dark to see very far. "Hello? Thank you for the flowers."

Billie smiled. *Looks like Lou has a beau.* If he's come a-calling, maybe he would be sufficient distraction for Lou, and then Billie could move back into town.

As she lit the lantern she decided the man might need some courting tips, though. It seemed his flowers were snipped off of someone's shrubs. A fragrant rose or a bunch of carnations might be more appropriate.

Billie resumed her rocking, but she could no longer look out the window. Instead, the glass window reflected back a wide-eyed girl with uncharacteristic messy hair and dirt smudged on her cheek. If she weren't so frustrated with the recent turn of events, she would have laughed at herself.

Who was she becoming? What was she doing helping her uncle try to invade her cousin's small claim, all in the hopes that she was hiding a magic mirror from the Snow White fairy tale? Her rivals back home would have a grand time gossiping about how low Billie had gotten.

As Billie examined her reflection, the surface of the window shimmered. It so startled her that she froze, and the hair on the back of her neck rose. Another storm must be on its way, charging the air with electricity again. She stood and tried to peer out the window looking for lightning.

Seeing nothing, she pulled the curtains for the night and prayed the little shack would survive the coming storm.

$\mathcal{B}$illie stood over her makeshift bed with her hands on her hips. It wasn't the worst place she'd ever slept—sleeping outside took that prize.

A tingle of alarm skittered across her neck. She glanced over at the cot expecting to see Lou awake and ready to grouse about something, but her cousin was snoring softly, a sliver of moonlight falling on her face from a gap in the curtains.

That won't do. The last thing Billie needed was for Lou to wake at the crack of dawn with the sunlight in her eyes.

Billie moved to shut the gap and as she reached for the curtains, every nerve in her body started firing, warning her that something was wrong. Was the feeling for real, or was she simply overly sensitive because of Winn's warnings to stay away from the shack?

Heart racing, Billie fought against her instincts to freeze where she was standing, but when she reached out to close the curtains, she saw her faint reflection in the window with another face appearing ghostly with hers.

She snapped the curtains together, certain it had been a man outside.

She considered waking Lou, but what could her cousin do to help with a bad ankle? Billie's fright was silly. The man could simply be Lou's mysterious beau, the one who left the flowers. Maybe he had shied away earlier but worked up the courage to talk to her now.

Billie would have to tell him to come back later. She only opened the door wide enough to call out. "Lou's asleep. Come back tomorrow."

Silence.

She closed the door tight and noticed there was no lock. Adrenaline flowed through her veins. She opened the curtain again, and the man was still there. Not a man close to Lou's age, but a young man. It was too faint to fully make out his features.

She opened the door a crack again. "It's too late. Come back tomorrow."

When there was no answer, she opened the door wider and peered into the darkness. No one was there. She slammed the door tight and then checked the window, peeking in from the side of the curtain. What game was he playing? She didn't like it one bit.

Billie grabbed the lantern and a shovel before marching out of the house. She held the light high and swung it around the desolate mountainside.

"Either come out and talk to me or go away. It's rude to look into people's houses." Her anger at Winn fueled her boldness. People should treat each other better.

Cicadas chirped as if nothing was wrong. Chirp wasn't the right word. The high-pitched hissing noise was more like the thrumming of tinnitus in her ear than a cricket sound.

Billie tread carefully around the corner, ready to throw the lantern in the man's face and run for it. Her light illuminated the scrub brush and caught the fluffy white tail of a rabbit bounding away.

No one could be fast enough to hide when she came out and

then be standing at the window again when she looked. Was it a ghost? She didn't believe in ghosts.

She went back inside and threw open the curtains. She pressed her nose close to the glass trying to see out. As she did so, the image became clearer and her fear subsided, replaced with irritation.

"It's you." Billie said, finally recognizing the faint image of Winn. That boy was exasperating. "Quit playing around. You don't scare me."

Indeed, her heart stopped racing. She was so glad she didn't wake Lou.

First Winn tells her to leave, and then he shows up at Lou's acting all spooky to scare her away. He was too much. She stormed outside to give him a piece of her mind, but he wasn't there.

She called out into the dark hills. "No use hiding, Winn. I've already seen you."

I can't believe he's doing this. Now she was truly irritated.

"You're being immature," she said.

Back in the shack, she went to close the curtains, thinking Winn must have run off for good, but he still appeared faintly in the window. Her reflection merged with his, only his face was devoid of emotion. Not gloating like he had pulled a prank on her. Not frowning like he was trying to make her leave. Vacant like he was frozen in place.

She waved her hand in front of his face, and he didn't move. Not even a blink.

No.

No. No. No.

She took a step back and examined the oval window. Her reflection. Not in a mirror, but in a window.

Billie placed her palm on the surface, and her fingertips tingled. *It couldn't be*. All this time it was right here in the wall of Lou's shack. Not hidden away in the depths of her mine behind two locked doors. No wonder they missed it. It wasn't at all what they were expecting.

The magic mirror.

Billie felt sick to her stomach. Not Winn. He wouldn't do this to her.

With dry lips, she quoted:

> *"Mirror, mirror*
> *on the wall.*
> *Who's the fairest*
> *of them all?"*

Her palm burned, and she snatched it away, taking two steps back. The glass rippled around the outer edge like it was melting. Soon the entire surface swirled, twisting her reflection. A white mist spread around a silhouette, and when the mist dissipated Winn was there waiting for her.

He grimaced, looking like a schoolboy caught smoking behind the outhouse.

She stared.

He opened his mouth, then went back to his grimace.

"Who are you, really?" Her voice was cold, her breath shaking.

Nothing had prepared her for this. Even though Winn, himself, had been telling her for days to get out of town. Insisting that his problem was so great no one could help him.

He had been warning her to stay away from Lou's because he didn't want her to find him in the mirror. He didn't want her to discover his true identity.

Unless this was a reflection made to *look* like Winn. Get her to let her guard down. A trick.

"Who are you?" she repeated. "Tell me, or I'll—" she looked around for something heavy. She grabbed the kettle off the stove. "I'll break the glass."

"You know who I am." His voice was resigned.

"No. I know who you are pretending to be." She choked back a sob. Not Winn. Please not her Winn.

"Show me what you really look like." She held the kettle higher in warning. She was expecting a glowing green face or an old wrinkly witch in a black hat to be staring back at her from the magic mirror. Not the cute boy she'd been flirting with since she came to town.

"If breaking the glass would have broken the spell, I would have been out of here months ago," he said. "It's unbreakable."

Billie faltered, but maintained her aggressive stance. "Prove to me that you're really him."

He smiled sadly. "The first time I saw you was outside the assayer's office. You looked spittin' mad—kind of how you look now—and you caught me staring. The second time was in the restaurant, and the third, you chased me through town until you had me cornered." He took a deep breath. "And yesterday, I held your hand, tight, so you wouldn't let go." He lifted his palm to the glass. "I'm real."

Billie slowly lowered the kettle. It *was* him. "So, you lied to me in town, on the mountainside? What are you?"

He waved his hands in protest. "No, no. I'm just like you. Was just like you. I got myself trapped in here a few months ago."

This was too much to process. Winn was trapped in the magic mirror, which really wasn't a mirror at all.

"But I've seen you. Touched you. How can you also be in there?" She pointed to the window-mirror.

"I'm not always trapped in here. During the day I can leave and live my life as something close to normal. You've seen that. But at night? I'm locked away."

Billie shook her head. "This makes no sense." No story of Snow White had ever said the mirror was, in fact, a window. It was always a mirror.

Mirror, mirror.

"*You* think it doesn't make sense?" Winn said. "I'm the one stuck in here."

"How do we get you back out?" she said, looking for a way to open the window.

"We don't. I'm sorry. I tried to scare you off. I should have tried harder, but you didn't make it easy."

A loud snore broke the silence. Any other time it would have gotten a laugh, but Billie and Winn just stared at each other.

Billie pulled up the rocking chair. "You better start talking, and don't leave anything out."

CHAPTER 24

Before answering, Winn looked around the room. "Lou isn't awake, is she?"

"Sleeping, a bit fitfully, but she's out."

He lowered his voice. "I figured, otherwise this conversation would not be happening."

Winn strained to look over Billie's shoulder. "She's going to kill me now that you know, but it's not as if I told you. I tried to be as still as possible, despite how hard you were making it for me."

Well, that answered one thing. Lou wasn't the innocent cousin. She pretended the value in her claim was the turquoise, but really, it was the mirror.

He cracked a smile. "It was quite charming how you were going after the intruder. Exactly how were you going to use that shovel?"

Heat rose up her neck as she realized the implications. "You've been watching me."

"Hey. I wasn't trying to. You're the one who likes to open the curtains."

Billie covered her mouth with her hands. This wasn't

happening. She shook her head. "I don't believe this. That really is the magic mirror? The one from Snow White?"

He shrugged. "Apparently. I had no idea the thing was real. Instead of reading mysteries, turns out I should have been reading fairy tales."

Billie cocked her head. "Is that your book over there?" She pointed to the library book of Sherlock Holmes.

"Yeah, did you like the story?"

"That's beside the point." She waved her hands to indicate the mirror. "So, you aren't the original..."

"The original chump? No. I suspect he got out of here a long time ago. Back in the Snow White days, I bet. No, I'm the latest fool to stumble into here." He patted around the edges of the frame as if looking for a way out.

Billie stood and touched the glass again. "You're in there for real? Not a trick like what I saw at the theater? Because I've seen you outside."

"Yes. I'm telling you the truth. I've no clue how this all works. That's my problem. From roughly sundown to sunrise I inhabit this space. Otherwise, I'm free to roam about the country, as far as my invisible tether lets me. Go too far, and well, you've seen what happens. As soon as the last hint of sun crosses the horizon I'm sucked back to my nightly prison. At dawn I land on my backside inside the shack. Lou usually keeps the bed below the mirror so it's a softer landing."

Accusingly, Billie put her hands on her hips. "Why haven't I seen you fall out?"

He chuckled. "I presume you've been in the outhouse when it happens."

"I just. I can't." Billie held her hands out. She and her uncle wanted to find the mirror so they could find a way to cure her mom. Some medicine or concoction the mirror could give them. "I had all these expectations about what the mirror was or could be. But...it's you."

Winn frowned. "Hey, now. I'm not such a poor find, am I?"

"Sorry. I didn't mean it like that." She was having a hard time keeping her voice quiet. She could hear her own panic as she tried to adjust her expectations. Her hopes. Her disappointment. "Are you magical?" she asked.

He laughed. "If I were, do you think I'd be stuck in here? No, I was a normal guy, still am, except for the obvious."

"So, what is the point of this magic mirror?" Seemed it had no good use at all.

"Shh. Don't wake Lou. She won't like us talking, and she'll close the curtains again. It gets pretty boring in here."

Billie refused to be shushed now. "That morning when Lou kicked me out before sunrise. I thought you were following me, but you had just come out of the mirror?"

"Yeah, and your cousin threatened me within an inch of my life to stay away from you. I tried to stay away. Really, I did. But you were so cute and helpless." He cleared his throat. "Wonder what she's going to do now."

"You thought I was helpless?" *And cute. He also said cute.*

He raised his eyebrows. "You're not going to tell me that you've had everything under control since you walked into town, are you? Remember, I've been watching."

Billie closed her lips tight. Had she done anything embarrassing in this room? When you think you are alone, you can do some unguarded things. Oh, no. That first night with Boston on her mind, she had pretended to be at the fall formal with Branson asking her to dance.

"Yeah. I saw that." He was grinning. Grinning so wide his face looked like it would burst.

He couldn't have known what she was thinking, but he'd seen enough unguarded moments it didn't matter which unguarded moment he was referring to.

"You're horrible! I can't believe you would watch a girl

unawares like that. I should have you arrested." Billie forgot to keep her voice down.

Lou startled and rolled over.

They watched, waiting to see if she would wake.

He held up his hands. "Look. It's not like I purposely crept up to your window and spied on you."

He had a point. And she did close the curtain whenever she needed privacy, so he hadn't seen *too* much of her. But how did he end up in the mirror?

Lou took a deep breath.

"Did she trap you inside?" Billie asked, glancing at Lou.

Winn shook his head. "No. Lou put the mirror in the wall, not realizing what it was, and then she discovered me accidentally, much like you did. When she saw me, she knew exactly what the mirror was. Apparently, your family has stories?"

Billie nodded. Did they ever. Minus some important details.

"Then Lou made curtains. Said she didn't like the way I stared."

"Are you awake in the mirror? You did have a vacant stare until I said the poem."

"I'm aware of things, but I can't interact until you say the stupid rhyme. I'm probably supposed to answer the question."

Billie couldn't help herself. She quirked a smile. "So, who is the fairest in the land?" she crossed her arms, arching her eyebrows in a challenge. She was partly teasing, but also serious.

"I don't know who's the fairest of them all. Besides the fact I think it's a bad trick for a mirror to have, I think that part is broken—the original spell maybe, because it doesn't tell me anything. Besides, what do I know about ultimate beauty? I like what I like, that's all I know."

Was that a blush creeping up his neck? Did that mean he did know and didn't want to tell her? Or was he awkward about girls? She'd circle back to the question later. There were too many other things to learn right now.

"But if you really want my opinion," he said, "fairest isn't about looks, it's about character. Who is fair, and who's in it for themselves."

Billie was taken aback hearing this from the boy she thought was a con artist Faro dealer. He didn't know how close he'd come to touching a nerve with her when he mentioned fairness. She'd been struggling over what she and uncle were planning. Was it fair to take the mirror?

Maybe the mirror wasn't broken after all.

She'd let it go for now. Instead, she took to examining the glass. It appeared to be a normal window pane except for its unusual oval shape. Looking at it with this new perspective, it was obviously mirror-shaped. It could have remained hidden from her and Uncle for months.

"Why isn't this an actual mirror? You know, 'mirror, mirror'?"

"Not entirely sure about that either. It acts like a mirror at night when you can see your reflection. During the day, it's a window." He looked around the frame and reached up to touch something. His hands came away with what looked like crumbling pieces of wood. "The thing is falling apart inside. It's really old. I suspect it will eventually crumble into nothing, and if it happens while I'm in here, I'm trapped. Or dead. If it happens when I'm on the outside, maybe I'll get to live a normal life?" He shrugged. "There's no instruction book for this."

Billie squinted, trying to see past Winn. "What *is* in there?" All she could see was swirling mist behind him.

"Nothing. I can understand why my predecessor wanted out." He looked over his shoulder. Sometimes there's a light. And sometimes I can hear music."

"Odd. Is it a room? Do you hit a wall?

"I've never found a wall. I've walked for hours in one direction and it's all been the same."

"So, you have a floor."

He nodded. "Dirt. And a window." He chuckled.

Billie smiled back. At least he wasn't completely bitter about his circumstances. "Can you ask it for things? Like a cure for my mom?" She felt callous for asking, but if he could help her mother, they'd get something good out of a bad situation.

"I wish." He looked all around the frame. "No, I'm powerless, trapped in this strange prison."

"Can't you get out the way the original person did?"

"I suspect I'll need to find my own chump to trick into the mirror. Know of anyone?"

Billie took a step back, senses alert. "You're not thinking of me, are you?"

His eyes grew wide, "No. I would never. At least not yet."

"What do you mean, not yet?"

He held up his hands in a stop motion. "If I get desperate enough there is no telling what I will do. That's why your cousin wanted me to stay away from you. Desperation makes people do things they normally wouldn't."

"But if I know about you and the mirror, how can you trick me?"

"That's why it would be a trick, now isn't it? But no, I'm hoping that staying on my best behavior can be my ticket out of here. You know, time off for good behavior."

"You're not making sense."

He took a deep breath before letting it out slowly. "This is like a prison. I thought if I changed my ways, I would be released. But nothing I've tried has freed me from this place. Apparently, I can't pay for my own sins."

"What do you mean?"

"Before you met me I was a thief. I stole things from all over this town. But with my wages from the Apple, I've paid back everything I ever stole and a little more. My last payment was the day you came into town. That's when I noticed you. I'd just come from the store and heard you and your uncle talking. I followed you and pieced together why you were here."

Billie didn't know what to think. She'd seen how angry he'd gotten with those children when he caught them gambling. But she was also having a hard time reconciling the fact that he was a Faro dealer. She couldn't only consider the things about Winn she liked. She had to see all of him.

"Lou wants me to stay away from you for many reasons, not just the mirror. She knew me before I was trapped. I stole from her."

"You certainly did," Lou said.

Billie jumped. She was so focused on Winn she'd forgotten her sleeping cousin.

CHAPTER 25

"*I* see neither of you heeded my warnings. Winn, didn't I tell you to stay away from Wilhelmina?" Lou struggled to stand. "And Wilhelmina, the same about Winn?"

"You stay off that foot." Billie rushed to Lou's side. "Here, I'll help you sit back."

Winn looked sheepish. "I didn't tell her. She figured it out on her own. You know I can't hide myself in here." He pressed around the edges of the mirror as if to prove his point. "When someone says the rhyme, I get pulled front and center to the frame. We've experimented."

"Can you get him out?" Billie asked. She fluffed up Lou's pillow before setting it behind her.

Lou swatted at Billie's hand. "Quit fussing. He'd be sitting in that chair if I could get him out. I wouldn't wish his fate on anyone. It's a high price to pay for foolishness." She looked at him with fondness, as a mother would a son.

Well, what do you know? Lou did have a soft heart beneath that crusty exterior. It just took Winn to bring it out of her.

Billie understood that sentiment. Winn had a way of getting

into a person's heart even when you didn't want him to. "What sort of foolishness did he do?"

"Not my tale to tell."

Billie looked at Winn for the answer.

"I'm not in the mood," he said.

"Fine. What do we do now? How are we going to get him out of there?" She couldn't tell her uncle she'd found the mirror without first getting Winn out of it. Uncle Dale wouldn't care who was in the mirror, as long as they could figure out the magic.

"*You* are going to do nothing," Lou said. "Now you know why you need to leave—before this gets more complicated than it already is. And make sure you take that uncle with you."

"I can't go away now that I know about this." She waved her hand at the mirror.

"For Winn's sake, you need to go. I know the real reason your uncle is here. I'd gone to Germany trying to find answers, and when I came back, Winn was waiting to tell me there was a man and girl asking questions about me. And they'd been to the assayer's office."

She looked pointedly at Billie.

"My uncle didn't tell me anything about his plans. All I knew was that we were coming here to give you that ridiculous watch, and then we'd be on our way back to Boston." She didn't know if that was a good thing or not. Had there been no watch, no Winn. But she would have been home by now and happily unaware of the existence of a magic mirror except for in the family bedtime stories.

"And yet, you're still here." Lou turned her head as the flowers in the vase finally caught her eye. She stiffened, her features narrowing.

So, the advances of the mystery man were not welcomed. Billie would have to ask about him later. Right now, there were more important things to discuss. And not about why she and her uncle were still in town. "Did you find answers when you went away?"

"No."

"What about this watch?" Winn asked. "What's so special about it?"

Lou leaned over to pull the timepiece out from under the bedroll. She winced when her ankle moved.

"Careful," Billie said.

Lou held it up. "Belonged to our other cousin who grubstaked my claim for me. The one who disappeared. Left all his things behind, including that mirror. I don't know how the watch ended up with Billie's father."

Billie wondered the same thing. Along with why Uncle thought the watch was special.

"Can I see it?" Winn asked.

Lou held it like a ball she was going to toss. "Ready?"

Winn nodded, and then Lou threw it through the mirror.

Billie gasped, expecting to hear a shatter. But the surface rippled like what happens when a pebble plops into a still lake. The watch passed through.

Billie blinked. "You can send things through the mirror?"

"When I found out the window was really the magic mirror and that Winn was trapped, I tried to smash him out of there, but everything I threw at it only went through. After that we had a bit of fun."

Staring at the watch, Winn said, "The longer I'm in, the more we figure out."

"But the less he can do outside the mirror. He's losing himself, Billie. Bit by bit the mirror is taking his life from him. If we don't stop it soon, Winn will be completely trapped. You can't let your uncle find the mirror. He won't care who is in it as long as he can find a way to use the mirror to his advantage. It would be best for all if you convinced him to leave town."

"But what about Winn? I can't leave him trapped in there."

She met his gaze and held it. He returned her concern with a slight smile.

"You can," Lou said. "Walk away. We'll figure something out."

"How long have you been trying to figure something out?" When her question was met with silence, she followed up with, "That's what I thought. You need help. Besides, I'm part of the family business, aren't I? The legacy of the mirror is that we're supposed to keep it hidden, isn't it? It's all making sense now. All those bedtime stories Dad told me were to prepare me in case something like this happened."

Lou laughed. "*Liebling*, you are about as far removed from the family business as you can get."

Billie masked her hurt. She was tired of everyone discounting her. She found the mirror, didn't she? She crossed her arms and stared Lou down. "Looks to me like I'm right in the center of it." Which is right where she liked to be.

Winn cleared his throat, but they both ignored him. They were like two gunslingers facing off on a deserted street in the middle of town.

"Listen," Winn said. "Since she knows, she may as well help. It's not like she's going to be able to forget about a magic mirror."

Billie lifted her chin triumphantly. Two against one. Billie sat in the rocking chair. "So, what now?" As she pressed her toe into the floor to start rocking, she remembered what the girl in town said. She flattened her foot to stop the movement. "Lou, you sit in this chair every night and talk to Winn, don't you? That's what those girls meant when they said you were seen talking to yourself."

Lou offered a small laugh. "I suppose I do look like I've lost my mind, sitting and talking to no one. It's a wonder they haven't run me out of town yet."

"How long have you known about the mirror?" Billie crossed her arms in accusation.

"Hey, kid. Don't get yourself worked up. I recently learned

about it, too. Fremont shows up from Germany and stashes the mirror in the mine. When he didn't come back I put it in the wall. No use risking it breaking back there, I thought. May as well use it, I thought. Lo and behold, I find out I've got a genie in there."

Billie gasped at Winn. "I thought you said you didn't have any magic."

"Well, I, she—" Winn sputtered.

"*He* doesn't. There's magic there, all right," she circled her hand around the mirror, "but it doesn't come from Winn. We need to figure out how it works so we can bust him out of there."

If they'd been experimenting, maybe Billie could help them experiment with finding a medical cure for her mom.

"Seems to me, this other cousin knows some things. Fremont? Perhaps we should be tracking him down." Billie pressed her toe to the floor to start rocking. "Tell me everything about him." She felt like she was back at home holding court with her friends. She liked to be in the know about everything, and finally, it seemed, she was getting answers.

Lou and Winn exchanged a look before Lou said, "Don't know what you think you can do that we haven't already."

"I'm part of this family, too, I keep telling you. No need to keep secrets. Can we start with the watch?"

Winn examined the pocket watch. "It's the last thing I tried to steal before I got sucked up into the mirror." His face turned red. "Sorry, Lou. I didn't tell you about this one. But I never even got it into my pocket before I was trapped in the mirror. One day I came up here for what was supposed to be a private Faro game—"

"In my house? Why would you think I'd allow a bunch of gamblers in here?"

"I didn't know this place was yours. Fremont had played at my tables before." He laughed sardonically. "I'd always admired his pocket watch. I'd hoped to win it off him one day, but he never got so low as to pawn it. When Matron told me there was going to be a private game, I hoped it would be my chance. But when I got here, there was no one around. She'd told me there was whiskey in the back and to bring some out. I never did find the whiskey, but I did find the watch. After wanting it for so long, I couldn't resist taking it. It's probably what finally condemned me. As soon as I picked it up, I landed in the mirror. Scariest experience of my life. I thought I was dying."

"You told me you didn't know how you ended up in there." Lou crossed her arms.

"I'm only speculating, since seeing this watch again. Do you think it was a trap set by Fremont? Maybe we've been going about this the wrong way. He did bring the mirror here. Maybe he was the one setting me up the whole time to take *his* place."

Lou sucked in her lips and thought a moment. "No. We're not wrong. He's involved somehow, but I don't know how, yet. I spent enough time with him. I would have known if he was going in and out of the mirror."

"Not wrong about what?" Billie asked.

Winn started to answer but stopped. He and Lou exchanged looks again, blocking Billie out of the silent discussion.

"Nothing," Winn said in a way that made Billie think it wasn't nothing. He continued. "Lou? Any clue if this watch is important?"

"It's got Fremont's name on the back. Nothing special about that. And I especially don't know why *her* father would have this watch. As far as I know Chester and Fremont never met." She looked at Billie for confirmation.

"Not that I know of."

"Can I keep it?" Winn held up the watch.

Lou laughed. "After you just telling me how you wanted it so bad you were fixin' to steal it? Don't think so. I need to study it further." She held her hands out like she was catcher behind home plate.

Winn took one last long look at it then tossed the watch back to her.

Despite seeing the watch fly into the mirror, Billie gasped when it flew out. It was like the wall vomited the watch from nowhere. "Can you jump out of the mirror like that?"

Winn shook his head. "No. Something holds me until sunrise."

Lou put the watch back under the mattress. "Fremont has always been the family outcast. He thinks it's because of his dwarfism, but it's really his attitude. He was born sour and never did sweeten up."

Billie raised an eyebrow. Lou was one to talk.

Lou scowled and shook her finger at Billie. "If I'm standoffish it's because I didn't want you to stay." She waved a hand at Winn. "I was trying to avoid this."

"Sorry I messed up your plans," Billie said, "but I'm glad I know. Maybe I can help."

"You going to be able to keep quiet about the mirror?" asked Lou. "No one can learn about the magic mirror. Miners can get vicious when new treasure's found. And this treasure is priceless."

Billie thought of her uncle and his unrelenting nature. He wasn't going to stop until he'd turned this mountain inside out. He would figure it out sooner or later.

"Sure. I can keep quiet about the mirror."

CHAPTER 26

$\mathcal{T}$here was no sleeping after discovering Lou and Winn's secret.

It was one thing to imagine there was a magic mirror, but quite another to discover one. Add to that shock, finding out that someone you knew was inside the mirror, and that about spoiled any chance for normalcy thereafter.

They talked until sunrise when Winn fell out of the mirror. Literally. One minute he was in the mirror, the next he was out. Lying on the floor like he'd been unceremoniously pushed out.

"I can see why you moved your bed," Billie said. "Winn would crush you."

He stood and brushed himself off.

"Billie, would you make us some breakfast? I normally feed Winn before he goes into town, but with this ankle." She indicated her propped-up foot.

"Of course."

"And Winn, the curtains, please."

He closed the curtains, hiding the mirror, which now looked like an ordinary clear window.

"Why close the curtains?" Billie asked. "It's always so dark in here."

"This is a hot summer, child. I only open my curtains in winter," Lou answered, rather quickly, her tone defensive.

The long night must be weighing on her. Billie made a mental note to give Lou a quiet afternoon so she could rest.

After breakfast, Winn stood to go. "I'll, uh, see you tonight?" he said to Billie. He looked so awkward and sweet. Not the usually cocky Faro dealer she'd come to know. *Sheepish*. That was the word. He didn't have a secret to hide anymore, and the mirror had humbled him.

Billie glanced at Lou. "I'll stay here a few more nights, I think. Until Lou is up and going again."

He smiled. "Great. See you then."

"Take the alpenroses away, please," said Lou. She handed Winn the flowers by her bedside.

"What do you want me to do with them?"

"Send them back." She glanced at Billie then looked away.

Once Winn had left, Billie began work on the dishes. "Who are the flowers from?" She gave Lou a conspiratorial smile.

"Never you mind. They aren't a romantic gesture, but someone trying to make a point."

"Oh." Billie turned back to her task. *Odd way to send a message.* Now she was more curious than ever to find out who sent them.

"Why—"

Lou gave her a stern look and Billie adjusted course. "I've never heard of the alpenrose. It's a lovely name."

"Also snow roses or *donnerblume* in German. Your papa ever tell you those names? They say the snow rose attracts thunder and lightning. No thanks. Now, make yourself useful and bring in some water for tea."

Billie bit her tongue. "Your water barrel is almost empty. How do we go about getting more up here?"

"It'll come up by mule today."

"Have you ever thought about moving into town?" Billie asked, folding the towel and hanging it to dry. "You can still work your claim, and it's much more convenient."

"*Bah*. You can't get more convenient than this." She waved to the mine behind her.

"That's not what I meant, and you know it."

Lou seemed to think she had to keep up her gruff image even after Billie had discovered her secret.

"You have to admit you are a little unconventional. Is it even legal for you to be living here?" Billie slid the rocking chair so they could face each other. "As you recall, our ancestors left their little cottage in the woods to go work their mine, leaving Snow White on her own." Billie opened her eyes wide. "That's the first time I thought of the storybook characters as my ancestors. I'm still having trouble believing it."

"Every family has its secrets."

Billie laughed. "Not like ours."

After a hesitation, Lou smiled and nodded. Finally, they'd connected, not just as distant cousins, but as family.

Later on, as the cabin heated up, Billie propped the door open to allow a breeze through. "That's better," she said, fanning her face.

"What is that man doing now?" asked Lou staring out the door.

Billie leaned over and saw Uncle Dale guiding two pack mules up to the shack. He waved. "Got your water, Lou. No sense in two of us coming up here when I was already on my way." He untied the dusty water barrels and deposited them outside the shack.

Lou immediately began to fuss. "I thought I told you not to come up here again."

"You're welcome, ma'am." He doffed his prospector's hat and was gone again.

Billie touched Lou's shoulder. "You just sit tight while I take care of the water."

But Lou wouldn't sit tight. She pushed herself up to get a better look out the door. "Is that mining equipment he's got with him there?"

Sure enough, Uncle had strapped, a pickax, a shovel, and several wrapped bundles tied with twine to the mules who were *clip-clopping* past the door.

Why hide it. Lou was bound to find out sooner than later. Especially if Uncle Dale used explosives.

"He, uh, made a claim next to yours."

Lou maintained a steady gaze out the doorway. "For what purpose?"

"He wants to try mining in this area. He figured since you were holding on so tightly to your claim there must be something to this mountain." Even as she was speaking, her words sounded false to her ears. How could she remain neutral to both sides until she figured out what was going on?

"*Ach*, what nonsense. He's after the mirror."

Of course, he was. Lou could have her theories, but Billie wasn't going to confirm any of them. Billie's loyalties to both sides of the family were strong, and she'd known her uncle her whole life. Lou, she'd only known for a short time.

However, with Winn tied up in it all, her interest leaned his way, and therefore Lou's. She couldn't trust herself to think clearly about anything. All she knew for certain was that it wasn't fair for Winn to be trapped in the mirror, and that he was her best chance at helping her mom.

The open door provided a clear view of Uncle Dale staking his claim. He piled up rocks indicating where his boundary met up with Lou's, not once glancing at the shack. With the sound of each rock hitting the pile, Billie felt Lou's eyes bore deeper into the back of her head.

Uncle seemed to be going out of his way to show Lou what he was doing. Billie thought it was a stealth mission he had planned, but evidently not. Every move was exaggerated.

"He's hoping I cave in and hand over my mine," Lou said pointedly.

"Yes, probably." That would fit her uncle's personality. He may have been involved in field work in his younger years, but when he joined the Bergmann's company his hands had gotten soft. It was too easy to spend the Bergmann money on hiring out the dirty jobs. If he could make Lou sell through intimidation, he'd try it.

What he didn't fully realize was that Lou had a determined streak in her that only got stronger when threatened, as Billie had learned during the Opera House fiasco. Lou would call his bluff by not doing anything, and he'd have to start shoveling and blasting to find a vein to cross over into Lou's mine.

Lou and Uncle Dale were playing their own version of the philopena, only theirs wasn't based on flirting, it was based on winning.

Such a waste of time and money, but Billie couldn't tell Uncle Dale she found the mirror while Winn was trapped inside. Billie would have to mask her true reality from her uncle if she was going to keep this secret. It would be best for her to keep away from him as much as possible. Uncle Dale had a way of reading people. He'd know something had changed.

CHAPTER 27

Three days into her stay with Lou, Billie was ready to go back to the hotel. Uncle had been taunting Lou every day with his over-the-top surveying of his claim until Lou was determined to get back on her feet to better monitor him.

Winn had made a crutch for Lou to hobble around on, and it seemed just the thing. With gritty determination, she was able to get out of bed, to the outhouse and back, plus fix herself something to eat. She wanted her independence back, which was fine with Billie. *I want my hotel maid service back.*

Besides, she'd avoided her uncle for long enough, and, despite being a risk, it was time to find out if he knew anything else about the mirror that might help free Winn. They simply weren't getting anywhere on their own.

"You don't mind?" Billie asked after she told Lou about her plans to return to the hotel. The three of them were gathered around the table for breakfast.

"Not at all." Lou said. "In fact, I welcome it." She tried to use the same brusque voice she always did when trying to push Billie away, but it came off as false this time.

Winn raised his eyebrows at the exchange, and for a moment

Billie had second thoughts, wondering if she should stay longer. Lou had started to let Billie into her life, but Mom had always abided by Benjamin Franklin's opinion that guests, like fish, began to smell after three days. It was hard for Billie to break free of her upbringing and stay longer.

"You can walk back in with me today," Winn said, voicing the final decision. He gave her a look that she understood to mean he wanted to talk to her alone.

Billie nodded. It had been wonderful, if not odd, to talk to Winn each night through the mirror and eat breakfast with him every morning. Always overseen by Lou. Even when it looked like she was asleep, they couldn't be sure, so they never talked about anything important. Anything personal.

And then the in-between times were long. Hours upon hours with little to do but watch Uncle Dale strut past the shack, and Lou gather steam like a kettle on the verge of a blast. Billie had never felt such cabin fever.

Housework was over quickly. The most time-consuming tasks involved cooking, but Billie knew few recipes, so they ate simple meals. When Winn wasn't around, the conversation became stilted. Lou was a recluse who liked living alone. A twisted ankle wasn't going to change that.

Billie was a city girl through and through. She loved the activity, the music, the food. Lou's shack was primitive, and Billie had no intention of getting used to living without modern conveniences. If the Almighty wanted her to live the pioneer life he would have created her for that time. But he didn't.

Besides, that electric feeling she got around the mirror never left. She expected it to go away when Winn wasn't in the mirror, but even in the daytime she still felt like someone was watching. When she tried to explain her feelings to Lou, her cousin brushed it off as Billie's dramatics. But it wasn't. Something wasn't right about that mirror.

At the door, Winn turned back to Lou. "The town is planning

all sorts of celebrations for the Fourth of July. You want me to get a mule up here so you can join us? Our first celebration since incorporation. Even the governor is coming."

"*Ach.* Last thing I want is to be mashed up with the crowds. No thank you. You can tell me all about it when it's over." She waved them on their way.

"What are you not saying?" Billie asked after they were out of earshot of the shack.

Winn glanced at her. "What do you mean?"

"I mean, you're guarded when Lou is around. It's like you're hiding something from her. Or from me."

They walked in silence for several minutes. Finally, Winn said, "She's from that family. It's her shack. I think she's got my best interests in mind, but I can't be sure. So, I'm careful."

"I'm from *that* family, too."

He smiled. "I know, but you're—don't take this the wrong way —an outsider. You're just finding out about the magic mirror, so you don't have ulterior motives, and you're not part of a conspiracy. I can tell because your face hides nothing."

"What?" Billie covered her cheeks with her hands. She prided herself on not giving away her true thoughts and feelings.

"Allow me to correct. Your face hides nothing from me."

Now, Billie's face flamed. She was hiding a few things from him, but apparently not her feelings. She didn't want Winn to know how much he was drilling his way into her heart. Bisbee was only supposed to be a quick detour before she resumed her former life in Boston. It wasn't supposed to change her life.

"You still haven't told me what you're hiding," she said. They were already halfway to town, so Billie slowed her steps.

"I'm suspicious of Fremont. I thought he was cagey because he's a gambler, but now that I've been trapped in the mirror, I think there was more to his actions than I realized. I feel like I got duped, and he had something to do with it."

"You tried to go down that path with Lou, but she stopped it rather quickly."

"Yeah and I dropped it, but I think Fremont might be the key. If we can find him, I think we can get our answers."

"Where did he spend his time when he was here? Have you talked to his acquaintances?"

"He was at the Poisoned Apple a lot. From what I gather, much of that time was spent talking about Matron."

Billie whirled around, almost losing her balance. "That's why you wanted me to find out about her?"

Winn reached out to steady her. "Careful. These paths are slippery. Don't want you twisting your ankle, too." He kept his hand on her elbow. "Matron knows everything that goes on in this town. She's well connected, and her reach is growing."

"You sound like you don't approve of a woman in business."

"Depends on the business. And how she goes about it. Matron isn't the plainspoken, honest type, and she's got aspirations."

"How do you know all this?"

"I work for her, remember?"

"If you don't like it, quit."

"Not as simple as it sounds. Look. I warned you from the very start to get away from this town. It's going to get worse before it gets better, and I know you want to go back home. If I were you, I'd work on talking your uncle into leaving."

"And abandon you to the mirror?"

He shrugged. "No one would miss me." He said it matter-of-factly. Not like he was feeling sorry for himself and looking for pity, more like he had analyzed his life and come up with the conclusion a while ago. "Maybe that's why I was singled out for the mirror."

Singled out. An ominous choice of words.

"Your dad. Those kids you look out for." She lowered her lashes. "Me."

He groaned and slid his hand down her arm until his fingers entwined with hers. "You're not making this easy."

"I'm having the same difficulty myself." Billie kept her eyes straight ahead on the path, but broke into a smile.

All her life she had an image of who she was. Who she would be. It focused on having the best of everything. Even Branson because he was popular with her group and being with him would mean a certain status.

But for the first time she was imagining a different version of herself. One that opened itself up to being less superficial. More real. The idea was so new she wanted to protect it and see what became of it. Like following a thin gold vein to see if it reached pay dirt.

The silence stretched between them, and Billie wondered if they'd both said too much. They were almost in town now, and Winn, for propriety's sake would drop her hand. She couldn't help but wonder if the growing closeness she'd felt these last few days would disappear once they stepped onto the first street.

She'd have to pretend in front of her uncle. He wouldn't like her getting sidetracked from finding the mirror. But neither could she let him guess that Lou had the mirror in her shack. It would be better for him to believe she was falling in love—hard and fast —than she was protecting the mirror from him. Sneaking a look at Winn's handsome profile, Billie didn't know if she could hide the fact that she was falling for him even if she tried.

CHAPTER 28

*W*hen they got close to town, Winn did indeed drop her hand, and then left her at the intersection where he turned up Brewery Gulch. She continued on to the hotel in search of her uncle. Since she didn't meet him going up the mountain to work his claim, she figured he must be taking the day off for the festivities.

Even though it was only the third of July, the town was already festooned with red, white, and blue bunting. The colors draped around almost every window and balcony, accented by the American flag with its forty-five stars.

An elaborate WELCOME sign with a large star on top hung across the road for all the expected visitors arriving for the weekend fun. Billie's heart swelled with pride over the displays of patriotism. *Good show, little town.*

At the Copper Queen Hotel, men perched on ladders putting up the finishing touches of bunting. Billie stepped carefully around their decorations, smiling her approval.

She found her uncle reading the morning newspaper in the hotel restaurant.

"The Governor will be here later today," he said, handing Billie the paper. "He'll be giving a reception. I want you to be there."

"Nice to see you, too," she said, sitting across from him.

"No need to be cheeky. Make sure you meet his wife."

"Seems an odd place for the governor to come. This faraway mining camp."

"He was only appointed governor a few days ago, and there's a lot of voters here he needs to win over before next election. Remember to say something about your family's business."

"Which business would that be? Mining or mirrors?"

He waggled a finger at her. "You've been spending too much time with Lou. Don't pick up her bad habits."

"Only her possessions, should I find the right one."

He glared at her. "Any progress on that front?"

"What exactly should I be looking for? Do you have a description for me?" She flipped through the paper looking for any news on the royals and avoiding her uncle's gaze.

"I don't know. Doesn't much matter. If you find a mirror, say the little rhyme and then you'll know."

"Okay, but then what? How do we get the medicine?"

"I don't know. Another rhyme? Seems like that's how fairy-tale magic works."

"Do you know any rhyming poems for Mom's illness?"

"You just take me to the mirror as soon as you find it. I'll figure one out."

"Of course."

Billie continued casually flipping through the paper, stopping at a poem by Susan Marr Spalding. As she read it, the blood drained from her face.

Fate

Two shall be born the whole wide world apart;

> *And speak in different tongues, and have no*
> > *thought*
> *Each of the other's being, and no heed;*
> *And these o'er unknown seas to unknown lands*
> *Shall cross, escaping wreck, defying death,*
> *And all unconsciously shape every act*
> *And bend each wandering step to this one end, —*
> *That, one day, out of darkness, they shall meet*
> *And read life's meaning in each other's eyes.*

She and Winn were born a whole wide world apart, not only across the map, but also in society. If the poem had stopped there, it might be a romantic notion for her to clip it for her scrapbook at home, but then the poem turned more desperate:

> *And two shall walk some narrow way of life*
> *So nearly side by side, that should one turn*
> *Ever so little space to left or right*
> *They needs must stand acknowledged face to face.*
> *And yet, with wistful eyes that never meet,*
> *With groping hands that never clasp, and lips*
> *Calling in vain to ears that never hear,*
> *They seek each other all their weary days*
> *And die unsatisfied—and this is Fate!*

Was this a warning that Winn was going to be trapped in the mirror forever? *Groping hands that never clasp...seek each other all their weary days...die unsatisfied!* Was it fate that this poem was published in today's paper?

"You getting all teary-eyed over that poem?" Uncle asked. He set his coffee cup down with an emphatic *clunk*.

Billie took a deep breath and blinked her eyes clear. She didn't believe in fate. Providence, yes. Fate, no.

She changed the subject. "I take it you're planning to meet the governor?" she asked, pleased that her voice came out clear and not shaking. She was worried about Winn and shouldn't succumb to reading portends where they didn't exist.

"Yes, I plan to meet the governor. Arizona is on track for statehood. He'd be a good person to know."

"Sounds like your focus has returned to business. Does this mean you're ready to go back to Boston?"

Wouldn't that be a change if her uncle wanted to continue on, and she wanted to stay here and help Winn?

"Not at all. I'm having a great time working my claim. What does your cousin think of my pursuits?"

"She's not impressed, and she's not backing down." Billie kept her gaze focused on the newspaper.

"She will. One way or the other, she will."

He tapped the edge of his coffee cup. Usually well-manicured, his fingernails were caked with dirt and his hands marred with darkened red scabs, cuts from working with the rocks.

The same waitress Billie had first asked about Cousin Lou came to take her order, but Billie waved her away. She was still full from breakfast at the shack. Not as tasty as the food here, but the company was warmer, and that accounted for a lot. Besides, that waitress was not her favorite.

"The governor is scheduled to arrive on the two o'clock train, and then take in the ball game. So shall I."

Billie flipped through the paper looking for something interesting she could do today. "There's a grand ball tonight at the Opera House. Do you think the governor and his wife will be attending?"

"Most likely. You want to go, don't you?"

She closed the paper. "It's not proper to go to a ball during the mourning period."

Uncle set his lips firm and shook his head slightly. "It's your choice. Your father didn't give much for mourning the dead, so he won't be offended."

"But mother, she wouldn't approve."

"She only wouldn't approve because she follows that so-called Madge of Truth who gets her ideas from Queen Victoria. New Era child, do with it what you will."

Uncle Dale had a point. Everyone who was anyone would be there, so she could ask around about Fremont, and see if she could piece together what happened to him. Lou wasn't the most connected person in town, so she probably hadn't asked around much. And since Winn couldn't be there, it wouldn't be like she would be having a grand time of it and forget herself and her mourning.

"I won't be attending," said Uncle. "There's an excursion train coming in from El Paso today, and I suspect the saloons will be full tonight."

Billie was about to make a comment about gambling but bit it back when she saw his look. He already knew what she was thinking. She changed tactics.

"How is your claim progressing? Found the start of a vein yet?"

"It might take longer than I expected. But the paper says the Tarr brothers are in town for the double-drilling contest tomorrow. Seems like I could offer them some work if they're willing."

"Who are the Tarr brothers?"

"World record holders. They're here for the five-hundred-dollar purse."

"If they win that, they'll not need to work for you."

"Five months' wages, yes. But any miner worth his salt takes work when he can get it."

Billie suspected the Tarr brothers wouldn't be too thrilled when they learned Uncle Dale was a one-man operation. But at least he was preoccupied and could be for a while. That gave Billie and Lou time to figure out how the mirror worked, so they could rescue Winn.

CHAPTER 29

Billie went to the station at two o'clock with half the town to welcome Governor Brodie and his wife. Spurred by an advertisement in the newspaper, she bought an umbrella for shade from the sun. Best decision she'd made all day for the train was late and the sun hot.

At noon a cry of "Fire!" had rung out, which made for a few minutes of excitement until it was discovered the smoke was from a smoldering manure pile.

Billie thought she'd seen her name-twin, young Billy, running away with a suspicious grin, but maybe not. Winn would be disappointed to learn the little boy was getting into trouble.

The brass band tried to keep everyone's spirits up, but two hours was a bit much, especially when the dust started to blow. The second time her umbrella popped in a gust, Billie decided she could wait for the reception or the ball to lay eyes on Mrs. Brodie.

She followed several others away from the station, but as soon as she started down Main Street, the band began to play in earnest. The train had finally arrived. She considered turning back but kept on to the drug store where they were selling the tickets to the ball. To keep her options open, she ought to have a ticket.

Despite the crowded town, she was the only one in the store as all the others had followed the excitement of the band.

With the ticket and a small bag of sweets in her reticule, along with another penny added to her collection, she returned to her room at the hotel.

If they were giving out a prize for best Fourth of July decorations, the Copper Queen would win. With all the bunting and streamers and flags, you'd think President Roosevelt himself was coming to visit.

All the pomp and ceremony of the day sparked a vague memory of watching a Fourth of July parade when she was a child. Perched on her father's shoulders she stared down at her mother's wide brimmed hat trimmed in patriotic colors. As if sensing Billie's stare, mother had tilted her head and looked up at her. "Exciting, isn't it, Wilhelmina?" Her voice was light and soft.

Most of Billie's recent memories were of mother wrapped in blankets in her favorite chair or stretched out on the couch. By the time Billie and her father had left for California, Mother was confined to her bed. It was too easy for Billie to forget her suffering mother when being out west seeing new things, meeting new people.

After unlocking her hotel door, Billie shoved it open in frustration. What a terrible daughter she was. Uncle Dale remained focused on healing his sister, no matter how absurd the cure seemed, while her head was getting turned by the fate of a boy she'd only known for a few weeks.

She tossed her reticule on the bed and immediately spotted a thick, rectangular box near the pillow. "How did you get here?" she whispered. There was a card on top which read:

Enjoy the ball,
-Matron.

How did she know? Eagerly, Billie pulled the lid off the oversize box. Inside lay a deep purple silk gown shimmering from top to toe, as elegant as any dress she'd ever tried to talk her parents into letting her wear.

If only she could use it tonight, but it hadn't been even three months yet. It wouldn't be proper to switch to half-mourning colors, would it?

Still, it was a thoughtful thing for Matron to do. The woman had been nothing but generous to her since the beginning. Billie had no idea why Lou and Winn were so at odds with Matron. Must be they didn't understand her interest in the finer things in life. Billie pinched the silky fabric, reveling in the cool softness. She'd have to find out where the businesswoman shopped; her style was impeccable.

There were no mourning rules about trying on clothes in the confines of one's own bedroom. She had to see how well it fit so she could properly thank Matron. Showing appreciation was proper etiquette, too.

Without a second thought she discarded her black crepe to exchange it for the purple gown. When she pulled the dress fully from the box, a pair of black-heeled shoes fell out. *Oh, bless her.* Billie could pretend she'd gotten used to her brown boots, but truthfully, their thick soles pulled her to the ground and made her feel common.

Before she'd even finished buttoning, she could tell the dress was special. Trying to see the full gown using the smallish mirror attached to the dressing table, she twisted and jumped to get a view from every possible angle. If this had been the magic mirror, she would have looked ridiculous from Winn's perspective.

She self-consciously stopped jumping and whispered the poem, "Mirror, mirror, on the wall." She waited for the swirling, the silhouette, or the smirking Winn.

Nothing happened. *Ha.* She resumed her primping, happy that this mirror was just a mirror.

The silk gown fit her like a dress measured exactly for her, even down to the length of the tulip skirt. It was too bad no one would see her in it. Maybe she should go ahead and wear it after all.

On the heels of that thought, the room began to tilt and Billie sat down hard on the floor. Beads of sweat broke out along her forehead. Heat stroke? Caught up in all the excitement of the day, she hadn't had enough water to drink.

The dress seemed to constrict around her chest, forcing shallow breaths. All she could think was she needed to get the bodice off, now.

Taking panicked breaths, she tore at the buttons. Off came the bodice, and she could loosen her corset. Billie lay still for a moment before turning on the faucet in her room and getting a drink. She'd not make that mistake again. Water with every meal.

With reluctance, she folded up the purple gown and returned it to the box. One day she'd wear it. But for now, that hard-to-breathe feeling reminded her that all was not right in her world. She was still in mourning, and Winn was in trouble. Her vanity almost won out again, but with her focus back, she set out to meet the governor's wife.

CHAPTER 30

$\mathcal{A}$s expected, the reception for Governor Brodie and his wife was a popular event. Billie only managed to see the top of Mrs. Brodie's hat and had to sit through the governor's political speech for the pleasure. On the bright side, it was a beautiful hat. Wide-brimmed with blue ribbons and violet flowers.

Billie made casual inquiries about Fremont, but most of those around her were not from Bisbee. They'd come in for the festivities from close-by Douglas and Naco and as far away as Tucson and El Paso. And many of them were here specifically to see Governor Brodie, former Rough Rider. Boston itself couldn't have drawn a more devoted crowd than this group, eager to join the sisterhood of states and make their wishes known to the governor, their hero.

When the sun went down, the time seemed about right for her to try to find Matron and thank her for the gift, even though she couldn't wear it yet. As soon as was appropriate in the reception, she made her way out the front door. "Excuse me," she repeated over and over until she managed to step out into the cooling air outside.

Soon, she spied Matron crossing the street near the drug store. Billie was surprised she hadn't gone to the reception seeing as though that's where all the powerful or soon-to-be powerful were. Just the type of gathering for someone like Matron.

Billie straightened her sleeves, tried to smooth out a wrinkle in her skirt, then hurried to catch up with her benefactress. "Matron!"

The woman turned, her face transforming into a smile at the sight of Billie. "Why aren't you wearing the gown? I had it specifically tailored for you."

"I love it and look forward to wearing it soon." She indicated her black crepe. "But I'd like to wait a little longer. Thank you for your generosity." She pointed her foot out from under her skirt to show she was at least wearing the black shoes. "You are my own fairy godmother trying to send me to the ball."

"Hardly." Matron glanced over Billie's shoulder in the direction of the Copper Queen. "Did you come from the reception?"

"Yes. Governor Brodie is promising the world, while his wife is a perfect picture beside him."

"Indeed. That is the way of politics." She inclined her head. "Has that cousin of yours taught you to be wary of those who make such promises?"

Lou was wary of everyone, especially so of Matron, but Billie couldn't reveal that. "How do you and Lou know each other?" It was her polite way of asking what their conflict was.

"It's a young town, with relatively few women. We all know of one another. Doesn't mean we all get along. But you're old enough to have figured that out on your own."

Matron saw right through Billie's attempt at polite meddling. "Yes, but we can still be friendly, can't we?" Lou could learn a lot from Matron, about how to get on in town. How to be a woman in business. Billie worried about Lou's solitary existence up on the mountain. It wasn't healthy.

"Let's not talk of Louisa. What about you? Looking so grown up tonight. What is it you want most from your time here?" Matron asked.

No one ever asked Billie what she wanted. It was do this or do that or meet this person or say this. Her whole life she'd never had a say in the big decisions. It was all expectations, no choices. She'd had no practice in wanting things she might actually get. Other than shoes. Maybe that was why she was so particular about fashion.

At Billie's silence, Matron continued. "I've made some inquiries. You're Chester Bergmann's daughter. Do you know what happens with your family business? It is passed from male heir to male heir. You think you're secure in your wealth, but wealth, like so many other things in life is fleeting. When your daddy died, so did your life as you know it. They'll not take care of you the way they say they will."

Billie was confused. One minute Matron was giving her gifts, and then the next talking about things she knew nothing about.

"You're mistaken. We've had women in charge of the company before." Lou's grandmother had once been in charge of the company. Not that that meant Wilhelmina wanted to be in charge now.

"Just watch. Your relatives in Germany will take over soon. They always do."

"Why are you saying this?"

"You've been coddled your whole life. Enough naive girls have passed through my saloon doors for me to recognize the signs. I hate that your family did that to an intelligent woman like you. If I can open your eyes in any way, it's my gift to the next generation."

Billie wanted to protest and defend her family, but there had been whispers and side looks at the offices in California that extended beyond the concerned stares of well-meaning employees. That, and the difficulty Uncle Dale continually had securing funds from the company—he'd had to go directly to his sister.

"No one knows you here, sweetheart. You can do anything you want and be anyone you want to be."

Matron stepped closer and stroked one of the curls framing Billie's face. "I can help you become the person you want to be, without the backing of your family." She smiled, her red lips curving broadly.

Billie couldn't smile back. She could only stare, stunned. At the start of this trip she knew what she wanted. She wanted to be back in Boston, reunited with her friends, and most especially, Branson. But now? She still wanted to be back in Boston, but not only had Branson lost his appeal, she had little idea of who she was anymore. In a few words Matron had taken the peeling edges of Billie's life, stripped her identity, and offered to give her a new one.

"Come to my office at the Poisoned Apple tonight."

Billie hesitated. A saloon during the day was one thing, but at night after the men had been drinking?

Matron held up her hand at Billie's shocked face. "Go up the back staircase. You won't have to walk through the saloon."

"Thank you, but I'm going to the ball tonight." However appealing Matron's offer to help, Billie was not comfortable meeting at the saloon. The ball was a good excuse to avoid it, and Billie made up her mind to go on the spot. She was glad she'd gone ahead and bought a ticket just in case.

"Yes, of course. That's tonight." Matron's eyes flicked to the front porch of the Copper Queen Hotel where the ladies of the reception committee gathered. "I may see you at the ball. You learn to make things happen for yourself in this world, Wilhelmina. Don't let a bevy of gossips get in your way."

"Ma'am?"

"Never mind. Enjoy the ball."

CHAPTER 31

*A*s the guests from the reception made their way over to the Opera House, Billie fell in line with her uncle. "I didn't think you were going to the ball," she said.

"I'm not. I was looking for you."

"Good, because I need to talk to you, too."

"I was only able to shake the governor's hand. I need you to try to get close to the wife tonight. See if you can secure an invitation to breakfast. It'll be too busy to talk to him during the tour of the power plant later. Too many of us are clamoring for a look at that new generator."

"Why do we want so desperately to meet privately with the new governor?"

"I have business to discuss with him."

"What kind of business? Surely not my father's because apparently that is going to be taken over by some distant relative in Germany." She paused for a breath. "Please tell me I'm wrong."

He led her off the boardwalk and onto a quieter street.

"Don't be upset. It'll all work out. What were you and your mother going to do with a mining company anyway?"

"Run it?" The idea popped out of her mouth practically before she'd even thought it. It was a reaction to people making decisions about her without telling her or asking her or even acknowledging her.

"Seriously. Your mother is dying, and you are a child."

She winced. He didn't have to be so blunt. She'd just lost her father, and here she was dressed in black and getting ready to go to a ball. It made her feel as shallow and naive as he and Matron had suggested she was.

Pick out what kind of shoes you want, but don't you dare think about what kind of life you could have.

"They're looking for the next male heir, possibly your cousin Fremont if they can find him, or someone in Germany. They're still mapping the family tree. I've been rejected."

Billie stood aghast. "Why didn't I hear it from you? Matron, a stranger to our family, was the only one who saw fit to tell me."

"Bergmann Consolidated has always transferred ownership via the males in the family. No one ever told you?"

She shook her head and pressed her hands over her churning stomach. "But Lou said her mother ran the company for a time."

"It was a very short period, and they codified the transfer protocols thereafter."

"So, what are the implications for me and Mother?"

"I'm sure you'll be cared for, comfortably, maybe not like you've been expecting."

"Who do I talk to about this?"

"Me, I'm afraid. They've made me the liaison between Bergmann Consolidated and the family."

That did not reassure her. "Isn't that a conflict of interest?"

"They thought it best that I explain things. I was planning to go over all the details with you and your mother together since it directly affects her."

"And me." She watched the strangers walk by on their way to the ball. Fancy gowns glittered from the electric lights. Modern society, made for her generation, yet she felt lost. Passed by. Ignored. Not needed.

He shrugged. "Indirectly. It only indirectly affects you."

Uncle Dale didn't understand. This wasn't his family or his heritage. Billie was waking up to the fact that there was so much more to her family than she realized. Their secrets and their business practices had all been hidden from her. For all those years she didn't care because she was happy growing up in her carefully maintained corner. She was content with her place in society, not noticing the wider world around her.

"I better go," Billie said, backing away from her uncle. "It's almost nine thirty. The ball will be starting soon."

Uncle Dale smiled as if relieved he'd gotten through to her. "That's a girl. Don't stay out too late." As an afterthought, he said, "Do you need an escort? I can drop you off and pick you up again."

After letting her loose on the town all this time, it was a little late for him to be thinking about propriety.

"I'll be fine. Thank you. I'll watch for a group going back to the hotel and leave with them."

She turned in the direction of the Opera House, following the last groups of revelers headed to the ball. She was no longer excited about the possibilities of the night.

She ought to send a telegram to warn her mother of the company's plans, but what good would it do? If she was in a bad spell, she wouldn't have the strength to care, and if she was in a good way, it would only worry her. Or, she might already know. Uncle had assumed Billie herself did. Maybe in all things, Billie was the last to know. No, not in all things. She knew where the magic mirror was.

Applying all her social graces, Billie smiled as she handed over her ticket and entered the room. Electric lights made possible by the copper pulled from the local mines shone brightly, as if sponsoring the night themselves. The room took on an entirely different look with all the chairs removed from the center, showing off the gleaming hardwood floor. Copious amounts of red, white, and blue bunting draped the walls, and the orchestra played a waltz for the dancing couples.

Immediately, Billie went for the punch at the back of the room so she'd have something to hold on to and ward off any requests for dancing until she could gather her thoughts. A young man standing near the exit noticed her right away. She turned her back, examining the finger sandwiches and hoping he'd get the message.

"Hello, name's Darren," said the fellow, walking around and planting himself in front of her. He spoke above the music in a deep, rich voice that she couldn't pretend she hadn't heard.

"Miss Bergmann." She spoke crisply.

"I've seen you in town with Winn. How's he been?" the fellow asked.

"Oh, are you friends?" she said, immediately warming up to him. She was supposed to be gathering information about Fremont but couldn't let an opportunity to learn more about Winn slip away.

"Used to be. Don't know what happened to him, but he's pushed all the fellas away. Hoping you could tell me how he's doing."

"You mean he wasn't always this way?" She stepped away from the refreshment table, leading Darren to a quieter corner of the Opera House where they'd have a better chance of speaking freely.

"Standoffish? No. We used to have great fun together, but then he started acting all strange. We'd make plans and he wouldn't show up, and then he'd have no reason. He stopped playing ball, quit trying so hard in school. We all know our future is in the mine, but he has other ideas. We were okay with that, but I guess he felt different, like he didn't belong with us anymore. I don't know. We stopped asking him to do things. He started acting all snooty, being a Faro dealer and all. We figured he thought he was too good for us. But we were seeing him go down a bad way. What's a fellow to do if his chum won't listen to him?"

"Did you ever see him with a man named Fremont? A German fellow?"

"Fremont? Oh sure, I know the guy you're talking about. I blame him for what happened to Winn. Final nail in his coffin, if you pardon my expression. Was a good tipper when he was drunk, so Winn made sure to treat him nice. Sorry for being so blunt. I know it ain't good manners to talk about such things in the presence of a lady." Darren shuffled his feet as if trying to figure out a way to backtrack.

"My uncle's a serial gambler. I'm not completely unaware of what goes on in a saloon."

"Hope it works out better with Winn."

"He's trying to get back. Be there for him, will you?"

At least if Billie had to leave before the business with the mirror was settled, she knew Winn would have someone besides Lou willing to stand by him.

"Sure. Tell him to find me if he needs help, then, okay?" Darren nodded, then excused himself.

He'd confirmed Billie's gut feeling about Winn, so she was glad she'd come to the ball. He'd also confirmed that this cousin Fremont was bad news.

CHAPTER 32

A twenty-one-gun salute shook the town awake the next morning.

Billie slung the pillow over her head until the noise ended. Was there ever such a thing as too much patriotism? *Happy Fourth of July.*

The grand ball had been a decent affair. After her brief conversation with Winn's friend, she'd finally been able to introduce herself to Mrs. Brodie, but to what affect, who knew? The poor woman had met half of southern Arizona that day and would be hard-pressed to remember any of them. The Mrs. G. B. Wilcoxes and Mrs. G.J. McGabes of the world kept her busy.

Matron had arrived shortly before Billie left, and Billie witnessed the cool looks the ladies from the Bisbee Women's Club gave her when she wound her way through them to meet Mrs. Brodie. The longer Billie stayed in Bisbee, the more untold stories she noticed. What did those women have against Matron?

For Billie, much like the governor's wife, the rest of the night was filled with strangers. And even though she'd danced her fair share with amiable young men, the person she wanted to dance with wasn't there. She'd asked all her dance partners if they'd known her cousin Fremont, but aside from Darren, none of them had.

Billie swung her feet out of bed next to her clothes puddled on the floor where she'd left them. She regretted her carelessness with them now, but last night all she wanted to do was crawl into bed. Had she been home in Boston she would have also raided the kitchen for cake or other comfort food before retiring.

She had ended the night long before the last dance, following a group of older folks who wanted to beat the rush out. The evening had clarified all that hung in the balance if she and Lou couldn't figure out a way to rescue Winn. A life without Winn was a life with a hole in it. Trapped in the mirror at night meant he would have no shows, no dances, no romantic walks under the stars holding a girl's hand. Life was too precious to miss out on even the small things.

With these thoughts, she went outside to wait for Winn on the hotel steps. As she arranged her skirt around her legs, she realized she'd never truly appreciated black crepe before, always associating it with sad old women. Funny, it was almost time to switch to half mourning when she was finally accepting deep mourning. Maybe that was how it was supposed to work. A gradual moving-on process.

In her melancholy mood she thought she'd have to force a smile when she saw Winn, but when his familiar hat and broad shoulders came strutting up the street, her smile was automatic. She couldn't not smile at the sight of him even if she tried.

"Met a fellow last night who said he was an old chum of yours."

"Oh, yeah? Who?"

"Darren. He says he blames Fremont for what happened to you."

"Yeah, Darren's a good guy, but I can't blame anyone but myself. Before getting trapped in the mirror I faulted everyone else for my mistakes. I've had enough time to realize that I was my own undoing. I was the one who made all the bad decisions that led me to the mirror. No matter what role Fremont may or may not have played in all this, it still falls on my shoulders for what I did."

How could Billie argue with that? "I'm sorry. Seems the night was a waste. Darren was the only one who knew of Fremont, and he doesn't know what's happened to him. We're not any further along than yesterday."

"I'm going to quit," he said, his face blank.

"No! Don't give up now. I'm sure we'll come up with a solution soon."

"I'm going to quit my job. What's the point of pretending I can have any kind of a normal life? All I could think about last night was you all dressed up and at that ball without me. All the fellas you'd be dancing with. Them with their hands—not mine—around your waist."

"Really?" Billie's stomach fluttered.

He smiled, looking down. "And if my life is going to be cut in half, why waste it working for Matron? She can find some other patsy." He spit at the side of the road.

"Indeed," Billie said, imitating Matron's mannerisms. But despite her growing fondness for Matron, she was thrilled Winn wasn't going to be a Faro dealer anymore. It never did make sense to her why he still worked in such a place. "Let's make every moment count, then. Shall we go see the special attractions above the floodgate?"

"You don't seem the type," he said.

"What do you mean? I love wild men. The advertisements said he was one of the cannibals who killed Dr. Livingstone. If you believe everything you read."

"Considering Livingstone died of dysentery, I'm already underwhelmed. Besides, I thought you'd be more interested in the snake eater. He bites their heads off in front of you."

Billie wrinkled her nose. She had her limits. "Maybe we could just get ice cream."

Winn laughed. "Let me talk to the manager, then we'll spend the day together."

"Great. I'll save us a place for the parade out front of the City Bakery."

The streets began filling up with parade watchers, and Billie kept her elbows out, making space for Winn. But when a brass band made its way down the street followed by soldiers celebrating the end of the Philippine-American War, he still hadn't shown up. There were floats and children and handsome horses with colored ribbons braided into their hair. The mayor and the governor rode by, but still no Winn.

She wound through the crowds to the Poisoned Apple and tried to see in the windows but couldn't make out a thing. She cracked open the door to see if they'd tied him to a Faro table. Already the room was full of patrons. So many men it was hard to find anyone. One man noticed her and smiled such a grisly smile at her, she jumped back, content to wait on the street.

She was about to give up and go back to the hotel when a flood of men poured out the door. They marched as one down the street, taking bets as they walked. *What in the world?*

Finally, Winn came outside. "Did I miss the parade?"

"All of it." She examined Winn's face for signs of why he was late. "Everything okay?"

"Lars tried to talk me into staying, but we both know he can easily replace me. He just might not get someone so honest." Winn chuckled. "I didn't have the heart to tell him how dishonest I started out."

"Are you glad you quit?" Billie couldn't tell.

"Yes. The saloon by day and the mirror at night wasn't giving me much of a life."

"I'm glad, too." She didn't know how glad until that moment. It would be a lot easier to introduce her mother to a boy trapped in a mirror than a boy who dealt Faro. "Now, where were all those men off to in such a hurry?"

"Drilling contest," Winn said. "Have you ever seen one?"

"No. The way the miners press in, there's never a place for a lady to watch."

"I know where we can go. You can't live your life and not have seen a drilling contest."

He looped her hand onto his arm, and together they wove in and out of the spectators until Winn led her through the door of Lacey's salon.

"Well, hello there Winn," one of the young beauticians called out. "Come for a manicure?"

"No thanks, Florence. Is it okay if we go on up? The drilling contest is about to begin."

"Anything you want, sweetie."

Billie opened her eyes wide at Winn, asking for an explanation.

"What? We both work for Matron, at least, we used to." He led her up a narrow set of wooden stairs, up to a second-floor balcony. Winn put his hand on the small of her back to propel her to a better position overlooking the contest.

Meanwhile, others in the beauty salon took note of Winn's plan and followed them up, pressing the two of them into the railing. Billie leaned back into Winn's solid chest with her pulse racing. *Happy Fourth of July.*

In front of the library, a large crowd had gathered around the granite block which was secured with wood scaffolding. It appeared the entire town had come out to watch, filling the plaza and flowing up the hillside.

"That there is thirty thousand pounds of Gunnison granite brought in for the contest," Winn said.

"I thought you weren't much into mining?" Billie tipped her head back to talk to him, turning her mouth inches from his.

"I like rocks. And I enjoy mining as a spectator sport." He looked down at her and grinned.

She grinned foolishly back. Who cared about a drilling contest when there was a boy who made her heart flutter standing so close? One who, despite being trapped in such weird circumstances, continued to go out of his way to make her feel special.

He broke her gaze and looked back at the contest. "They're starting."

She reluctantly turned around but leaned back into him. The double drilling contest was a race between pairs of men to see who could drill the deepest in a given amount of time. One man held a drill bit, the other a mallet. The one with the hammer swung with everything in him while the man holding the bit would turn it after each strike. It was loud and exciting with the crowd cheering them on until the whistle blew, and then it was dead silence while the holes were measured.

Winn pointed out the Tarr brothers waiting for their turn. Uncle Dale stood behind them within an arm's reach. They were the local favorites and the team Uncle wanted to hire to help with his claim. Wasted time and money, but Billie couldn't tell him so without revealing she knew where the mirror was, and that it had trapped the boy she was falling head over heels for.

Winn shifted, putting his arms around her to touch the railing, encasing her in his arms as he leaned over her shoulder for a better view. The team that just finished had come all the way from Canada. Strong mountain men from the mining town of Rossland, British Columbia.

"The team of McNichols and Ross set a new world's record," the judge said before his voice was swallowed up by the roar of the crowd.

"It's going to be hard for the Tarr brothers to win, now," Winn said in her ear. "Told you it was worth watching."

Billie nodded. She agreed, but for different reasons. As she nestled in his arms, she wondered if there could be a more perfect boy in all the world. They just needed to figure out a way to free him from the mirror.

After the final team failed to beat the new record, the crowd began to disperse and Billie reluctantly followed Winn back down to street level. She already missed the secure feeling of Winn against her back. There had to be a way to get him out of that mirror for good.

"I've got something for you," he said. "Follow me."

CHAPTER 33

*W*inn led her through the crowd and down the street until they were in front of the assayer's office.

"Where we first met," Winn said. "Now, close your eyes and put out your hand."

She did, and he placed something cool onto her palm.

"This is the main reason I was late to the parade," he said, "I had to pick up your surprise without you knowing about it."

She opened her eyes to find a gorgeous turquoise cabochon attached to a plain silver chain. The stone was the deep sky-blue she'd seen before, in Lou's mine, but this particular one was half blue, half chocolate brown swirled in.

"I made it for you," he said, grinning. "Lars at the Apple has a grinder he lets me use. Do you like it?"

Like it? "It's amazing." The stone was a bit wild, somewhat unpolished, like Winn himself.

"The turquoise is unique to the Mule Mountains. They find all kinds of it in the mines around here, but they don't want it, so they dump it. I rescued some rocks and tried my hand at cutting stone. The color is called Bisbee Blue, since you can only get it here. Something to remind you of the town when you're back in Boston."

Billie touched his hand. "It'll remind me of you, not the town." She held up the necklace and asked him to fasten it around her neck.

He spun her around, and after he'd adjusted the clasp, rested his hands on her shoulders. He whispered in her ear. "Philopena."

Her breath caught, and she pulled away to look at him. "Winn! I don't believe you. I'm usually so careful." *Something undervalued, overlooked, yet precious.* He'd tricked her into accepting his philopena gift.

He won using the German version of the game, and she was never gladder to lose a game of wits.

She fingered the turquoise pendant, marveling at the beauty of the stone. "I'd forgotten all about our game. No fair. You were in a magic mirror. How was I to remember a game of wits when dealing with that?"

"You're probably the only girl in the world who could find me stuck in that mirror and still want to be friends."

She raised her eyebrows. "It was a shock." A shock lessened by the stories she'd been told growing up and of Uncle's quest to find such a mirror. Imagine if she'd come in blind to the realization that such a thing existed? Could give a person a fainting spell, if not a heart attack.

He leaned against the assayer's wall. "You wouldn't have liked the person I was before I got trapped in there."

She started to protest but knew that what he was saying was true. She would never have gotten to know his full story based on first blush. She was glad circumstances made her stop and take a closer look at Winn.

"How did you start dealing Faro?"

"My dad knows Lars. He's from Norway, came over with the same recruiter my dad did. One of his dealers was sick one day, and I talked them into letting me deal. I've always liked playing with cards; I know some tricks. They liked my style because it drew a crowd. It was the best night the Matron had ever had, so she kept me on the payroll."

"What about the future? If you weren't stuck in the mirror, and you could do anything, be anything, what would it be?"

He looked away, studying the mishmash of houses clambering up the hill. "You'd laugh."

"I wouldn't."

"Have you heard of the City Beautiful Movement? Warren Manning?"

She shook her head.

"It's about creating beautiful spaces for people to live in. No more tenements one after the other, cramming people in. But planning for parks and landscapes in the city."

"Why would I laugh at that? Sounds wonderful to me."

He shrugged and then pulled a weed that had grown through a gap in the boardwalk. "Yeah, well, it's not mining or smelting. That's what matters around here." He started breaking the weed into pieces. "I thought you might have heard of Warren Manning since he's from Boston, and he studied under Olmsted, the man who designed Central Park in New York, not to mention several places in Boston. You must have seen their work."

"No wonder you were so interested in Boston. One of them probably created the Emerald Necklace, a chain of parks. I always liked that name." If only Winn could go home with her to see it all.

She gasped and grabbed his arm. "Has Lou ever tried to move the mirror? We could move you to Boston." Why didn't she think of this before? It didn't get him out of the mirror, but it brought the mirror to her mother.

His forehead wrinkled as he thought. "No, can't say we tried that. But I don't see how it would help me. Pretty soon I'll be stuck for good anyway." He shook his head. "No, I couldn't risk it."

"What if you could apprentice with Mr. Manning?" She smiled sweetly, trying to think of ways to talk him into it.

"Maybe he would take me. As a landscape architect, he thinks we should use plants that are natural to a place. He says he takes out what doesn't belong, fixes up what's there, and makes it all nice to look at. I like that idea."

Billie noted the twisted walkways, the vertical stairs, the smeared dirt paths that connected one wooden building to the next. "This town looks like it sprouted out of the ground. Everyone was focused on getting a roof over their heads, not knowing how long the mine will hold."

"Exactly, but the mine's been proven. Buildings are turning to brick and becoming permanent. Cities need someone to see the big picture and help people work together to make the place look good. You don't think that's a waste of time?"

"There's nothing wrong with being beautiful." Billie said.

"Every time I step out of that mirror, I appreciate how beautifully created our world is. Let me show you." He led her off the low boardwalk to an open area still covered with desert plants. "Take the prickly pear for example." He pointed at a cactus with flat pads. "It's the party cactus. You should see when it flowers. It produces a violet-purplish fruit that makes the plant look like it's decorated for Christmas. And you can eat it. The pads and the fruit."

Winn's face came alive as he talked about the land he loved. Could he love Boston as much?

He caught her staring. "What? Too much?"

"No. I like learning about this side of you. I would never have guessed; you keep it close."

He shrugged. "Sometimes an idea needs time to sprout, and if you talk about it too soon, well, someone is bound to talk you out of it."

Billie gasped. "I've felt the same way. Like I need to figure out who I am before everyone else tells me."

He took off his hat and the wind blew his hair. "I thought all my dreams were over when I got trapped in the mirror, and then here you come along—from Boston. Lou told me over and over to stay away from you, but you were irresistible."

Billie smiled at the complement, heat spreading up to her ears. "Did you take it as a sign that Boston was the right choice?"

"Signs can be hard to read, so I don't put much stock in them. But if you were in Boston, I would have one more reason to pursue my dreams there. That is, if we get me out, and if my pop forgives me."

"Have you told your dad about the City Beautiful Movement?"

Winn shook his head, looking off in the distance. "Won't matter what I say if my actions can't back it up. I tried to get him to meet me at Lou's cabin so I could show him what had happened to me, but he wouldn't come."

Suddenly, his eyes grew wide, and he yanked her between the buildings.

"Hey! I like my arm thank you very much. What was that for?"

"Shh." He pressed flat against the wall and poked his head around the corner. When he turned around his face was pale, his expression confused.

"What is it? You look like you've seen a ghost."

"I kind of did. I saw Matron, but that's impossible." His voice was quiet, like he was talking to himself.

"What are you talking about? I see her all the time."

"At night. Haven't you noticed? You only see her at night."

CHAPTER 34

*B*illie twisted her lips as she watched Winn hiding around the corner. What was he getting so worked up about? Matron was always about town.

"Are you afraid she'll give you a hard time for quitting?" she said. "What can she do? She can't make you work for her."

"Shh!" Winn waved his hand indicating she should stay quiet and hidden.

Billie ducked down with him and took inventory of all her meetings with Matron. The first time they met was in the ladies' parlor at the hotel. Next was at the theater. Then she saw her after the governor's reception. All at night.

"She's a businesswoman; she works during the day."

Winn shook his head. "No, no, no." He held his hands out and examined them.

"What *are* you doing?"

"Looking to see if I'm all here."

"Winn, you're scaring me. What's going on?"

"She's supposed to be in the mirror. She's there during the day. I'm in there at night. If she's found a way out during the day, why am I still here?" Winn's voice was filled with panic.

Billie stood in shock. "Matron is trapped in the mirror, too?" She quickly processed any instant where she could have suspected. "Why didn't anyone tell me?"

Instead of answering, Winn peeked around the corner again. "I don't see her now. Not that it means anything. She was fading in and out. Invisible in the light, but when she stepped into the shadows she was translucent, like a ghost. She could be anywhere."

Billie was still stuck on Winn's first revelation. "How did she get in the mirror?" Billie asked. "And why didn't you tell me?"

"Lou."

"Of course. She *really* doesn't want me involved, does she?"

"She's protecting you."

"And why didn't Matron tell me? She knows I'm related to Lou. Why didn't she say something? Ask for my help? Is Lou silencing her, too?"

"The opposite." Winn scowled. "We suspect Matron is the one behind all this."

Billie's stomach dropped. "The one who tricked you into the mirror?" *It couldn't be. She's been so kind.*

"We think she meant for me to replace her, but that didn't happen. And as long as she was still in the mirror, I had hope. That's why I stayed close to her. The reason I kept working at the Poisoned Apple was to learn everything I could about her."

"And?" *Why didn't Winn tell her sooner? Didn't he trust her?*

"She's a mystery. To everyone else in town, she's a wealthy woman who surrounds herself with expensive goods. She has a knack for getting anything she wants. Her private quarters are filled with exotic items from around the world. Last week I found evidence she's set her eyes on taking over Copper Queen Consolidated. She's been buying up shares and is poised to have control soon. It's making everyone nervous on the one hand, and then they pander to her on the other.

"Lou has tried to pull information out of her, but Matron

won't talk about herself, or why she is in the mirror. At first, she gave us this sad story, but as we got suspicious that she was lying about it, she gave up any pretense and now just smiles and laughs at us." He hit the wall with his palm. "It's infuriating."

Billie's arms erupted in goosebumps. Matron, the one who had been so nice to her. Treating her to beauty salon treatments, theater tickets, clothes. Giving Billie exactly what she craved and gaining her trust. All this time, Billie's guard had been up against her uncle and Winn, but it was Matron who was the con the whole time.

Winn pressed his back against the wall. "When you returned the watch, it triggered a memory, suggesting Fremont might be the one to blame. That maybe he tricked both Matron and me into the mirror. I was willing to be wrong about Matron." He shook his head. "But this. I don't know what to make of it. How can she be out during the day?"

"I'll find out for you. She's invited me to her office at the Poisoned Apple. I wasn't going to go, but maybe she'll talk to me."

Winn shook his head. "No. There's no telling how dangerous she is. You think you two are the same, that you share some kind of high-society bond. But you don't. You're not the same. She's a fake, and I don't trust her."

"Then trust me. She reveals things to me without realizing it. I know she feels rejected by the women in this town, in particular, the Women's Club members. But now I understand because I know how these things work. Besides the shadiness of her saloon business, she's unavailable during the day for tea and planning meetings. I can help her get in with them. She'd open up. I could ask her to help you."

"Lou tried to talk to her, but the woman only wants what benefits her. Lou thinks Matron played on my desires to trick me into the mirror."

"But you still don't know how you ended up in the mirror?"

"No. But I've seen how Matron has been plying Lou's desires for luxury."

Billie laughed. "Lou? She lives in a shack with her only luxury being a set of books about mining."

Winn sat on the edge of the boardwalk, stretching his long legs out in front. "Lou is a private person and her business isn't mine to tell, but your safety is my concern. There is so much more going on here that I don't understand. Lou is right. You need to go back to Boston before you're pulled into this web, too. I'm sorry that I let you get so close. Lou was right. It wasn't fair of me."

"Oh, so now we've gone back to wanting me to leave, have we?" Billie crossed her arms, reminded again of how little choice she had in her life. "I understand you've been keeping things from me because you're trying to protect me, but you have to share all of what you know if I'm going to properly help. I can get to Matron in a way that you and Lou can't. I realize I can't trust her, but I do understand her. I've seen what she wants."

Billie thought back to the expression on Matron's face while she watched the women coming out of the governor's reception. Matron wanted power and acceptance. Power she had, but the way she got it made the other women in town resentful.

Winn reached for her hand and pulled her down to sit with him. "Do you understand that she seeks out a person's weakness and uses that against them?"

"Yes, and because I know it, I'll be ready for it."

"What is your weakness?"

She had several but didn't want to list them out in front of Winn. Matron had been playing off her vanity, so that's what she'd have to look out for. Starting with not accepting any more flattery or gifts.

She touched the turquoise cabochon Winn had given her. Bisbee Blue. Winn shouldn't be a mere memory once she returned to Boston. She wanted him fully living, night and day outside the mirror. He was worth taking a few risks for.

"I'm a visitor here," Billie said. "There aren't any expectations about me, and when I leave, no one will even remember I've been here. Right now, that is a strength. I've always been too concerned about what my friends will think, or how my behavior will reflect back on Bergmann Consolidated. My freedom to act can make me bold when I normally wouldn't be. I might be your only chance."

He licked his lips. "I'm going to regret this."

Billie clapped her hands. "No, you're not." She was going to save the day. "Let's go find Matron and let her know we know," said Billie. "Come at her directly and take her off guard."

Winn looked like he was about to disagree, but his curiosity was obviously piqued. "Let's start with finding her, and then we'll decide what to do." He gently tucked a stray hair behind her ear, slowly running his fingers along her jawline. "But if this is going to be my last day out of the mirror, I want to enjoy it." His low voice and intense eyes sent a shock of electricity down Billie's spine.

She cleared her throat, forcing herself to look away. "You don't know it's your last day. You said yourself she looked like a ghost. That means she's not completely free, correct? I think if she was, you'd have been pulled in to fill the void. Maybe I should run up to the shack now and see what she looks like in the mirror. We can ask her what's going on."

Winn grabbed her hand. "No. Let Lou take care of that. I already told you Matron just laughs at us. You are staying away from that mirror. It's too risky right now. Last thing I need is for you to accidentally fall into it."

"What do you mean by 'fall in'?"

"That's what it feels like. Like you tripped and can't catch yourself. You fall and you fall."

Billie thought about the claustrophobia she felt whenever she stepped into a dark mine and she shuddered. "What if Lou fell in, and that's the change you're seeing? You said yourself Matron had been working on her."

"If that's the case it's already too late for us to do anything there. We should do what we can in town." Winn stood.

"First, come with me." She led him to the nearby haberdashers. "You need a disguise, so you're not having to dart around buildings again."

CHAPTER 35

"May I help you?" the gentleman at the counter asked when they walked in.

Billie quickly scanned the displays and pointed at a bowler hat and a Stetson. She'd been wanting to rid Winn of his prospector's hat for ages, so this was as good an excuse as any.

The clerk found Winn's size and positioned a mirror in front of him.

"Stetson," Billie said. The bowler made Winn look too citified. She wanted him to stay rugged Winn and the Stetson was perfect.

Winn took out his wallet, but Billie had already paid the clerk. "Don't let me buy you a philopena." She winked, feeling brash.

"Why do I get the feeling you've been after my hat all along?" He tipped his new hat at her and her heart skipped a beat.

"Now that suits you," she said. But they had a job to do. Outside, she said, "Where would Matron want to go during the day if no one could see her?"

"Where the powerful people are. She's always trying to get close to the company executives. Their wives have rejected her, but her sights are still set on power. I wouldn't be surprised if her ultimate goal was to take over the town. She has an uncanny ability to make money, so she can try to buy her way to what she wants."

"Where's the governor?" Billie asked. "Everyone of importance will be near him."

"The next public event is the yard races at five o'clock. They're probably meeting privately right now at the Copper Queen offices," Winn said. "We have no way to get in, but if she is as transparent as a ghost, she could."

"No harm in walking by, is there?" She looped her arm through his and merged with the other pedestrians on the boardwalk.

"Now what?" Winn said, eying the office building like it contained unexploded dynamite.

"I'll be right back." Billie crossed the street, and then marched through the doors as if going in to meet with her father.

"Hi, I'm Wilhelmina Bergmann," she said to the secretary at the front desk. "I'm looking for Matron, the owner of Lacey's?" Billie pointed and moved past the desk as if she knew where she was going.

The secretary stood in her way. "No, miss. Only men in the boardroom at the moment. The governor's wife is freshening up at the hotel, and I haven't seen Matron today."

"Does she come here often?" Billie asked, paying close attention to the shadows. *If Matron was ghostlike, would she be able to go through walls?*

The woman shook her head. "I've not seen her."

"Thank you." Billie took one last sweeping look around the neat and tidy front office. "What perfume do you wear?" Billie asked. "I can't put my finger on it."

"Pear's soap?" The woman looked at Billie as if she were trying to patronize her.

That wasn't the scent that caught Billie's attention. Matron's scent was citrus and lavender, and it lingered in the air.

Winn waited across the street, leaning with one leg up against the wall in the shade. Billie sidled up beside him.

"She was there," Billie said, "but I didn't see her. Her expensive perfume gave her away."

"I saw her. She went that way." He pointed up the street.

"And I've got a hunch where she's headed," Billie said.

Winn stood. "All right. Let's go."

Billie shook her head. "Even with your new disguise, you'd stand out where I'm going. Women only."

He mouthed "Oh" and took a step back. "Then while you're doing that, I'll go check on Lou."

"If everything is fine will you come back right away?"

He doffed his new hat. "I want to spend as much time with you as I can today, Wilhelmina Bergmann. Meet me at the Waldorf when you're done, and I'll romance you one last time."

His voice had turned husky, and it melted her insides. If this was to be his last day outside the mirror, she would certainly help him make it a good one.

They parted ways, and Billie hoofed it up Quality Hill. She knocked at the door of a building that looked like a quaint family home. The Women's Club. If Matron wanted to spy on anyone it would be these women who refused to invite her into their circle.

A woman wearing a pretty pigeon waist and matching pink tulip skirt opened the door. While she was here, Billie needed to find out where these women were buying their clothes. Certainly not at the Fair in town.

"May I help you, dear?" she asked.

"Yes, I am Wilhelmina Bergmann, daughter of the late Chester Bergmann, of Bergmann Consolidated, based out of Boston. I'm here on business with my uncle, and it seems we're going to be in town for a time."

The woman took a quick sweep of Billie's attire and said, "I'm sorry for your loss. Please come in. Most of our members and their daughters are busy around town today with the festivities, but I'd love to show you our brand-new home, the first Women's Club in Arizona to have our own building."

The woman led Billie into their main meeting hall, a spacious room with a proscenium arch at the far end and a beautiful baby grand piano on stage. Two other women sat at an oak table, deep in conversation.

"Pretty piano, isn't it?" the woman asked, noting it had drawn Billie's attention. "The Knabe was a gift from a gentleman at the Phelps Dodge company. They own the Copper Queen and have been very generous to the town. Do you play?"

"Yes," Billie said. She'd been taking piano lessons her whole life. This trip was the longest she'd ever gone without playing. "Perhaps I could come back and play a little, if you don't mind."

"I'm sure we could arrange something. Today isn't a good day as we have so much to do with the governor here, and our cake auction down at the library is about to begin. A few of our ladies haven't left yet, and they'd love to meet you. Bergmann Consolidated you said?" She raised her voice to garner the attention of the two women.

"Mrs. Dobbs and Mrs. Frankle, I'd like you to meet Miss Bergmann, from Boston. She'll be in town for a period of time and is looking for companionship. Mrs. Dobbs, is your daughter still here?"

Mrs. Dobbs nodded politely at Billie. Her Gibson pompadour hairstyle poofed out dramatically, framing her face like a hat. "Yes, my Hazel is playing checkers in the kitchen with one of her little friends."

"What work do you ladies do here?" Billie quickly asked, changing the conversation to where she wanted it to go. "I'm curious what a small-town society can do as compared to the important work of the women's clubs in Boston." She kept her tone light and lilting while she appealed to their pride in hopes they'd forget about sending her out to be with the children.

Mrs. Dobbs leaned forward slightly. "I'm sure you will find

this club of the highest variety. We take on projects for the betterment of the women and children in this community and therefore raise up the entire town. Should you remain in Bisbee long, you will no doubt be touched by our endeavors."

Billie nodded, though she was distracted by a movement in the hallway. Matron? She couldn't see her, but sensed movement. Now was Billie's chance to show how useful she could be.

"I may have met one of your members. She certainly is busy in the town. A woman they call Matron? She's been very kind to me since I arrived." *Did the shadow come closer?*

"She has applied," the first woman said before being cut off by Mrs. Dobbs.

"We do not discuss membership applications."

"She's quite clever." Billie said, "I'm sure she would do you ladies credit." There. If Matron was hovering she'd hear that Billie was on her side.

Mrs. Dobbs rose. "Come meet my daughter. She'll introduce you to proper society. You're here with your uncle, you say? The men don't always know proper upbringing. Your instincts were good to come here, child. We'll take care of you."

Billie felt a change in the air. A slight version of the electricity she felt at the shack. If pressed to name what Matron was feeling, she'd say Matron was angry instead of pleased that Billie was speaking well on her behalf. The electric air dissipated, leaving Billie chilled. What had she done?

"Oh, good, here's my daughter now."

The door to the left of the stage opened, and the girl from the street walked into the room. The one who'd insulted her in front of Winn. The girl's eyes opened wide, but she smiled as she'd been trained. Her friend ran in behind her and smiled and waved in acknowledgment.

"Hazel, meet Wilhelmina, she's new in town."

"How do you do, Wilhelmina. Did you want to play checkers?" Hazel dutifully asked.

"Another day," Billie said. "I'm meeting Winn Harris at the Waldorf." It was petty to bring Winn up in front of the girl, but she couldn't help it.

The girl's look turned sour before the pasted smile returned.

"Oh, my. Winn Harris?" said the first lady. "There are plenty of other young men we could introduce you to. Others more suitable."

"Excuse me," Billie said, extracting herself from the conversation. "I must freshen up for the Waldorf."

here was too little time for her to freshen up at the hotel, so Billie quickly used her handkerchief to blot the beads of sweat from her forehead while she waited for Winn in front of the Waldorf.

He arrived wearing a suit and his new Stetson.

Her heart melted even more. He really did think this was the end. She blinked back tears before he could see them.

"Impressive," she said, putting on a big smile.

"You always look so beautiful. Was about time I cleaned up, don't you think?"

"You clean up very nicely, Winn Harris. I'm proud to take dinner with you."

Winn adjusted his bow tie, and Billie tried not to laugh as he made it more crooked than it started out.

"Where did you get that?" she asked as Winn held the door open for her.

"Your uncle. He saw me cleaning up at a water barrel and asked what we were doing tonight. He told me I better have one of these or they might not let me in."

"My uncle? I don't believe it." Either he had a plan, or his heart was getting soft.

Winn picked at the bow tie some more. "It cuts off my air supply. Be ready to catch me if I faint."

"Oh no. I've learned my lesson. You're staying within the radius of town."

The restaurant was all white linens and crystal glasses. They ordered some sort of beef, although Billie had forgotten what kind by the time it arrived at the table. Every time she looked at Winn her stomach performed somersaults. She'd never been so tongue-tied before. She couldn't think of one intelligent thing to say.

Winn didn't seem to be doing much better at carrying the conversation. They eventually settled on talking about the food. A neutral topic after they tried to put so much importance on this one dinner.

It was the kind of dinner at which you'd expect to talk about the future, but doing so would only remind them of how bleak the odds were that they'd have more dinners like this. She wanted this meal to be special for Winn, but it seemed to be falling short.

Under the table, Winn shifted, and his leg touched hers. She smiled. He grinned back. Their legs remained touching for the rest of the meal, and Billie couldn't be happier. He seemed to be feeling the same awkwardness that she was. It opened her heart, and she told him all about growing up a Bergmann, her mother's illness, and her worries for the future.

"My uncle and I had our hopes set on the mirror being able to make the medicine we needed to cure her."

At the mention of the mirror, Winn shifted uncomfortably.

"I'm sorry, I know we were trying to stay away from talking about it."

They lingered over a shared chocolate cake before finally giving up their seats in the restaurant. When he got his change, Winn handed her the pennies and smiled. Pennies from their special dinner to go toward her wedding shoes. She slipped them into her pocket, glancing away.

"I wish you could see the fireworks with me," Billie said they stepped outside. As soon as she said it, she wished she hadn't. It was another reminder that he'd be back in the mirror tonight, maybe for good.

"I'll spend as much time with you as I can."

"Let's go somewhere away from the crowd, so when the mirror pulls you back no one will notice."

"The best location to watch is over there." He pointed at a spot up the mountain. "But it doesn't matter where I am. Somehow all the witnesses have amnesia afterward."

"I didn't."

"You're special," he said.

"Why do you think?" she asked, not fishing for a compliment, but trying to figure out how the mirror worked.

He thought for a moment. "Might have to do with your family's connection to the mirror. Or maybe because you notice me while the people here have already written me off. No thanks to Matron. She's probably the one who started the rumors about me, and because I dealt Faro for her, they were easy lies for people to believe. That, and she was exaggerating what I was actually doing, so there was a piece of truth to it. People like to believe the worst in others."

"Well, you're not dealing for her anymore, and we're going to get you out of the mirror soon, so the other unexplainable happenings around you can stop. And in a town like this, people will move on and new folks will come around. The stage will get robbed, and all attention will be elsewhere again." She spoke with more confidence than she felt.

"And you are a stranger, so you could disappear and no one would notice. You need to be careful."

"No talk like that tonight. Let's end our day celebrating."

They settled into a clear spot on the mountain as the light

faded to near darkness and Billie realized Winn was still with her. *Winn was still with her.*

"You should have been pulled in by now, right? What if the mirror has broken for both of you?"

Winn examined the sky. "You're right." He grinned. "I've not seen beyond a sunset in months. I could kiss you for that, Miss Wilhelmina."

He leaned in, putting his hand at the back of her neck and pulling her close. "Happy Fourth of July."

Billie panicked. She'd never been kissed for real before, and it was happening too fast. Did she want it to happen? She'd been waiting for Branson, always imagined he would be her first kiss. And shouldn't she be doing something with her hands besides squeezing them so tightly together?

She closed her eyes, licked her lips, and leaned in before she completely ruined the moment. Winn's hand suddenly left her neck, and she opened her eyes.

She was alone on the hillside.

Billie blinked back tears. Winn had been pulled into the mirror.

No, no, no. It wasn't right.

A fairy tale should stay in a book, not have fingers that reached out through time to wreak havoc in the lives of regular people. She raised her knees up to meet her forehead as she curled tightly into a ball. Her black crepe was not only for mourning the death of her father but the death of her hopes. How could they fight something they couldn't see or understand?

The first *pop* of a firework cracked the air. Soon there was a barrage of pops and whistles, followed by startled shouts, and then a call for the fire department.

Billie stood to see what was going on when she noticed the young boy Billy running off into the night. If there was a disaster nearby, that child was bound to be front and center.

"A spark lit all of the fireworks at once," said Matron from behind.

Billie jumped. Matron must have just come down from the mountain, the mirror having exchanged her and Winn.

For Winn's sake, Billie masked her anger. She wanted to fly at the woman and make her fix things. Make her release Winn. But there was too much they didn't know. Was Matron to blame, or was she as stuck as Winn? As long as Matron didn't know all that they had learned, Billie had to pretend nothing had changed. It was the best way to catch Matron off guard.

"What a mess," Billie said watching the fireworks explode too low to the ground. "Something so beautiful that was meant to be shared with the town is now ruined." She was talking about Winn's life, but Matron didn't need to know that.

"Yes. It's unfortunate, but life presses on. Why don't you meet me in my office in an hour? Go around back; it's at the top of the stairs. I'd like to talk about your future." Matron continued her way down the mountain without waiting for an answer.

Meanwhile, the fire department scrambled to contain the fireworks and keep a fire from starting, while the crowd watched with interest.

Matron had extended another invitation, which meant maybe she was impressed with what Billie had said at the Women's Club. But that didn't lessen Billie's worry about the meeting. What future could Matron have in mind when she knew Billie was here with her uncle and would leave as soon as he did?

Billie's time in Bisbee would be nothing but a dream that would haunt her for her entire life. The tragic meeting of a boy trapped in a magic mirror.

She held on to her turquoise cabochon. If she couldn't change Winn's fate, this stone would be the only proof that this special summer ever happened.

CHAPTER 37

*A*t night, the player-piano music seemed louder, the gamblers, wilder. Billie skittered around the back of the building like a mouse seeking a hiding place, only to find the lack of lights made the night dark indeed. She didn't linger but raced up the stairs as soft on her toes as one could be in clunky work boots. Funny how she'd gotten used to wearing them. They were so practical in this town.

She knocked on the back door and waited, listening to the cicadas' eerie chirps. Below her a door in the adjoining building opened, and a man stepped outside. She suddenly felt vulnerable and tested the handle.

It was open, and a light shone into the hallway. *Matron did say to meet at her office.*

Billie slipped through the outside door, keeping her eyes open and her ears pricked for any suspicious noises.

She made her way down the narrow hall and passed a powder room, its door ajar. The next door was shut and Billie listened intently. She heard nothing, but noticed the sliver of light under the door, and so she knocked. Quietly at first. She couldn't help feeling she wasn't supposed to be here. All her training was screaming that no society girl should be sneaking up the back staircase of a saloon at night. It made her jumpy beyond belief.

"Matron?"

When no one answered, Billie tried the door, and it too, was open. *I really hope this is the right place.* She pushed into the room.

Red silk curtains draped the window at the back, and the electric light came from a crystal chandelier, of all things. A sitting area with a plush sofa and chair created a cozy nook with a small mirror above a table laden with fresh flowers. Matron had mixed bold solids and stripes to lovely affect. Less of an office and more like a sitting room, if it were not for the imposing oak desk in the middle. A room the Women's Club would be proud of, if Matron were ever able to get a representative to visit.

No one was around, but the scent of Matron's perfume lingered. Billie noted a small bottle of *No. 4711* on the desk beside a bottle of ink. Now she recognized that blend of citrus and flowers. She was in the right place, and Matron had been there recently.

Billie tried to find something to fault Matron on, but by all appearances everything she did was first rate, even how she decorated her office.

Time was running out, so Billie zeroed in on the imposing oak desk to look for anything nefarious. Music from the saloon below beat against her boots and masked the sound of anyone who might be approaching. She had better be quick, or she'd be caught with her hand in a drawer.

Based on the paperwork left out, Matron was in the midst of filling out purchase orders. Her pen lay perfectly perpendicular to the document, itself situated at an exact right angle to the edge of the desk. Would an evil mastermind be filling out purchase orders?

Billie gave herself a chill thinking about it.

She slid out the top drawer to reveal a variety of fountain pens and squat ink jars filled with India ink. The deeper drawer to the right contained more papers pertaining to the saloon. Closing one, she opened another. More business dealings, including notes on stock purchases of the Copper Queen. Matron *was* planning to buy them out.

None of this provided any clues for Winn's freedom, though. He'd said his attempts at restitution didn't save him, so what could save him if a changed life wasn't enough to free him from his prison?

The story books taught a lie. They said good people won. Evil was vanquished because good won out. But if being good wasn't enough, what else was there?

Frustrated, Billie put her hands on her hips and surveyed the room. The piano music came up through the floor, and she tapped her toe along with "Maple Leaf Rag."

She hadn't much time before Matron would return.

There had to be a secret drawer or hidden box with evidence of Matron's clandestine activities. The woman was too clever to leave anything out where her employees would stumble across them.

A noise sounded in the hall, and then the door opened. With no time to find a hiding place, Billie dropped to the ground, scrunched under the desk, and pulled the chair back to its original position. As she did so, her feet struck Matron's shoes, discarded under the desk.

Billie held her breath as the door closed, leaving a small gap as if someone kept their hand on the handle.

She chided herself. *Why did I hide?* A guilty reaction. She should have stood where she was, like she'd been patiently waiting, taking an innocent look about the room. Too late to correct her mistake, Billie held her breath and did the only thing she could. She eavesdropped.

"I tried to get her back into the store, but she waved me off."

It was Miss Brooks from the salon. Billie had met her in the street during the parade and Miss Brooks had tried to get her to come in for another beauty treatment.

"Be more insistent next time," said Matron. "She craves pampering. Play on her vanity, and she'll be a loyal customer."

"She'll need to be a loyal customer for one of the other girls. Remember, I'm leaving at the end of the summer to go back to California."

"Yes, so you've said." Matron's voice delivered an edge that cut. "You weren't a good fit anyway. Don't bother coming into work anymore."

"But we're still saving up for travel expenses. I can finish like I said." Miss Brooks sounded confused, hurt.

"It's already decided. Leave me. I don't want to see you again."

Maybe Matron had tried to trick Miss Brooks into the mirror and failed.

Billie shifted her weight and bumped into the shoes again. They were the deep red shoes that she had admired so much. She'd looked all over town for these shoes, but they weren't in any of the stores.

"Matron!" called a male voice from downstairs. "It's broke again."

"Imbeciles. Can no one do the job I ask?" Footsteps sounded away from the office and Billie quickly scrambled out from under the desk. She'd sit on the couch like a normal person, waiting for Matron. Seconds turned to minutes, turned to endless waiting.

Billie paced the room. Maybe she should go. This was a mistake from the start. She took one last look around to make sure she'd not made a mess of things and noticed one of the red shoes she'd kicked earlier was now sticking out from under the desk.

Oh no. Matron was so particular, she'd notice. Billie went to shove the shoe back under, but instead, reached for the other. They glittered in the light so tantalizingly, begging to be tried on.

Dare she? Before she fully realized what she was doing, she had one boot off already. It was just like the time she and her friends snuck into Jane's older sister's room and tried on all her fancy clothes.

Quickly, she pulled off the other boot and slipped both feet into the dainty shoes. As her toes slid in a feeling of warmth began spreading rapidly up her legs, her torso, her arms, her head.

A falling sensation gripped her, and she reached out to catch herself, missing the edge of the desk and falling into the room.

But it wasn't Matron's room she fell into. Unless Matron's room had suddenly been enveloped in smoke from a fire below or a mist from the mountains.

She thought she saw Matron come through the door, a look of surprise, followed by a smile, but then she was gone, drowned by the fog.

The ground came up to meet her and Billie smacked down hard. The fire in her body died back the way it had come, leaving her breathless. She stood and turned around but the room was gone. White mist landed on her with a cooling sensation, floating around her legs, her arms, her fingers. Everywhere.

She stepped tentatively through the swirling air, not confident of the ground beneath her. The air smelled stale, strange. Adrenaline coursed through her body. *Where was she?*

She kept walking forward. Her steps were muffled and there was no other sound. No more piano music from the saloon, no raucous voices.

Panic began to well up to choke her. She'd seen this white mist before. At Lou's cabin.

No. It couldn't be.

She had been cautious. Careful. Matron hadn't tricked her.

Billie stopped walking so she could focus on her breathing. *Stay calm.*

"Hello?" She called in all directions, but her voice died out on her lips. There was no one out there. No one to help her.

She was trapped in the mirror.

CHAPTER 38

$\mathcal{B}$illie felt a pulling sensation, leading her to turn to the right, face forward. As she walked, the mist began swirling in earnest, clearing a path for her and showing her the way. The motion felt purposeful, like someone was guiding her.

She walked for ages it seemed before she came to the mirror frame, suspended in the air. There was no wall, just the frame floating as if of its own accord. It was a very old, gilt frame with a verdigris patina, possibly caused by the heavy mist surrounding it. Intricate carvings of fairies and flowers wound all around the frame, and at the bottom was a pomegranate with two little fairies on either side leaning on the fruit with impish grins.

Her mouth went dry. It was true. She really was in the mirror. A fairy mirror.

"Winn?" she called. "Are you here?"

Her heart beat, beat, beat.

Silence.

"Winn!" She stood close to the frame and tried to peer out, imagining the inside of Lou's shack. "Winn!" The mirror was dark. Did that mean she couldn't see out, or that the cabin was dark? She touched the surface and then jerked her hand back. It was so cold it burned.

If she was in the mirror, that meant Winn was out. He would know something had happened and would come to the mirror to find out what. She had to remain calm and wait for him to recover and then call her.

She'd never been so alone before. Not a sound. Not a soul. Not a hope.

No. There was always hope. She stood firm in front of the mirror and said:

> *Mirror, mirror*
> *on the wall,*
> *Help me escape;*
> *Outside let me fall.*

Not a bad rhyme for making it up on the spot. She waited, but nothing happened. Maybe the person inside the mirror couldn't ask for something. Or couldn't ask for their freedom. She tried again.

> *Mirror, mirror*
> *On the wall,*
> *Medicine for mother?*
> *My request is small.*

She clasped her hands and waited. Still nothing.

Billie paced in the small space in front of the mirror, the red shoes glittering brightly against the white mist. Red on white. Blood on snow. A memory sparked.

The shoes.

Her father's voice came to her: *"The evil queen couldn't stay away. When she learned where the wedding was to be held she came to see for herself how beautiful Snow White had become. But before she could enter the chapel and ruin the ceremony for everyone, the townspeople stopped her. They'd had enough. Their fear had finally been overcome by courage. They forced her to put on red-hot shoes of iron. The shoes were so painful she danced and danced until she fell to her death."*

Billie had always thought that was a strange thing for the villagers to do. They should have just taken away her mirror and put her in jail. Who came up with the idea that shoes would be the death of her?

She fell to her death. That's what Dad had said. *Red-hot shoes. Fell to her death.*

Billie gasped. The evil queen fell into her mirror. Billie was sure of it. The tale had lost some of its telling over the years. The queen probably danced her way back to the mirror to try to save herself but fell into it instead and became trapped.

And if that was the case, what if Matron's red shoes were those same shoes? Matron's final play for Billie's vanity which pulled her into the mirror.

Billie's head pounded with the possibilities. What happened to that queen? Did she ever escape? It was entirely possible that Matron was the evil queen from the Snow White story.

The more she thought about it, the more sense it made. The mirror was real. The queen was still alive, and the red shoes were now on Billie's feet.

Realization crashed into her, and she pressed her hand to her chest.

Matron did it.

The evil queen was free, while she and Winn were trapped.

She felt sick. If only she could go back five minutes and make a different decision. Matron had left out the shoes to tempt her. Winn warned her Matron would use her greatest weakness against her, and she did. Her vanity.

Billie reached down to take the shoes off, hoping they were the key to getting out of the mirror. They were hard, like iron. She tugged and pulled, but they wouldn't come off. Matron must have added the red crystals to the shoes to mask their true nature as iron shoes and make them look pretty instead.

Billie would have cried if she weren't already beyond tears.

Ironic. She'd discovered Matron's secret, but by doing so, fell into her trap. Now Billie was condemned to a life tied to the mirror. Since it was night, she must have switched positions with Winn. Unless she was the only one inhabiting the mirror now. She choked out a sound. She might have freed Winn only to take his place forever.

He had never said how oppressive the atmosphere was behind the mirror. She could barely breathe. She collapsed in front of the frame and stared at the ground while she tried to catch her breath. How would she survive this?

She would not give in to despair. She would not. She forced herself to look up.

A light flickered in the mirror. Billie pushed herself off the ground and feeling grit, looked at her hands. Traces of dirt, like she was outside. She brushed it off and stared into the mirror. The window to her world.

The surface was no longer black, but it was still dark. She leaned in, watching the dim scene unfold before her. The flickering light was a match, followed by the flair of a lantern. Winn's face, angled away from her was illuminated by the lantern he held. He turned to look into the mirror and his expression was wary. That meant he couldn't see her. She could see him, but he was probably viewing his own reflection.

Oh, Winn. It's me. Call to me.

"Mirror, mirror on the wall," he started.

The mist around her became alive again. It swirled and twirled, attacking the glass itself while Winn recited the poem. Small ice fragments stung her skin as the whiteness rushed past her. Tiny prisms that swirled colors onto the mirror's surface.

When the mist spun away and the air cleared there was nothing separating her and Winn.

Except everything separated them.

His eyes widened. He'd seen her.

They just stared at each other, adjusting to the reversal of fortunes. Letting the truth seep in.

"Are you free?" she finally asked. She swallowed the lump in her throat.

He gasped. "Wilhelmina, what have you done?"

"I'm not entirely sure," she said, giving him a half smile. "One minute I was in Matron's office, the next in the mirror."

"You pushed me out." He looked pained. "Why did you do that?"

"I didn't mean to. It just happened."

The reality of her situation sank into her bones. She blinked rapidly. She couldn't fall apart now, not when she'd helped Winn.

She examined her surroundings again. The mist remained, but it had stepped back as if it couldn't get too close to the opening, yet still had to stand guard against her.

"I felt that way myself—that it happened without warning. One minute I was pocketing Fremont's watch, the next I was falling into the mirror. I hadn't a clue what was going on. For a time, I wondered if I was dead and what it meant that I was in this place all alone. Then Matron called me to the mirror and explained." He laughed, a dull sound. "She thanked me."

"Are you free?" Her voice came out hard this time. She had to know if her unwitting sacrifice did anything. Right now, nothing else mattered.

Winn took a step forward. "I'm not going to thank you. I wish you wouldn't have done it."

"Winn, tell me. Are you free? Can you tell if you'll get pulled in again?"

His face was in shadows since he stepped away from the light. She couldn't see his eyes clearly.

"I don't know if the mirror will call me back in or not, but I'm not free if you aren't. I could never leave you alone in there, Billie. Never."

Despite her fear of being trapped in the mirror her heart sang. Winn truly cared for her. "Thank you," she managed to choke out.

Winn nodded, but his shoulders closed in, like he had already given up.

The front door opened, and Lou hobbled in. She dropped her cane when she saw Winn out of the mirror and Billie inside.

"Wilhelmina." Lou shook her head. "A fine kettle of fish you've gotten yourself into." Winn picked up Lou's cane and helped her over to the bed.

Billie could only imagine what she looked like to Lou, hanging on her otherwise bare walls. Her black crepe gown standing out in stark contrast to the white mist and her despondent face staring out at them. A pitiful sight, for sure. They needed to know what she'd found out.

"I think I know who Matron really is," Billie said. "She has the red shoes."

Winn looked at her like she'd spoken in German, but Lou cocked her head, her eyes narrowing as if the information struck a chord.

"She danced in red-hot shoes," Lou said, recalling the story.

"One of you please tell me what you're talking about." Winn said, exasperated.

"In the Snow White fairy tale, the evil queen was forced to wear burning-hot shoes that made her dance to her death," Billie explained to Winn. "But now I know it wasn't her death she danced to. She danced into the mirror. Being trapped in the mirror was her punishment, a living death."

"And you think that person is Matron?" he said. "How long ago was that?"

"It has to be centuries." Billie looked to Lou. "The stories are old, but not recorded in the history books. They weren't supposed to be real."

"And she lives on," Lou said, "Trapped in the mirror she used to try to destroy Snow White. There's justice for you." She smiled as if pleased at the punishment.

"How can we use this information to get her back in the mirror for good?" Winn said.

"Wish I knew." Lou hobbled into the kitchen and put the kettle on. "Fremont is the one to ask, but he's missing."

"What changed do you think?" Billie touched the glass separating her and Winn. Her fingers burned and froze at the same time. She snatched her hand back. "Why is the mirror acting differently after all these years? Is it the mirror itself, or did Matron learn how to get out?"

Winn took another step closer to the mirror, filling the frame with his earnest look. "All I want to know is if Billie has taken Matron's place."

"Because if it's Matron's place I've taken," Billie said, staring into Winn's kind eyes. "Then she is free, and one of us will always be in the mirror." She swallowed, thinking of the poem she read in the newspaper. *Fate*. "We'll never be together again."

CHAPTER 39

*A*ll night Billie was afraid to leave the frame which was her view into the world she had left. If an opportunity for escape presented itself, she had to be ready.

Winn and Lou kept vigil with her, taking turns pacing and trying to come up with something to talk about that didn't lead back to the mirror. No one wanted to hint at anything that might upset Billie any further.

For Billie, it was an eerie business. She could only see a limited portion of the shack, watch them walk in and out of her field of vision, blurred around the edges like a vignette photo.

To be present, but not. A part, but not.

She couldn't imagine living like this for any length of time.

Alive, but not.

No one would miss her. The folks in California had said their goodbyes, not expecting to ever see her again. Her friends in Boston didn't know she was on her way home. She never did get around to sending Jane or Suzanne or Holly a telegram. Only Uncle and her mother, Lou and Winn would notice her absence.

Billie Bergmann had never felt so unseen in all her life. Growing up as Chester Bergmann's daughter, she was always aware of who she was, and that people were watching. Now who was she to be? A fairy tale that no one would ever read?

She was just beginning to figure out her life in preparation for her return to Boston, and now she might never return. She'd have to tell Uncle Dale she'd found the mirror, and why they could never leave Bisbee. *How would that conversation go?*

At some point in the early hours of the morning, Billie was thrust from the mirror with a force akin to a steam train. She tumbled onto the bed that Lou had graciously placed under the mirror in the hopes that Billie wouldn't be stuck forever.

As soon as she regained her senses, she looked for Winn. Where was he? Where was he? She couldn't see him. "Lou? Where is he?" She didn't want to look in the mirror.

But then strong hands lifted her up from behind, and she gasped with relief.

"You're out," Winn said, and held her tight. "We both are."

"Well, yeehaw!" Billie laughed and cried all at once. She nestled into Winn, drawing strength from his arms. She shook from shock, from fear, from relief.

The air smelled spring-morning fresh after the cloistered mist, and Billie breathed and breathed, trying to rid herself of the stale smell that had also seeped into her clothes. No wonder Winn preferred the outdoors like he did.

Lou thumped her cane on the floor as she moved to the mirror. She got up close and peered in. "Mirror, Mirror, on the wall, who's the fairest of them all?" she said tersely.

The mirror swirled and whirled while everyone remained riveted to the spot. Soon, a faint version of Matron was revealed, barely visible at the dawn of day. She was scowling.

"I am, of course."

She scanned the room until her gaze landed on Billie. "Found my shoes, I see," she said looking down.

The ruby slippers faded from Billie's cursed feet and disappeared, leaving behind a burning sensation.

"Where'd they go?" Billie asked.

"Child, where do you think? Back onto my feet." She looked down as if admiring them, but the edges of the mirror cut off the view for the rest of them. "I do hate them so, but they are irresistibly pretty, aren't they?" She frowned. "And unpredictable. I hoped I'd not see this side of the mirror again."

"They're the portal that pulls you into the mirror," Billie said.

"And you, now, too."

"I'll never put them on again." Billie crossed her arms. Lesson learned.

"Doesn't work like that," Matron said. "They were only the final piece. To tip the scales so to speak. I hoped they'd stay on your feet, and I'd finally be free." She narrowed her eyes. "Something about you is interfering with my plan, but don't worry, I'll figure it out. There's still time. Once the mirror has you, it doesn't let go easily. Right, Mr. Harris?"

Billie didn't know how to respond. She didn't like being part of Matron's plan, but if there was something about her interfering with that plan, she wanted to know what it was to make sure she kept doing it.

"I never got near your shoes," Winn said, standing close to the frame. "How did I get pulled into the mirror?"

Matron shrugged. "You were just trouble waiting to happen and a happy accident for me."

"Aren't you the one in charge of the mirror?" Winn said.

"If I were in charge, you think I'd still be in here?"

"Then who is in charge if not the queen?" Lou said.

Matron twisted her lips as if amused.

"We figured out who you are," Billie said. "You're the evil queen who tried to have Snow White killed."

"Evil now, is it? That must have been added to the story after my time. No one called me evil. Ambitious, yes." She waved her hand nonchalantly. "It wasn't much of a stretch for you to figure out. Yes, yes. I'm the queen, and you lot are descended from those nasty dwarfs. Except my card player here, who found himself in the wrong place. Bully for you. Doesn't change anything, though does it?"

Billie's eyes widened at the shift in Matron's demeanor. If she'd acted like this from the start, it would have been easy to understand why Lou didn't like her.

"Actually, it changes a lot," Billie said. "I've got the full picture now."

Matron laughed. A big, gut churning chortle that sent a tingle up Billie's spine.

"See what I mean?" Winn said. "You'd think a woman stuck in a mirror for centuries would have learned some humility by now."

"Silly child. You've only got as much of the picture as you've figured out, and what they've told you," Matron said. "I gave you a chance. I told you I could help you become whoever you wanted to be. Instead, you fell to temptation. I knew your vanity would be your undoing."

Billie let out a small gasp. She wasn't silly, she just believed life was meant to be enjoyed. Sure, she might place a little too much on outward appearance, but that was no reason to trap her in the mirror. "You planned for me to take your place from the moment you knew I was in town."

Matron pursed her lips. "Yes and no. You were always a possibility, but as a Bergmann, you could have been just as useful to me outside the mirror as inside." She waved her hand in a circular motion. "I could have set you up to do anything you wanted in this town, but you chose to associate with these people instead of me. Wrong decision."

"No," Lou said. "She made the right decision. You're buying up the town and putting people out of business out of spite. No one wants to be a part of that."

"As queen, I'm used to owning everything." Matron stated it simply, as if there were no other way. "If I'm going to live here, I ought to be comfortable. These immigrants are used to a hard life, in fact, they crave it, moving from one mining place to the next. A town finally begins to get decent, and they move along to the next mining boom."

With each taunt Matron threw out, Billie grew angrier. She wanted to say something to show that Matron hadn't won. That the fight wasn't over. To take back control from her, even if they didn't know what they were doing yet. She wanted to do something to disrupt Matron's life the way she had disrupted Winn's and now her own.

An idea began to form in the back of her mind that would completely disrupt Matron's position in town and leave her near as vulnerable as the rest of them.

"Why don't we move the mirror?" Billie said, turning her back on Matron. "If we're all trapped within its radius, we could move it away from here. Take it back to Boston."

"You shall not touch this mirror." Matron's voice boomed into the room.

Billie and Winn exchanged a look.

"You'll regret it if you move the mirror," Matron said, her voice once again in control.

Billie faced Matron, sensing the upper hand. "Why?"

"It's in flux and if you move it, we will all be destroyed. This mirror is in the exact place it needs to be."

Lou got up close to the mirror again. "What about this place is so special?" She touched the edges of the mirror as if trying to figure out how to pop it out of the wall.

"Every generation there is an opening. A window of opportunity when the mirror becomes clear like glass. The first time it happened I didn't know what was going on, but the world felt closer, like I could almost touch it." She reached out her hand like she was imagining plucking a flower. "But then it closed and became a mirror again."

She focused on Lou. "I was never quite able to get out of the confines of this prison. It's the copper in these hills providing a powerful conductor stretching the portal and making it thinner than it's ever been." She arched an eyebrow. "Passable."

"How long do these windows of opportunity stay open?" Winn asked, his voice betraying his hope.

Matron shrugged. "It's never stayed open this long. Perhaps we can go along like this for years. Perhaps days." She stood close to the frame and peered down at Lou, who was still examining how to remove the mirror. "Until the portal closes, you can't move it. You'll risk losing your impetuous little cousin or the boy to the mirror. One of us will remain inside."

"You would trade your life for one of these young ones, wouldn't you?" Lou said.

Matron straightened her shoulders, growing in height. "Youth is easier to sway. I tried to pull you in, but you would never accept my gifts."

"We should move the mirror this instant." Billie said. "While she's in there, let's get it away from the copper so the window will close and she'll be trapped."

There was a rush, as of a wind, and then Matron was standing in the shack, her thin hands gripped around Billie's neck.

Billie went up on her toes to lessen the strain Matron was putting on her windpipe. Panicked, she looked around for help, but Winn was back in the mirror, waving his arms, trying to keep his balance. He looked completely shocked, as did Matron.

"Not so fast, missy. I may not be completely free, but I know more about how that mirror works than either of you."

"Let her go," Lou said, cane raised.

Dismissing Lou, Matron leaned her face close to Billie's. "Did you like how you felt in the mirror? An impression hard to describe, isn't it? A longing for what you can't touch, perhaps? The world as you know it is so close, but you can't quite grasp it. When it becomes a full mirror again, you will be locked in with no freedom. You'll choke from the oppression, like being in one of these mines with all of the mountain closing in on you and you have no escape. It won't be me. I've worked too long and hard to fail now. Tread carefully, child." With a shove, Matron let her go.

Billie struggled to bring in a breath. Not because her airway was being restricted, but because she was scared. Her pulse raced as her body reacted to Matron's words. She knew the feeling Matron described all too well. It was the way she felt in the mines. If she could never escape the oppression, had no hope of escaping, being trapped in the mirror would drive her mad. She couldn't let it happen.

"No. We can't move it," she said quietly. It was too risky. They'd need to find another way.

CHAPTER 40

"*W*ilhelmina, look at me."

Billie did. Winn was inside the shack, on the other side of the mirror from her, but his face did not reflect the fear that was surely displayed on her face.

She and Winn had been in and out of the mirror countless times now, as puppets Matron moved around at will to show them she was in charge of them, if not the mirror. Whatever it was that had happened the day they confronted her, Matron had learned a new skill.

And every time Billie was in the mirror she had to fight the panic attacks Matron's description had implanted in her mind. She was sure the window would turn into a mirror while she was in it, and then what would she do?

For her whole life and beyond she'd be locked away from the rest of the world. What would she eat? How would she find a drink? These were the mundane things that she focused on, and it was so crazy she didn't know how to stop until she looked into Winn's eyes. Winn's gentle eyes that looked back at her with sadness and guilt. She couldn't pull him down into this pit with her.

"Better?" he asked.

She nodded, her heart palpitations slowing. "Yes. It's almost over."

It had been hard for her to let Winn see her panic attacks at first, but after he'd shown her such tenderness and stayed with her, she learned to trust him. His granite exterior from when they first met was so different from the boy she'd come to know.

Boom.

Another blast went off in Uncle Dale's mine, rattling Lou's teacup in its saucer.

Lou wasn't complaining much, but the proximity of her claim to Uncle Dale's must have been bothering her. She was one who enjoyed solitude, but Billie's uncle had increased his work on the claim by hiring an experienced hard rock miner. The Tarr brothers weren't interested in working such a small claim and had gone back to Globe.

"This attack was longer," Billie said. "I don't know if I'll have much time to look around today."

Since their confrontation with Matron they were working together to explore the unending mist to see if there was another way out, or if they could learn more about how the mirror worked.

Since Matron seemed to have the ability to control more of her time out of the mirror, they were more determined than ever to figure out how she was doing it. Winn would sit with Billie and talk her through the panic attack, then talk her through exploring areas he'd not been in yet.

"Lou was thinking we should examine the frame again, anyway. When Matron attacked you, she was standing right there."

"We've both looked at it a million times."

"Maybe a million and one will do the trick." He smiled encouragingly.

Fine. The frame hung suspended in space with nothing supporting it. Billie walked around it, but from the back, she could see nothing. Literally, it disappeared. The first time she'd discovered this, she'd worried that the frame was gone, but it can only be viewed from the front. From behind, she could reach her hand out to touch where it was supposed to be, but her hand went right through empty space.

When she went back around to the front, the mirror was visible and solid again.

Billie gripped both sides and tried to move the frame. She didn't want to rip it away, lest she tear the boundary between worlds and be trapped inside, but she wanted to see how permanent it felt. It was as solid as the mountains. Perhaps they should try dynamite to blast the thing open.

Next, she looked at the top of the frame, examining each individual fairy and flower.

The winged fairies were the classic-looking creatures, the size of hummingbirds next to the flowers, and with impish smiles ending in tiny dimples. Carved from wood with thin copper hammered in place, the frame would have initially had that shiny copper color, but was now a dull green patina, with pieces flaking off.

The inside frame was so different from the plain outside frame. Had the side facing the shack been sporting fairies from the beginning, more people might have stumbled across the mirror. It might have been valued for its art, if not its more mysterious qualities.

Billie tried to pull off the tiny fairy with the widest grin, but it was firmly attached. Maybe with more pressure it would detach, but breaking the frame probably wasn't a good idea. Another little fairy had a cute, upturned nose which Billie rubbed. She blew a puff of air on a third.

"What are you doing?" Winn asked, amusement in his voice.

"Trying things. I don't know what else to do."

"All I see is your head bobbing in and out." He laughed and demonstrated what she looked like from his point of view.

"I'm glad you find it amusing when you do the same thing when you're in here."

"I know, but I'm not as adorable as you."

She made her way round to the pomegranate on the bottom and what she saw made her heart skip a beat. "Winn?"

"What?"

"The fairies at the bottom moved."

"What do you mean?"

"I'm pretty sure these little twins used to be leaning forward with their elbows on the pomegranate, but now they're leaning backward on it. Do you remember what they're supposed to look like?"

He disappeared from her view.

"Winn?"

He came back with a pencil and paper. "One way to find out. Let's sketch the frame each time we're in there and compare notes. Ready?"

He made like he was going to toss her the items.

She nodded. She'd never caught anything through the mirror before.

"Pencil first." He tossed it to her. As the pencil pierced the glass, the surface rippled like water and allowed it through.

Winn tried to pass the paper next, but each time he brought it to the mirror it would bend, not pass through. In the end, he crumpled it into a ball and tossed it in like a baseball pitcher. "I used to play on the high school team," he said. "Before all this."

She caught the paper ball. "Darren said you were good. Maybe you'll play again when this is all over."

"I'm better at ball than drawing. We'll see if my fairies look like anything other than stick people."

"Stick people with wings," Billie said.

He laughed, and the door opened. They both jumped as they weren't expecting Lou back for hours yet. She'd insisted on going into town herself for some supplies and with the way she was hobbling, they expected she'd be gone for hours.

Knock, knock.

"Hello?" It was Uncle Dale tapping on the already opened door. He stepped into the room, taking his hat off. "Thought I heard voices."

Winn closed the curtains. "That was me," Winn said.

Billie squinted, trying to see through the curtains. What was her uncle doing here? She'd been sure to visit him each time she came out of the mirror so he wouldn't become suspicious.

"Lou around?" Uncle Dale asked.

"In town. She'll be back soon."

"And Billie?"

Winn didn't answer so he must have shrugged.

"It's tough to catch her sometimes. Hope she isn't settling in too much. You know we're not staying long in town? She's got school to finish. Her parents had plans in place for her. Plans they've had since she was a child. That's not going to be a problem, is it?"

Billie's face grew hot with embarrassment.

"No, sir," Winn answered automatically.

"Send her to my claim when you see her next. I've got something to show her."

"Yes, sir."

The door clicked shut.

"Wait a moment," Winn whispered. "I'll make sure he's gone."

Meanwhile, Billie sketched the mirror. She was pretty sure the only fairies that had moved were those two at the bottom, but she wouldn't know for sure until she mapped them out.

"Tell me your secrets," she whispered to them. "Are you alive? Trapped like me?"

They remained frozen, their tiny mouths sealed shut. As Billie sketched the twins, she compared them to the other fairies. They wore the same draped bits of clothing, flowers in their hair, identical double wings, and their tiny faces carved to show details right down to eyelashes and everything.

"Imps," she said, hoping to get a rise out of them, but nothing.

With their new plan to sketch the position of each fairy in the frame, they'd know soon enough if the carvings were significant. But before Billie could complete her mission of creating the first mirror sketch, she was unceremoniously pushed out of the window. She landed on the bed, her place in the mirror now occupied by Matron.

Winn helped Billie up, and after closing the gap in the curtain, they exited the shack. There was no use staying there when they knew Matron could be listening in.

"Uncle Dale is getting close with his mine. He said he found a vein that he thinks crosses down into Lou's. Once he realizes there is no mirror hidden in there, he'll be ready to move on. I'll be forced to tell him I've decided to stay here. With Lou."

"What about your mother?" Winn asked.

Billie searched his face. He knew too well what an awkward conversation that was going to be. But Billie had the advantage that her mother had heard the same stories she had growing up. She should be able to tell the truth and have her mother believe her. But then would her mother tell Uncle Dale? If his niece was trapped in a magic mirror, what would he do? It was best to keep the mirror a secret as much as possible.

"For one, we haven't figured out how to get anything from this mirror, so I've no medicine to offer her. Secondly, school is starting soon, so she'll want me back in Boston. I'll have to tell her. She knows the stories, so she might believe me."

"Would you believe unless you'd seen it?"

Billie shook her head. *No way. How could anyone believe this?* "She'll think I want to stay because of a boy."

Winn nudged her. "And don't you?"

Had she not been tied to the mirror, would she have completely changed her life for a boy? For Winn? Maybe, not yet.

Even she wasn't irrepressibly romantic enough to deny everything in order to stay close to him. Her practical side would have kicked in and agreed to write copious letters to each other until they were older. But that wasn't what Winn wanted to hear. He wasn't even asking it.

She nudged him back and smiled. "I better go see what my uncle wants."

"Don't take too long. We've got plans in town."

CHAPTER 41

*U*ncle Dale paced outside the hole he'd carved into the mountain, peered deep inside, then resumed pacing, wringing his hands.

Billie had never seen him so anxious.

"There you are," he said, hearing her approach. "I've booked our trip for this weekend. It should give you enough time to say your goodbyes to the ah, friends, you've made while we've been here."

Too soon! Billie knew it was coming, but there's no way she could leave. "What about the mirror? Mom's medicine?"

"Today's the day." He held up a piece of paper, blindingly white against his dusty hands. "Right of Apex. I found the vein, and Lou doesn't have the money to go to court over it. I've got permission to cross over into her claim. We should know within minutes what she's got in there."

Billie stood stunned. Should she tell him about the mirror or not? Crossing over into Lou's mine would be harmless as far as the mirror went, but Lou would be so angry to have him barge his way into her mine. Despite it being legal, it didn't feel right what he was doing.

"I'm not going back to Boston," she said to stall for time. "I've decided to live with Lou."

He folded his document and shoved it into his shirt pocket. "You're not serious. You really think you can live in a shack up on a mountain tucked away in a forgotten territory and be happy? You? Never."

He knew her too well. "Arizona will be a state soon, you said so yourself."

It was the only comeback she could think of. No, she didn't want to live on the side of the mountain. She'd stay at the hotel, but that couldn't be a long-term solution.

"It's that boy, isn't it? I never should have let my guard down. I didn't mind you spending time with him, to help pull you out of your grief. I thought having a distraction would be good for you, but you can't think you've got a future with him. What will your mother say?"

At that moment, the miner Uncle Dale had hired scrambled out of the hole.

"Stand back," he said, his horseshoe mustache covered in a fine layer of dust. "Should be the final blast."

They quickly moved away, and Billie covered her ears. *Boom.* A cloud of dust floated out of the hole. Well, one positive, thing: if that was the last blast, Lou would get her quiet life back.

Uncle Dale told his hired help to wait while he went in first to see if the way was cleared. He was gone awhile, leaving Billie and the miner outside with nothing to say.

"Looks like we might get some rain," the miner said, staring up at the sky. Dark clouds gathered past the mountaintops.

Billie focused on the churning clouds. "Looks so," she said. The clouds contained shades of white to gray to black, with golden patches where the sun shone upon them. Pretty, but ominous.

When he came out, Uncle Dale looked shocked. He hid it well for the hired help, but Billie recognized the furrowed brow for what it was. He shook the man's hand and dismissed him. "I'll see you at the Fish Pond later."

Once the man was out of sight, Uncle Dale extended his arm. "Ready? Maybe you can help me make sense of this."

Billie wasn't exactly thrilled to be going into a recently blasted mine, but her curiosity was piqued. She clicked on her carbide light and took a deep breath. For Lou. She'd do it for Lou, to make sure a bad situation was handled well. She could report back all that her uncle did and help put Lou's mind at ease.

Billie began her ritual by stepping just inside the entrance, picturing Winn's face and hearing him saying "breathe." How did miners do this day in, day out for years?

Uncle Dale waited, her problem being no secret in the family.

When she looked up at him, he said, "Ready?"

She nodded. It was easier this time.

"Watch your step." Uncle Dale pointed to the rubble from the latest blast. Piles of jagged rocks, both big and small, littered the area with only a narrow path cleared through into the darker cavern of Lou's mine.

Billie shuddered at the close quarters, the walls and ceiling close enough to touch, heavy with granite, streaked with minute traces of copper and gold. This must be the vein that crossed over into Lou's. It wasn't that spectacular, and she was surprised her uncle managed to make a case for it.

"Look what's hidden here. Can you understand any of this?" Uncle Dale asked, shining his light onto a cache of household items better suited for a living room than an underground mine.

Billie's pale light followed his, spotlighting on paintings, candlesticks, silk pillows, furniture. She took a stunned step forward.

"If Lou's so rich, why is she living the way she is?" Uncle Dale said, voicing Billie's thoughts. "The old bird. She's either more devious that I gave her credit, or she needs help. Sure as the sun sets, if she's got the mirror, this is where it would be. Start looking."

Lou did say Fremont had left some things in the mine, but there were far too many luxury items to all belong to the missing cousin from Germany. But why would Lou have a cave of hidden treasures? Billie was missing something. Something Winn had said. What was it? And then something that Matron said about gifts, that Lou had refused all of her gifts.

A side table that wasn't there before.

A vase of flowers left at Lou's bedside and rejected.

These were from Matron. She was giving gifts to Lou, trying to link her to the mirror somehow.

Billie couldn't go into the cavern. This space represented Lou's strong will. Her fight against Matron. The sheer number of gifts, piled floor to ceiling was overwhelming. How could Lou stand up to the pressure for so long?

"Quickly now," Uncle Dale said, "Before she gets in here and moves things." He shoved a rock off an object, and then held up a golden candlestick. "Amazing quality. The blast didn't even scratch it."

A rock that size should have at least dented the candlestick. With renewed interest, Billie wandered the rows, amazed at what she saw. The magic mirror, despite its age and slow degradation had proved to be indestructible. What if Matron had been getting these items from the mirror?

The mirror could give her the medicine for her mother after all.

Billie glanced at Uncle wondering that he didn't hear her; her thoughts were shouting.

She made a show of searching through the treasures, but her mind was down the tunnel and on the other side of Lou's locked door. Uncle had been on the right track, justified in his search, though questionably not his methods.

As she looked at the treasures, another thought hit her hard. Winn and Lou already knew they could get things from the mirror. The evidence was all around her. They already knew and hadn't told her.

That's why Matron laughed when Billie boasted she had the whole picture. After all she'd been through, and they still didn't trust her?

Her heart was crushed that she was still being left out. How were they to work together if they didn't tell her everything they knew about the mirror?

Uncle systematically scoured the cache on his side of the room, then came over to Billie's and did the same. "Double-check me over there," he said, pointing her where he wanted her to go.

Each piece she looked at was lovely, but Billie knew she wouldn't find what he was looking for. She marveled over all of Matron's gifts until she thought of her own gifts from Matron and felt a chill run down her back.

Matron got her exquisite objects from the mirror.

Winn had warned her, but Billie thought she was strong enough to come close to temptation and not fall. How foolish she had been. Item by coveted item, she had been drawn into Matron's web, which was tied to the mirror.

After they'd seen every bauble and brick-a-brack, Uncle Dale raised his empty hands. "Well, that's it, then. No mirror here. I'd still like to check out the rest of the mine, if you don't mind keeping Lou out of here for me."

Billie nodded absently. "That might be hard to do once she sees what you did." Billie shone her light at the hole blasted in the wall. "Can't hide that." Nor could Billie hide that she knew what Lou was still keeping from her.

"I can't predict anything that woman might do." Uncle Dale's gaze took in the room, his light shining on each item one by one. He shook his head. "Sorry I gave you hope. I guess those stories of your dad's were just that. Stories. I can have things wrapped up here today." He pointed at her. "Don't say I don't know how to cut my losses. Be ready to leave this weekend."

CHAPTER 42

*W*inn waited outside Lou's, sitting on the ground and leaning against the dried, splintered wood of the shack, his Stetson pulled low. Billie had a hard time looking him in the eye. *Why didn't he tell me? He knew how important finding a cure for my mother was.*

"My uncle broke through," she said. "He's doing one final sweep for the mirror." She tried to keep her voice casual, like nothing had changed, but she must have failed, given the way he looked at her.

"Guess he'll be disappointed, then. No hidden magic mirror deep within the mine." Winn stood, brushing the dirt from his trousers.

Winn had to have known about the stash hidden in the mine. He knew the flowers came from Matron because Lou told him to give them back...to her.

"No, but he found some other things back there that Lou was trying to keep hidden." She searched his face for his reaction. He looked at his boots.

"Oh."

"Is that all? Oh? I can understand not telling me before I was trapped in the mirror with you, but now that I'm fully involved, shouldn't I be fully involved? You know what I want from it."

"Yes. I'm sorry. Lou is still looking out for you."

"And you go along with her. Every. Time. Why?"

He took a deep breath. "The mirror is in her house. It's her responsibility." He lifted his hat and ran his fingers through his hair. "And I think she's right."

Billie twisted her lips.

"She didn't want you to be tempted more than you were able to handle. In all fairness to her, if you knew that you could get whatever you wanted from the mirror, would you have been more focused on figuring that part out, or working on how to escape?"

"Escape, of course." *Or both*. Both. If she could figure out how to get her mother's medicine before the window closed...or if she could talk Matron into getting it for her...

"Billie? Are you listening?" Winn waved his hand in front of her face.

"Yes. What?"

"I was saying that our time is so short we have to stay focused on the one thing. You can still do that, right?"

She nodded. Yes. Time is short. She groaned, remembering what Uncle Dale said. "My uncle wants to leave this weekend."

Winn raised his eyebrows. "I'd like to see you try."

"What do I tell him?"

"Nothing. The mirror will take care of everything."

"Can you imagine what would happen if I disappeared on the train, or if the train hit another camel when I tried to leave?"

"That was probably the last camel in Arizona."

She tried not to laugh. "You know what I mean."

Winn reached for Billie's hand. "You can't tell him. It makes no sense unless you see it. And if you show him the mirror, what do you think he would do? He bought the claim next to Lou's for crying out loud and blasted his way in. You know the fever that sets in when someone finds treasure." He pulled her forward, and they started walking down the mountain.

"Take the town of Bisbee, for example," he said pointing in the direction they were walking. "The first guy to find evidence of mineral deposits told two people, and they staked a claim together. Then he grubstaked another guy by the name of Warren to find more. Instead of keeping it between them, Warren told his friends, and they staked a bunch more claims, leaving the first guy out of it altogether. Nowadays most folks think of Warren as the founder of the camp. No one can keep a secret, so how many more people do we want to know about the mirror? Your uncle has seen what the mirror can produce. If he makes the connection, and that kind of information spreads, there'll be a boomtown thrown up at Lou's front door."

"So, there's our answer. We don't tell." *And see what happens when I get on a train.* "Are we sticking to our plan then?" she asked.

"Yes. This is no way to live. We keep on Matron until we uncover her secrets."

Once in town, they made their way to the back of the Poisoned Apple and snuck into Matron's office. The dark clouds gathering outside made for dim light inside, but they couldn't risk turning on the chandelier.

Winn went straight for her file cabinet, and Billie looked through the desk again. They both completed thorough searches before moving on to other areas in the office, turning over pillows and looking behind picture frames.

"I'm not finding anything," Winn said.

"Me either. There's got to be something." Billie started for the closet, but on her way there she stopped and stared at her reflection in Matron's mirror. "Huh," she said. "What if?" Billie looked around for a hefty object. She settled on a deep blue azurite paperweight from off Matron's desk.

"What are you doing?" Winn asked.

Billie paused, the paperweight aimed at Matron's mirror. "Just a hunch."

When a roll of thunder sounded outside she threw the azurite. The mirror shattered. She frowned. "I thought for sure."

"You were testing to see if it was another magic mirror? You could have just asked it."

"But then she might have seen us in her office."

What was bothering Billie was that she'd tried on the shoes in the office but fell into the mirror hanging on the wall at Lou's. If Matron could make, or ask for things from the mirror, wouldn't she think to make another mirror to use as a portal?

"Come on," Winn said. "We better get out of here. Someone will have heard that."

They scrambled outside without getting caught and made their way to the front of the building.

"The items Lou stores in the mine are unbreakable," Billie said. "The blast didn't affect them. All that dynamite and rock? They were undamaged even when they got hit. I thought maybe..."

"No. If that mirror were magic, don't you think Matron would use it for convenience sake? She's not the type to hike down a mountain every night unless she had no choice."

Winn had a point, but the idea wouldn't leave. She needed to think about it some more. In comfort. "I'm going back to the hotel," she said before stepping out onto the street. Another flash of lightning lit the sky, and suddenly buckets of rain dumped down before she was halfway across the street. The roar of millions of raindrops splatting against tin roofs and hard-packed clay was louder than any train rushing into town.

"Run for it!" Winn called as he went the other direction.

Instantly drenched, Billie dashed through the mud and into the nearest hotel with everyone else running from the rain. By the time she'd made it inside, the bottom of her skirt was caked in wet clay. What a mess they had all brought with them into the lobby. It looked like a river delta spreading out, the way their muddy shoes dropped the dirt at the doorway.

She squeezed her way to a place at the window so she could watch the downpour. There was no sign of Winn, so he must have ducked under shelter somewhere else.

Those who had sought refuge on the sidewalks under awnings were soon standing in water and had to clamber for higher ground on stairs or in buildings. The streets became puddles, became creeks, became rivers. Billie had never seen anything like it.

"Where's all the water coming from?" Billie asked as she watched the waters race down the street.

"Floods. We get them sometimes," said a waitress, taking a break from her customers to watch the excitement outside. "Runs right off the mountains, gets channeled through the valley and into town. Always makes a mess." She looked out the window. "I've never seen it this bad."

Several pieces of wood floated and churned on top of the brown water. Then larger pieces floated by, a lamp shade, and then possibly curtains zipped by.

"It got a house," someone said, excited.

"It won't flood in here?" Billie asked, eyeing the water rising higher and higher up the steps. Would they be swept away?

"Doubt it," said a man watching at the window beside her.

"There's someone stuck in the water," a little boy said, pointing up the street.

"He's right," another said. "Hurry."

At the top of the road, a head was bobbing, arm flailing while the figure gripped a piece of debris floating on the rising water. He latched onto a tree caught between buildings and it looked for a moment like he was saved, but the panic on his face revealed he was losing his grip against the waters trying to sweep him away.

Several men raced outside. A rope was procured and tossed to a gentleman across the street. They held it taut and called out to the poor soul fighting for his life. "We'll catch you."

Billie held her breath. It was difficult to tell if the man noticed the rescuers. Could they be heard above the noise of the water? The crowd forming on the porch began calling to him and gesturing to let go.

He did.

Seconds after releasing the tree he was hurtling toward the rope. He latched on with both hands, as water surged up around him and over his head.

"He's going to drown," a woman yelled.

A burly man, who Billie recognized as one of the firemen in the parade jumped into the water, using the rope to guide him. The men on either side of the road strained at the added weight.

For several seconds it looked as if they would both be lost, but the fireman fought the current, lugging the half-drowned man slung over his shoulders until they reached the steps of the hotel.

"Stand back. Give him some room."

They dragged the man across the threshold where they paused to let him get his bearings.

Safe, he lay in the mud of the entryway, panting to catch his breath. Wet black hair plastered to his skull, and his clothes dripped a wide puddle around him.

Quickly, someone handed over a wool blanket to wrap him up. The water outside was comparatively warm, but shock was setting in, and the man visibly shivered.

But above all this, what caught Billie's attention most was that he was a dwarf.

A coincidence? How many dwarfs were common to remote mining towns?

With her heart beating hard against her chest she hovered at the edge of the crowd, not taking her eyes off the newcomer. She feared if she glanced away he might disappear again, and now that she had found him, she wasn't letting him go.

"Are you well?" Someone asked him.

He nodded, rubbing his beard. "*Ja.* Yes," he said with a thick German accent.

Billie sucked in a breath. It had to be him. Her missing cousin, the owner of the watch and, hopefully, the missing piece in this whole mirror mystery.

CHAPTER 43

Since Billie and her distant cousin Fremont had never met, he couldn't know who she was, but he had definitely noticed her staring. He kept checking to see if she was looking, and of course she was. Billie didn't care if she was making him uncomfortable.

She had to wait until the crowd around him left, and she could speak privately. She wanted to run and get Lou, but aside from the danger of going outside with the flood rising, that would give him an opportunity to slip away. The way his gaze shifted to the door and the flood waters rushing by seemed like he was contemplating throwing himself back in to get away from all the people hovering over him.

She inched closer in case he decided to try his luck in the water.

Eventually, the curious started wandering off for more excitement in watching the flood, and Billie saw her opportunity.

When he looked at her again, she said, "We have your watch."

The man flinched, and after a moment of staring at her, darted for the door. Wrapped the way he was in a blanket, he had trouble with balance, slipping on the mud, and landing with a *thud*.

"Whoa there, cowboy." A man with a handlebar mustache stopped Fremont from leaving and handed him a towel. "You ain't goin' back out in that." He forced Fremont to sit back down. "I'll be right back with some dry clothes."

Billie stood protectively with Fremont while the man made his way around the room gathering whatever the men were willing to give up. Billie wondered how he planned to talk a pair of pants off someone.

"Lou's been worried about you."

"Who *are* you?" he said.

"Chester Bergmann's daughter. Wilhelmina."

"Ach du lieber." He dried his hair with the towel. "It is a family reunion then? Where is the old man?" Fremont's accent hit the consonants hard.

"My father passed away a few months ago."

Fremont took in her black crepe as if seeing it for the first time. *"Ach.* I am sorry. What are you doing here?"

"Bringing your watch back to Lou, but I guess now that you're here it should go to you?"

He paused, looking uncomfortable. "Ja, it is mine."

"Does Lou know you're back? You know you disappeared without a ne'er-you-will."

Fremont cleared his throat. "That could not be helped."

"Care to elaborate?" Billie shifted her position to stand between Fremont and the door.

Meanwhile, the helpful man returned with a surprising amount of donated clothing for Fremont, who excused himself to get changed. Billie followed to stand guard at the bathroom door. No chance was she letting him get away.

When he came out wearing the mismatched and ill-fitting clothes, he rubbed his hands together. "If you will not leave me alone, how about you feed me?"

"I can do that." She indicated that he should walk ahead of her to the small restaurant where a table had just opened up.

Fremont ate bowl after bowl of chili until Billie was sure he would explode. She peppered him with questions, but his mouth was always full of food. It was something to behold. It was like he hadn't eaten in weeks.

"Where is my watch?" he finally said, leaving a smear of chili drippings on his white napkin.

"Lou has it," Billie said.

Fremont stood. He tossed his napkin onto his plate and stormed out of the restaurant.

Billie threw some money on the table and ran out after him. He couldn't be serious about going back outside in the storm.

"What's the hurry?" Billie called as she hurried to catch up in the lobby.

"It is mine; I want it back."

"But the flood."

She followed Fremont outside, and was pleasantly surprised to see the bulk of the storm had passed, and the river in the street had subsided to mere creek status. People were out on the sidewalks again, but the street was still impassible with the muddy, swirling water. *Winn?* She searched up and down the street, but there was no sign of him.

Billie set her lips and chased Fremont out of town and up the mountain.

What a sight they must look. Billie's long skirt was now fully caked in brown mud, despite the fine sprinkling of rain washing her from above. She slipped and fell several times while climbing the mountain but Fremont never stopped to help. *What a gentleman.*

Lou must have seen them coming for she was outside the door, shock registering on her face. "Fremont?" Her gaze darted to Billie and then back to Fremont. "Where did you go? All your belongings were left behind. I thought maybe you were dead. I even sent word back to your family in Germany that you were missing."

He marched into the shack, his gaze roaming the room. "Did you leave everything where I left it in the mine?" he asked. His tone indicated a weighted question.

"Almost everything," Lou hedged. "There was a window I put in the wall when mine broke.

"Was not my window. Can I see my things?" He approached the mine door, but halfway across the room he stopped, noticing the oval window. He froze.

Lou walked over to the magic mirror. "You sure this wasn't yours?"

Fremont squinted at the frame, listing his head to the right. He made a move as if to go closer, but then took a step away like it repulsed him. "What happened to it? It is supposed to be a mirror."

"The magic mirror from Snow White?" Lou said. She put her hands on her hips, rising to her full height. "You could have told me before leaving. You have no idea how much trouble that thing has caused." She jabbed her finger in its direction.

"*Ach*. I did not leave by choice. She tricked me."

"Didn't you think to give me some warning?" Lou said.

"That's not something you spring on someone right away, now is it?"

Lou frowned like she wasn't buying his excuses. "Tell me now. Why did you bring the magic mirror here? You owe us an explanation."

"You're family. If something happened, I knew you could step into my role."

Billie and Lou looked at each other.

"What role?" Billie asked.

"Protector of the mirror."

Billie sucked in a breath, reminded of an earlier conversation when Lou said the name *Wilhelmina* meant protector. A sense of foreboding settled into the pit of her stomach.

But they weren't looking at her, they were too busy staring angrily at each another.

"The world thinks the evil queen danced herself to death in those iron shoes. But she didn't. She danced herself right into her magic mirror."

Knew it. Billie nodded, pleased she'd already figured that part out.

"Ever since, our family has been guarding the mirror to make sure the queen never hurt anyone else again."

"But she has." Billie couldn't stay quiet.

Fremont glanced her way. "Matron was getting inside my head." He pulled at his hair in frustration. "I had to get away from her before it was too late. That's why I brought the mirror to you here. I thought I could bury it in the mountain, so far away from our homeland that I could keep us all safe."

"Thanks a lot. If you had said something I would have known to leave it back there." Lou crossed her arms.

"Would you? Wouldn't you have wanted to test the mirror out first? See if it really was the magic mirror from Snow White? Curiosity can be a dangerous thing, cousin."

"Yes, I would have left it alone."

Lou said it with such conviction, Billie believed she was speaking the truth. Especially so after seeing all the luxury goods stored inside the mine, bribes that went unheeded.

But Fremont scoffed. "The queen probably broke your window so you'd replace it with the one in the mine. You can't beat her. She's relentless. She works you over and over until the next thing you know, you're trapped in the mirror yourself."

Billie gasped. "You were in the mirror, weren't you? You never left town at all."

He turned red and nodded.

"How? Why didn't any of us see you?" Billie said. "I've been all over that misty land and it's empty."

Now it was Fremont's turn to look shocked. "You were in the mirror, too?"

She nodded, then pointed to the magic mirror while raising her eyebrows at Lou. *Who is listening in?*

"Go ahead. It's Winn."

"Mirror, mirror on the wall." Billie completed the poem and Winn's face became clear.

"Took you long enough to call me." His eyes shot daggers in Fremont's direction.

The cousin startled. "You, too? How many people are in there?" He peered in as though looking for more faces.

"Only one at a time, we thought," Winn said. "We keep changing places. It used to be pretty consistent between me and Matron, but since Billie joined us, it's all over the place."

Fremont scratched his beard, but when he remained quiet, Billie wondered if he was hiding something.

"How could you be in the mirror, and we not know it?" Billie asked. "Shouldn't you have landed back out in Lou's cabin? Please, don't keep secrets. We're desperate, and you're the one who's responsible for bringing the mirror here."

Fremont paced from the mirror to the kitchen and back again, as if wrestling with what to tell them. "I found another portal."

CHAPTER 44

"Is like a back door," Fremont said to his stunned audience. "One that is not controlled by *her* or that big mirror."

"I knew it." Billie clasped her fingers together and brought them to her lips. *There was another way out.* She met Winn's gaze and smiled. He didn't return her optimism.

"Where is this other portal?" Winn asked. "How do I get to it?"

"You will not find it."

Winn's eyes grew angrier. "Try me." He looked like he wanted to jump out of the mirror and pin Fremont to the floor.

"I cannot."

"You mean you don't know," Billie said. She guessed that Fremont was as clueless as they were. "You stumbled into it by accident."

Fremont scowled. "I might be able to find it again, but I cannot give you directions. Is not like there are road signs in the mirror. Look around. That mist is everywhere. Nothing changes except the sounds."

Billie's time in the mirror had been void of sound, simply a vast ocean of white mist. "Winn said he heard music sometimes. What sounds did you hear?"

Fremont shrugged. "Like I said. Cannot help you."

"Were you able to leave at will, then, or did the mirror push you out?" Winn asked. "We have no control here."

"Oh, I left at will. Stepped right out a few days ago. It was the best feeling I have had in a long time. To be free after one has been a prisoner." A smile lit his face for the first time.

"Where did you land when you stepped out?" Billie asked. If she were a gambler she'd bet it was at the Poisoned Apple.

"I was not paying much attention," he said, but his eyes shifted away. "Some saloon in town. The first thing I did was get away in case she found me."

"Can you describe anything?" Billie tried to impress on him the importance of his answer in her tone. "Even the smallest detail might help us."

"I landed inside a closet in an office. That is all I know. It was dark, and when I ran I hit the corner of a desk." He rubbed his side. "Left a hefty bruise."

Matron's office? Billie looked pointedly at Winn.

"Since you left by this other portal, have you stayed out?" Winn asked.

"Has been a few days. I think I am clear." He folded his arms like he was cold. "Except I am back here standing in front of it. Thanks to that flood washing me out of my hiding place." Fremont turned to Lou. "What day is it today? Or rather, how many days have I been gone?"

"Days? You've been gone for months."

"*Ach.* Longer than I thought. Where are my things?" He pointed to his ill-fitting clothes. "I would like to dress."

"Wait. What direction do I start walking in?" Winn asked, looking over his shoulder at the mist.

"No, no, no. That is the wrong question to ask. It is too late."

He pointed at Winn. "Something is wrong. That is supposed to be a mirror. Not a window."

"Matron said it was a window of opportunity when the portal became thin."

"Yes, but even then, it has always been a mirror." Fremont cocked his head, thinking. "How long has it been like that?"

"I don't know, but I put it in my wall early spring."

"Matron said the window has stayed open for a long time because of the copper in the hills," Billie said.

Fremont nodded. "When I learned copper was a good conductor of electricity, we began researching its other attributes. Our theory is that copper, as a conductor, would stretch the boundaries of the mirror to allow for breaks in the portal where one could pass through. It would magnify the alternating charge. In theory."

"Who is *we*?" Billie asked, more interested in relationships than a talk on electricity.

Fremont looked skittish. "My English; is wrong pronoun." He cleared his throat. "Back to properties of copper. These hills are filled with copper and *I*—" he bugged his eyes at Billie, "underestimated the effect it would have on the magic mirror. Looks like my experiment had mixed results."

"Your experiment?" Lou said. "I thought you planned to bury the mirror, never to be found again?"

"Ja, ja. But I wanted to see what the copper would do to it first. I did not realize it would be so unpredictable. Gone for months, you say?"

The way he was talking raised alarms for Billie, but she didn't know why, yet.

He turned to Lou. "Where is my watch?"

"Don't worry, it's here somewhere."

"The watch is the portal into the mirror, isn't it?" Winn said. "The way the shoes were for Billie."

"How would you know?" Fremont said.

Winn didn't answer, so Billie did. "He found your watch near the mirror back in the mine, and when he touched it, he fell in."

"Interesting. Why were you in Lou's mine?"

Winn let out a long breath. "Matron told me to meet her for a private Faro game, but when I got here the place was empty. She had told me to go through into the mine to bring out some bottles of whiskey stored in there, and that's when I saw the watch. She knew I'd be tempted to take it. Billie was being kind, but the reality was I was going to steal it."

Winn paced, working out what happened. "But why me? If she had already put you in place to take her spot in the mirror?"

Fremont snorted. "You cannot blame your sticky fingers on her. That is your own moral downfall. You could have walked away, but your envious heart sold you out."

"The instant I touched it," Winn said.

Fremont nodded. "Matron thought I would replace her, but it only half worked. She needed another to finish the job. Meanwhile, I was doing everything I could to get out. I tried mailing the watch to Chester to see if distance could break the spell on me since the mirror would not let me leave town. I suppose it almost worked, but not in my favor. That must have been when I got locked in for those months away."

Billie started to speak, but Fremont held up his hand.

"Before you ask, I chose your father because I knew that if I needed the piece back, I could contact him for it. If my theory was correct, he wouldn't be tied to the mirror, so I wasn't putting him at risk."

"Lou kept catching me in her mine, and I could never explain to her why I was there," Winn said. "It was just happening, and it was always dark, so I didn't know what was going on. Matron told everyone I was blacking out from drinking, but I knew I wasn't. I really thought I was losing my mind until Lou put the mirror into her wall and discovered me."

Fremont chuckled. "That I would have liked to see. Lou chewing you out for breaking into her mine I mean."

"I'll show you a chewing out, Fremont," chided Lou. "What are you going to do to help these young people?"

"Me?"

"You're the one responsible. If it weren't for you, the mirror would be tucked away in the family mines in Germany, and these kids would be free to live their lives."

"I had my reasons. I thought this was the best way. I made a mistake, all right? Is that what you want to hear? Can I have the timepiece now?"

"Why do you want it so badly?" Lou said, her eyes narrowed.

"The queen gave it to me. I should never have accepted it. But now I need to check something."

Lou opened up her mine and returned with the pocket watch wrapped in a cotton towel. "Now that I know what it is I'm not touching it," she said.

"Does not work like that," Fremont said. "Give it to me."

"First, you said you had a theory. What is it?" Lou asked.

"I think the mirror trap works on those who covet. Matron wanted to be the fairest in the land; she coveted Snow White's beauty. Young Winn there coveted riches, and my watch was his final undoing."

"What did you covet?" Billie asked as she repositioned a hair pin. This one piece of hair had fallen down and was bothering her.

"None of your business," he said, "but I can guess your downfall." He pointed at her.

Billie's face warmed, and she lowered her hand. *Can't a girl fix her hair?* "If we all have...issues, then why hasn't the mirror released Matron with us in her place?"

"Seems it's got a hold on her in a way that it can't hold us, but she's trying, and I think getting closer." He turned to Lou. "The watch?"

She started to hand it over, but then stopped. "Listen. It started ticking."

"What does that mean?" Billie said.

"The timepiece is tuned to the mirror, so now that it is ticking again it means the window of opportunity is closing." Fremont avoided their gazes. "Is going to become a mirror again, soon. And when it does, whoever is inside stays until the next window opens."

Everyone began talking at once: "What do you mean?" and "How much time do we have?" and "How do we stop it?"

"One at a time," Fremont said, holding up his hand. "You cannot stop it, and I do not know how much time you have. Once it closes, you cannot open again."

"It's like the law of apex," Billie said. "Whoever is tops in the rotation when the window closes is trapped. We need to force it so that Matron is in the mirror when the window closes."

CHAPTER 45

illie took Winn's place inside the mirror at some point during the night, and by early morning, before the sun was up, they'd devised a plan based on what they knew about Matron and the mirror.

Billie made a mental checklist of what they knew:

The window was closing.

They could speed the process by getting the mirror away from the copper in the hills.

Whoever was in the mirror when the window closed would be trapped until the next opening.

Matron didn't have all the secrets but knew more than they did.

She was able to push herself out of the mirror seemingly whenever she wanted; a new and frightening development.

Matron was still tied to the mirror, however tenuous those ties had become.

Minute to minute, Billie still spent the least amount of time in the mirror than either Matron or Winn, as if the mirror had trouble holding on to her.

There was a back door, and only Fremont knew roughly where it was.

He thought he could find it again. If he had to. Okay, he would do it, leave him alone, already.

Fremont also knew the secret of how to get inside the mirror. *Ach*, no, he wouldn't tell. That was not information you gave out to people, but Matron knew, too.

And one thing that Billie knew, but still hadn't shared: She was going to try to get a cure for her mother.

Billie figured the others wouldn't agree to try to get the cure for her mom, not because they wouldn't want to help, but because they wouldn't want her to get it from Matron, who could not be trusted.

Billie had also come up with a theory about what made herself so disruptive to Matron's plans. It all centered around copper.

"You know how Matron said there was something about me that was preventing the mirror from doing what she expected?"

Billie held up her reticule into the center of the frame so the others in the shack could see it. Her collection of pennies represented hope and planning for her future. "I carry more copper than the average girl. Do you think that might have something to do with it?"

"What is this?" Fremont perked up from his slump in the corner and scrambled to the mirror. "I had a lump of raw copper in my pocket when I went in that last time. Winnings from a game. I wonder if that is how I got out. You think having copper on your person prevents the magic from taking full effect? Have you tried leaving the mirror?"

No, she hadn't. Imagine if, after all this time, all she had to do was step out of the mirror.

"Try it," Lou said.

Billie jabbed her hand at the mirror, stealing herself against the icy-hot feeling. The surface bent with her hand, causing ripples to spread toward the edges. "I'm pressing into it, and if feels like it's stretching. What does it look like on your side?"

"Hard to see now that the sun is rising, but your hand isn't coming out," Winn said. He sounded disappointed. "Take a running leap at it, like how we can toss items through. Maybe it needs some force with it."

Run and fling herself at a mirror. It went against every instinct she had. But if she closed her eyes and thought of it as a portal, perhaps it would work if she didn't think about crashing into a hard surface.

"Okay. Here I come." She backed up and ran, diving forward at the last second and squeezing her eyes shut. The mirror stretched and stretched but snapped her back. She landed on her backside.

"I bet that looked like the fairest of them all," Billie said sourly.

"It was worth a try," Lou said.

"No, no. This is important," Fremont said. "We know something that I bet *she* doesn't know." He laughed. "We can use the copper against her."

"Looks like I need to start collecting pennies for my wedding shoes." Winn wiggled his eyebrows at Billie.

"That's actually a great idea," Billie said. "I can sew pennies into all our hems. Maybe it'll keep the window from closing while we're inside. A safety net in case our plan fails."

Fremont stopped laughing as if the full realization of their plan had hit him. He was free, but he'd be sacrificing his freedom to help them catch Matron.

So much depended on him, and there was a risk that he would end up trapped in the mirror. Lou handed him her carbide lamp. "Let's get you hidden in the mine. We don't want her knowing you're back."

Billie and Winn looked long and hard at each other through the mirror.

"It'll work," he said. "We'll get out."

"Do you think Fremont will do it?" asked Billie.

"I don't know. I wish we could find the portal ourselves, and then it wouldn't matter."

"Except we've been looking for days and haven't found another portal inside the mirror, nor another mirror in Matron's office," Billie said. They'd torn that office inside out. "We need him." She lowered her gaze as she tried to keep the *what if's* out of her mind. That's when she noticed the frame inside the mirror had changed.

"Winn, did you see?" The words came out in a rush. "The fairies moved from where I last sketched them." The two little ones at the bottom were now leaning one elbow each on the pomegranate. She got nose to nose with them.

"Please tell me what to do. We're running out of time."

The figures stared back at her, smiling their sweet smiles. A quick glance at the other fairies was enough to show her that these were the only two who moved.

"Fine, don't say anything, but I caught you. Won't take me long to learn more." *I hope.*

"At least we know where in the frame to focus on," said Winn. "Hey, look, there's all this condensation on the edges of the window. Must be cold this morning."

Billie examined the edges. "Doesn't look any different on this side."

"That's not condensation," Lou said, closing the mine door. "The window is turning back into a proper mirror."

Billie and Winn locked eyes.

"I noticed it earlier but didn't want to scare you."

Billie's mouth went dry. The mirror was changing, and she was the one inside.

"We can't wait any longer then," said Winn. "It's got to be today."

They all nodded their agreement.

Fortunately, Billie didn't have long to wonder if the window would close in on her. Before Winn and Lou had finished breakfast, she was shoved out of the mirror and Winn was back in.

"What's going on?" Billie said, spinning back to the mirror. "Matron is next in the rotation."

Lou studied the mirror. "I don't know, child. Maybe she figured it out, and that's why the window is closing."

Billie didn't want to accept that answer. "Winn? Are you okay?"

Because of the light, his face was faint, like he barely existed. "Same as always."

"Don't worry. Fremont and I will find the other portal today."

Billie called Fremont out of his hiding place and explained to him what had happened.

He scratched his chin. "Hmm. Sorry to see that. We better get started. Later, Lou!" Fremont casually strode out of the cabin.

"Keep an eye on him," Winn said. "He's awfully light-hearted about all this."

"Right. I don't trust him, either."

Too much of their plan was riding on Fremont.

CHAPTER 46

*A*fter stopping by her hotel room to collect all her pennies, Billie took Fremont to the back alley of the Poisoned Apple. "Is this where you came out?"

He cringed. "Ja."

"Up you go, then."

It was a risk that Matron would be in her office, but what else could they do? They needed that other mirror no matter what it took to get it.

When he got to the top of the stairs, Fremont looked down, and Billie waved him on encouragingly. "What is she going to do to you in her office?" she whispered. "We need that mirror, and you're the one who has any clue as to where it's hidden."

She waved him on again, and he entered the second floor. After ten minutes had passed and he didn't come back out, Billie grew worried. What if Matron could do something to Fremont?

She quietly made her way to Matron's office. The door was ajar, and she could just make out Fremont's arm as he stood before the desk.

"You really think I would fall in love with the likes of you?"

Matron said, using the voice and tone which revealed her true nature.

Billie gasped. *That's what Fremont was hiding.* He had fallen in love with Matron. So, his copper experiment had been about helping her escape. They were right to be cautious with their trust.

"I failed you once, but this time, I know what I am doing," he said.

Billie balled her fists. She had to put a stop to this. Winn's life was at stake.

"How could you?" Billie said, storming into the room before Fremont could reveal their plan.

Fremont whirled around. "No. No, it is not what you think." He held up his hands. "Ja, okay some of what you are thinking. I felt sorry for her. I am softy at heart, and a damsel in distress is my weakness. She had all these ideas about how she could break the spell. She sounded so remorseful I thought she had changed, and then our family could finally release this burden. Not all of us want to be miners and live on the edge of civilization, you know. I researched the old family stories and learned we needed a conductor. Copper, and lots of it to interfere with the boundaries of the mirror."

Matron looked bored.

"But it did not work out the way I thought it would. I think *she* knew it all along." He cast her a scowl. "Lou was always so strong. She should have been the one to protect the mirror from the start, not me."

Fremont spoke directly to Matron. "I believed that people could change, and I thought you had had enough time to learn from your mistakes. I should have buried you in that mountain and never looked back."

Matron cackled. "Doesn't matter anyway. One of those kids is going to end up in the mirror. Soon, by the looks of things. I'd have given you a role in my kingdom if you'd shown more loyalty than this. You left as soon as things got uncomfortable."

"Your kingdom?" Billie said. "There aren't kingdoms anymore."

"Doesn't matter what you call it, I'm well on my way to taking over this town. The mirror has provided me the funds I need to buy the shares in Queen Consolidated. Conquest may not happen with armies in this land, but it still happens. This entire town will soon be mine. Now get out. I don't need you anymore. Either of you."

"Wait." Billie stalled for time. With the hope that Fremont was still on their side, she needed to create a distraction so he could find the second mirror. He was already meandering around her office, picking up pieces and setting them down in a different spot. Not how Billie would have gone about it, but at least he was headed toward the closet.

"I have a proposition for you."

Matron's eyebrows shot up. "I don't know what you have to offer me that I want. I don't need anything from Bergmann Consolidated, even if you had the authority to give it."

"Once you're out of the mirror, you can't get any more objects from it. Am I right?"

A twitch in Matron's otherwise superior smile gave her away. She apparently had thought about that.

"A mirror that reveals who is the fairest of them all? *Really*." Matron smirked. "They thought they were punishing me by making me wear those red-hot iron shoes, but I've had the last laugh. After I danced my way into the mirror, I turned them into ruby slippers, and have been living like a queen ever since."

Matron's words rang hollow. If she was living so grandly inside the mirror, she wouldn't be trying so hard to get out.

Being in the mirror had changed Winn for the better. Just like the sun could melt ice and at the same time hardened clay, Winn's heart melted but Matron's hardened like Pharaoh's of old. And Billie could use that to her advantage.

"I need you to teach me how to get objects from the mirror, and then if I'm the one trapped at the end of all this, I'll continue to help you. But if you refuse, I won't give you anything at all."

Fremont was now behind Matron, at the closet door.

"Greedy little thing, aren't you? Just like your mother."

Billie paused, confused. "W-what do you mean? You've never met my mother."

Matron's lips curled into a snarl. "Once. I almost had her, but the barrier wasn't thin enough, then. Her hand went through the glass as she tried to grab a trinket she wanted."

"I don't believe you. She was never here."

"Not here. Your father's office in Boston when Fremont was on his way to this mining town. How is she, by the way?"

Billie pictured Mother's mottled purple skin that had started on her hand but had spread up to her elbow. How she had covered all the mirrors so she wouldn't be reminded of how she looked. But that wasn't why she covered the mirrors. She was afraid of mirrors not because of what they reflected but because of what they represented? Or what they could do?

Matron continued talking as if what she had revealed hadn't shaken Billie.

"Although, I'll grant you that living inside a mirror isn't so bad when you add furnishings." Matron glanced around the office. "You can—"

Billie stopped her. "My mother was the first one you tried to trap in the mirror, wasn't she?"

Matron waved her hand as if it was of no consequence. "I've been running my experiments for years. Some have been more successful than others. Take you, for example." Matron leaned back in the chair. "Bit by bit your vanity and greed have been binding you to the mirror. You can have anything you want in there, except freedom. Just wait, you'll be trapped by your vanity, and then forced to wallow in it. *If* you can figure out the proper way to ask the mirror for what you want."

Billie struggled to control her anger. It wouldn't do to become too vulnerable. "You don't know what I want most from the mirror, but it's nothing for my vanity, as you say."

"Hmm. Curious. Freeze Fremont." Matron flicked up her index finger. "Don't you take another step."

He turned at the closet door and met Billie's gaze.

"Men?" Matron called out.

Two bruisers with matching horseshoe mustaches filled the doorway.

Where did they come from?

"Escort these two out, please, and don't let them back in. They're banned from the premises."

The bouncers insisted on gripping their arms as they shoved them through the hall and down the outside stairs.

"I'll go on my own," Billie said, trying to get free, but the man holding her only squeezed harder until they'd descended the stairs.

Fremont scowled at his escort as the man shoved him on his way.

"You heard the lady, you're not welcome back," one said, before standing guard at the bottom of the stairs.

After Billie and Fremont returned to the main street, Fremont dusted his arms off, "She knew I was in town. I don't know how, but she was expecting me."

"I was afraid you were going to tell her our plan."

"No, I was trying to lull her into thinking I was still trying to get her out."

"And did you know about what she did to my mother?"

Fremont vehemently shook his head. "That I did not know. I cannot watch her every second of the day."

"Miss Bergmann! Miss Bergmann!"

Miss Brooks, from Lacey's beauty salon, ran down the street

toward them. She wore a greasy apron and had hiked up her long skirt with one hand so she could run faster.

"Wait here," Billie said, and went to meet Miss Brooks.

"I saw what happened," she said. "At back of Matron's place. Horrible woman. There was no need for those men to shove you down the stairs like that."

"I'm fine, Miss Brooks. Thanks for checking on me. How are you? Working somewhere else?" Billie automatically slipped into her polite-charm-school small talk but couldn't help stealing a glance at Fremont. They had to find another way into Matron's office.

"Yes, but that's not why I stopped you. I'm working in the restaurant up the street and was tossing out some trash when I saw you getting flung out of the Poisoned Apple. She always treated you like something special, and I didn't like seeing her turn on another gal like that, specially one like you who's in mourning."

"Thank you. But I could say the same for you, too."

Miss Brooks shook her head. "Doesn't matter what she done to me. I'm leaving town tonight, but I want to give you something before I go. I'm not normally one to be so spiteful, but Matron has soured enough people in this town, and I don't mind getting her goat a little. You can decide what to do with it."

Billie reached out and touched Miss Brooks's arm. "What are you talking about?"

"Follow me."

After a few minutes, Billie realized they were going to Lacey's, and she'd also lost sight of Fremont.

Miss Brooks looped her arm through Billie's so they could talk easier without being overheard. "I saw her hide something last night. I was saying my goodbyes to the gals at the beauty salon when she came in. They hid me in the back since they knew there had been trouble, and so I saw her put something behind the filing cabinet. Made me suspicious since what she was hiding used to be in her office at the saloon, and here she was acting all sneaky-like. It might be something you could use."

Billie couldn't dare to hope it was what she thought it was. But if Matron realized Fremont was back, she might have guessed they knew about another portal.

Miss Brooks breezed through the beauty salon to the back room, and then reached behind a tall filing cabinet. With a little bit of effort, she pulled out a mirror.

It was oval and shared the same patina as the frame at Lou's. Billie's heart skipped a beat. *They found it.*

"I don't know why she hid it back here instead of putting it on the wall," Miss Brooks said. "It's such a pretty thing; the customers would love it." She gave the mirror one last glance before handing it over.

Billie licked her lips and accepted the mirror. "Thank you, Miss Brooks. I know just what to do with this."

Billie hugged her tight.

"Oh, goodness." Miss Brooks became flustered. "Weren't that big a deal."

"To me it is. Best wishes on your new life in California," Billie said, squeezing her one last time.

Billie practically skipped outside with the mirror, the beauty salon girls exchanging looks and preparing for gossip as soon as the door closed.

Fremont stood waiting on the street, a bit out of breath.

"We got it!" Billie said.

"I had a feeling. So, I inquired about the next step in the plan. Good news. The touring company you told me about left their glass at the Opera House. It was the end of the run on that show and since the glass is delicate to transport, they left it behind. I may have hinted that Bergmann Consolidated might become a benefactor if they let us use their building today."

Finally, their plan was lining up nicely. Billie hugged the mirror. "Can I trust you to bring this to Lou?"

"*Ach*. How could you ask?" Fremont gave her an exaggerated hurt expression.

She raised her eyebrows.

"I promise. Hand it over before her royal highness sees us."

"Take these, too. Have Lou sew them in for you." Billie poured a handful of pennies from her reticule into his hand.

"I can sew." He tugged proudly on his collar. "Bet Lou can't."

"Tell Winn I'll meet him at the Opera House."

Fremont didn't look back but waved, whistling a happy tune as he headed up the mountain to Lou's mine.

Could they count on Fremont to do the next, most important step?

CHAPTER 47

Mr. Moore at the Opera House welcomed Billie inside. "I've got it all set up for you, Miss Bergmann" he said. "Any time we can be of service to Bergmann Consolidated, let us know."

"That's very generous."

"Is there anything else before I leave you?"

She shook her head. "No, thank you. I'll just get set up on the stage."

After Mr. Moore left, Billie poured out all her copper pennies onto the stage and set to work. She didn't want to risk dropping her reticule and leave herself vulnerable, so the fastest way to protect herself was to create a new hem, with the pennies sewn in. It was most efficient to create pockets for lumps of coins around her skirt. She needed to work quickly in case the mirror pulled her in next.

Good thing skirt lengths were getting shorter or she'd feel out of fashion with her hem above her ankles. When she finished, the skirt would look terribly rumpled and off-balance. Her friends in Boston would be wide-eyed over her lack of attention to detail.

How long had it been since she'd thought of her friends? If all went well today, she'd be seeing them soon.

The way she figured it, she had about forty minutes until she would know if Fremont was able to pull off his part in the plan. She swept up her extra pennies, put them back in her reticule, and waited for Winn at the location marked with an X on the stage.

So much was riding on this plan. Winn had suffered long enough, and Billie certainly didn't want to be trapped forever in that mirror. Fremont found his way out once, so hopefully he would again. Billie could almost feel bad about Matron being trapped in the mirror, but then she remembered Matron's hands around her neck.

Billie reached for Winn's philopena gift. Bisbee blue turquoise and so like Winn. Their plan had to work.

Soon, the door to the Opera House burst open, letting in the late afternoon light. It was Winn and Lou.

"You made it!" *Thank you, Fremont.*

"I did, and you look like a ghost," Winn said. "The same way I saw Matron." He grinned widely, but the way he rubbed his hands belied his nerves.

"We're all set," Lou said. "Fremont looked terrified, but he did it. I'm so proud of him. You kids sit tight while I go get Matron."

"How did he do it?" Billie asked Winn.

"He wouldn't let me see. Doesn't want us to know."

"That's probably for the best. You know what Matron told me? She tried to trap my mother in Boston. Apparently, my mother reached into the mirror for a trinket before the window had fully opened, and it poisoned her somehow."

"Billie. I'm sorry. I wish we could have figured out how to get a cure from the mirror."

"Yeah. Me, too." She handed him the pennies she'd reserved for his pockets. "Are you sure the stage looks real?" Billie asked. "I look like a ghost?"

Winn nodded. "As real as when we saw Matron out in the daylight. It'll be hard for me to keep a straight face when she realizes that you've figured out her secret." He laughed.

"I wish I *had* figured out her secret. We're still assuming she'll react a certain way, but she might not. I'm just glad she missed the first act of the play, so we might trick her fine."

"It's a risk, but I think we've set it up right. Besides, this is going to be fun." He put one arm around her waist and drew her closer. "She'll see us together. Me in the flesh. You as a mysterious ghost walking around outside the mirror." His other arm encircled her waist. "Matron will be so furious she'll march right up to Lou's place to put a stop to it, and then we'll have her."

He pulled Billie close, and she automatically wrapped her arms around his neck, her pulse racing. She loved being held by Winn; the sensation made her light-headed and weak in the knees just like the romance novels said it would.

"We should practice being in love so it's convincing. Remember the night of the fireworks?" Winn asked.

Billie bit her lip and nodded.

"I don't want to miss out again," Winn said. He bent his head toward hers.

This time Billie didn't hesitate. She tilted her chin up, signaling to him that she was ready. She took a shaky breath as Winn leaned in, pressing his lips to hers.

She kissed him back, trying to pour out her fears of what might happen next.

He pulled away with a goofy grin. "You're not just putting on a show for Matron."

"No, this is real." So real it scared her to think of what she might lose.

"Then let's make it work. We need to take our places."

She let her arms drop from his neck. "Of course." Her voice came out higher than normal, and she blushed at his grin. He backed away and went to his spot on the stage.

From the door where Lou and Matron would enter, it should look like Winn was walking in to meet Billie. For her role, all she had to do was look like a lovesick girl waiting in rendezvous for her love.

That would be easy.

No acting necessary. Her dreamy expression would come naturally as she relived the kiss over and over again. She was so caught up in the memory of two minutes ago that she didn't notice Lou and Matron had arrived until she heard Matron's voice.

"What is the meaning of this?"

"I told you they'd figure it out," Lou said. "It's only a matter of time, now."

Matron stood backlit in the doorway. When neither of them answered her question, she raced out, Lou at her heels, letting the door slam shut behind them. The auditorium echoed the slam, and then fell silent. Billie and Winn froze, gazes locked. The plan was in motion. *Dare they hope?*

Winn checked outside while Billie waited, her heart pounding.

"She's headed to the shack. Let's go."

They followed at a distance, not wanting Matron to catch them.

"Did you see her face?" Winn asked.

"No." She'd been focused on Winn. Memorizing him in case this was the end.

"What?" he said. "You've got a funny look on your face. You're worried, aren't you?"

"Aren't you?" she said.

"I am the most hopeful that I've been in months. Until you came to town, I thought this strange existence was going to be the rest of my life. It's one thing to choose to stay in a town, another to not be able to leave, ever. It makes you want what you can't have."

His gaze made her blush.

"If this does work out, what next?" she asked. She hoped he knew what she was really asking because she didn't have the courage to come right out and ask it. In her polite society they talked around the issues. That's what made the philopena game so much fun. In the game, everyone acknowledged the subtext, and you were supposed to seek out the truth.

Winn, on the other hand, always got straight to the point.

"I have to fix things with my dad, and depending on how that goes, I'd like to find an apprenticeship like the one I talked about, if someone would have me."

"I'm sure there'd be one or two in Boston who might be interested in taking you on."

"One or two?"

"At least one."

"All it takes is one."

Billie turned away and smiled. They were no longer talking about apprenticeships. Winn would fit in with her friends at home just fine.

They rounded the last corner before the shack and ran into Uncle Dale.

"Hi," Billie blurted, glancing at Winn.

"How're you kids doing?" Uncle Dale tipped his hat at Winn.

"Fine, don't let us keep you, sir," Winn said, stepping aside in the path.

"No, I suppose you're up here to say goodbye to Lou. I just popped in myself, but she wasn't there. If you see her, tell her goodbye from me, too. I'll be at the power plant. The engineer promised to explain the relationship between the copper and the magnetism and electricity. Faraday's Law of Induction. Fascinating stuff." He waved as he continued down the path.

Billie shot Winn a worried look. *Where was Lou?*

Hopefully they weren't too late.

CHAPTER 48

They opened the door to an empty shack. But then the creak of the mine door broke the silence and Lou came out of her mine carrying the second mirror. She was whistling.

Billie and Winn both released a big breath.

"Quit standing around and help me tie these mirrors together," she whispered. "First, we have to get that one out of the wall. You two do that while I hold up this other in case she tries to escape. If it doesn't reflect her back inside, we're lost."

"She went inside the mirror?" Billie whispered.

Lou nodded once before putting all her concentration into holding up the second mirror against the first. "She couldn't stand not knowing what was going on."

"Excellent." Winn handed Billie a crowbar and took one for himself. "And Fremont? Did he make it out?"

Lou shook her head.

"How long should we wait?" Billie asked.

"We don't. Fremont told me to take care of things. If he got stuck, he would get out at the next window opening." Lou shook her head. "Surprised me, too."

"That's...kind of him," Winn said. "Ready?"

"Shouldn't we wait a little longer?" asked Billie.

"There's no time," Lou said. "He made me promise."

Billie nodded. Her stomach was tied up in knots. Once they started attacking the mirror, who knew what would happen next? They had to work fast.

"Go." Winn jammed his crowbar into the wall.

Billie followed suit, and it stuck fast. She pushed with all her might, wiggling the wedge to make it go in deeper, but it wouldn't move. She thought it was her lack of strength, but Winn had the same problem. "We need the mallets." She handed one to Winn.

She pounded harder, feeling the reverberations travel up her arm. "Nothing. You?"

"No."

"Now what?" Billie asked. She yanked out her wedge and examined the tiny gash she'd made.

"We could take out the wall."

"What is Lou going to do without a wall?"

"I don't care as long as we get rid of this mirror," Lou said. She shifted her grip on the second mirror.

Winn hauled back the mallet and slammed it into the wall.

Nothing happened. Not even a splinter. *Wham*. He struck the wall again and again, frustration etched on his forehead.

Billie's heart sank. They had to get the mirror off the wall before Matron—"

"Children," Matron said from within the mirror.

She'd materialized without them saying the poem to call her out.

"You seem to be playing at a game that you can't win."

With Lou holding up the second mirror they couldn't see Matron, but that made the concern in her voice all the more noticeable. If Matron was nervous that meant they were on the right track.

"We're pretty good at playing games." Winn winked at Billie before trying the crowbar again. This time he was able to gain some leverage as he shoved the wedge farther between the frame and the wall.

Billie hoped Winn was as confident as he looked, because inside, she was panicking. There were too many unknowns. Matron still held too many cards and they too few.

Matron's arm jutted out as a loud *crack* sounded. Lou stumbled back while Matron's arm felt around the frame until she grabbed hold of Billie.

"Winn!" Billie cried out. "She's pulling me in."

He dropped his crowbar to help Billie pry off Matron's iron grip.

Meanwhile, a tiny glimmer in Matron's pupil drew Billie's attention. A flickering light that appeared to be coming from the bottom of the frame where the little fairies were. *That's it!*

"Winn, I know how she controls the mirror. Let me go, and I can try to get the cure for my mother."

Matron pulled harder and Billie winced in pain. She didn't know how long she could stand it.

"I don't want to hurt you." Winn said. "I'm losing my grip,"

"It's okay. Let me go. I'll get back."

"No, Billie. The window is closing. You can't risk it. We'll never get a chance like this again."

"Exactly. Give me time. Please." She knew she could do it. Matron didn't know what Fremont was doing, so they had an advantage. Plus, she had the pennies sewn in her skirt. The mirror would have trouble closing on her.

Winn searched her eyes before giving a slight nod. He let go.

Lou cried out, "No!"

Billie felt the tug as both the mirror and Matron pulled her in. She'd expected Matron to be kicked out when she came in, but when she gathered her wits she realized Matron was still holding on to her.

"We're both in here." Billie rotated herself closer to the mirror.

"Appears that way." Matron dropped her arms. "The window of opportunity has been open too long, and the mirror is getting...impatient."

"The mirror is a being?" Goosebumps erupted on Billie's arms.

Matron thinned her lips. "No, it's just a magic mirror. It can only do what it was created to do."

Billie tried to examine the frame without Matron noticing. She had to get what she came for and leave before Matron did. Back in town, Matron had given away a clue when she said: *if you can figure out the proper way to ask the mirror.* Well, if the mirror worked how she suspected, Billie could have both the medicine she needed for her mother and still trap Matron in her prison.

But not with Matron watching.

Billie turned her attention to Winn's worried face. *Do something to distract her, Winn.* She tilted her head slightly.

He gave her a nod, and then resumed his attack on the frame. Each time he jabbed the wedge into the frame, the ground shook. Billie spread out her arms for balance. No wonder Matron called for them to stop removing the mirror.

Matron wobbled her way over to the frame, arguing with Winn while Billie focused on the bottom of the frame at her two little fairy friends. The pomegranate between them was open, a flame flickering out of it like a candle. The flame must have been the glimmer she'd seen in Matron's eye. And there were those impish fairies, smiling and looking up at her to see what she would do.

"You two know what happened to my mom, and I know you can fix it." She hoped her own made up poem would be enough. She whispered:

> "*Mirror, mirror,*
> *inside the wall,*
> *Help me heal Mother*
> *once and for all.*"

She held her breath while the flame flickered.

Meanwhile, Matron continued to shout at Winn, oblivious to what Billie was doing. That is, until the mirror started to change. The surface turned molten gold around the edges, shimmering like a golden river flowing around and around the frame.

Matron cocked her head, watching for a moment. "You." She turned to Billie. "What have you done? The gifting only works once a day. Did you waste the wish on something frivolous? A new frock? A pair of shoes like mine? You stupid—that was my way out."

"I wished for what I want most. A cure for my mother."

Beyond Matron's shoulder, the mirror had stopped swirling, and an intricate purple glass bottle floated in the middle of the frame. *It worked.*

"Are you seeing this, Billie?"

Winn. She had forgotten that he and Lou were there. They had both stopped what they were doing and stared at the bottle.

Billie reached out and plucked the bottle out of the mirror at the same time Winn reached in and wrapped his hand around hers. Billie's eyes flew open. They had crossed the barrier together. *Thank you, fairies.*

Winn's face registered shock as well, but only for a second before his look became determined. He yanked, and Billie felt herself falling into the shack, and into his arms.

"*N*o!" Matron screamed.

Lou slammed the second mirror up tight against the first and began lashing them together with a rope. "Help me!"

After sharing a warm look with Billie, Winn began to tie the mirrors. While Billie had been in the mirror, Winn had managed to pry it out far enough for them to be able to tie the two mirrors together. Now, if their theory was correct, Matron would ping back and forth between portals if she tried to get out.

"What about Fremont?" Billie said.

"I am fine."

Billie spun around to see Fremont stretched out on the floor staring up at the ceiling. "Made it out of the smaller mirror, thanks to your little trick in there. The mirror wasn't built for so many people." He turned his head to look at her. "How did you get it to make you something?"

A flicker of greed lit in his eye and Billie froze.

She'd seen something like that in Matron's eye back in her office when they talked about Matron not being able to access the fruits of the mirror anymore.

"We need help!" Lou called, snapping Billie back to the needful thing.

Mist floated into the shack like puffs from a steam engine as Matron tried to escape. Lou continued to press the mirrors together while Winn bound the ropes, but Matron was proving to be too strong for Lou.

Billie and Fremont jumped in to help, pressing the mirrors together until Winn could secure the many ropes encasing the mirror.

"Done," Winn said. "Back slowly away, and let's see what happens."

The mirror hung off the wall like a tooth dangling from a child's mouth. Matron's screams reverberated throughout the shack, but her body stayed within the mirror world.

"That's not going to hold for long," Winn said. "Look at how she's making it shake. We need to force it to close now."

"How?" asked Lou. "We won't make the last train out."

"We need something to disrupt the energy keeping it open," Billie said. She thought of her uncle's interest in the power plant. "Do you think the generators would do it?"

"Faraday's Law of Induction?" Fremont nodded. "The changing magnetic field might be strong enough to close the window."

"Let's finish getting it off the wall," Lou said, giving Billie an odd look. Then Lou handed Fremont a crowbar before pulling Billie outside.

"I think you should be the one to take the mirror," Lou said in all earnestness.

Billie gaped. At the beginning of summer, this was what she had wanted. A chance to see if the mirror was real, and if it could save her mom. Back then, if Lou had said, look, here's the magic mirror that can give you all that you've been wanting, she would have taken it on the spot. But now that she knew the trouble it could cause, it was the last thing she wanted.

Lou continued. "I saw the look Fremont gave you when he realized you'd figured out how to get something out of the mirror. If he knows how to go in and out of the mirror of his own free will, and also learns how to get things from the mirror, it would be too much for him. I fear he'd be trapped and Matron would be released."

From what she knew about Fremont and other gamblers like him, she knew Lou was right. But what Lou was asking her was huge. To be the one in charge of protecting the mirror was a big responsibility. Could she handle it?

"Why don't you keep it?" Billie whispered. "You've done such a great job already."

"With all the copper in these hills, I'd have to move away or always be on edge, checking the mirror to see if it's changed. Now, it might not look like much to you, missy, but this is my home. Once Matron gets out of my hair, I can make it right comfortable again."

"But my uncle would know what it was. He's spent all summer looking for a magic mirror, and then I bring home a souvenir mirror? He'll be suspicious, and what if he tries it out? Can you imagine if my uncle met Matron?"

Lou put her hands on her hips while she thought. "We'll figure it out. I just need you to determine in your heart what you're going to do."

"I—I"

"Wilhelmina. Famous protector. It's in your name."

"My mother named me. She had no idea this would happen."

"Your mother didn't need to know for Providence to set you on your path."

Lou was convincing, but the fear was still there. "I don't know. I don't like knowing it's so close. That *she's* so close."

"What if you and I take it back to Germany together? You would need to leave with it on the train tomorrow, and then later you and I will return it."

"Fremont won't like it."

"No, but I'll talk to him." She glanced over Billie's shoulder toward the shack. "You and Winn take the mirror away now and finish closing that window."

"Hey," said Winn hanging out the door. "I stalled as long as I could, but we're done in here."

Lou marched into the shack. "All right, kids, get out of here. Fremont, let's talk about what you're going to do next."

"I'm going to take the mirror and skedaddle," he said. "Thanks for having me. Sorry about the trouble." He gave them a salute and made a move to pick up the mirrors. But Winn was faster and was halfway out the door before Lou stepped in to block Fremont's path.

"Let them go. They know what to do next."

"So do I."

"I don't trust you to stand firm against her wiles."

Matron yelled through the mirrors, "Let me out! Fremont!"

"See?" Lou said. "The window is still open. She's only temporarily trapped from leaving. You sit right there where I can see you while they finish what we've worked so hard to end."

They listened to Lou lecture until they had walked far enough down the mountain that her voice was lost on the wind, and it was the two of them, alone again.

"How did you know to grab my hand and pull?" asked Billie.

"Instinct. I saw your hand dart out of the mirror to take that vial, and I reached for it. Then I thought about how Matron pulled you in and thought maybe I could pull you out. Now that I think about it, I figure all the copper sewn into our clothes stretched the portal around us like a giant bubble."

She smiled, liking the idea of them being in their own private space.

Town was quiet as they went through, giving Billie hope that they'd make it to the electric plant without being noticed.

"Look," said Winn, "it's past sunset, and I'm still here. I could get used to this."

"So could I," Billie said.

A strong-looking man in miner's gear, dirty overalls, dusty boots, carrying a metal pail crossed their path.

"Dad." Winn stopped, holding the mirrors up like a shield between them.

"Son." He nodded once and glanced in Billie's direction.

"This is Wilhelmina Bergmann. She's visiting from Boston."

Mr. Harris tipped his hat, obvious curiosity about what they were doing splayed across his features.

"Nice to meet you, sir."

Father and son looked at each other. Billie held her breath wondering if Matron would cry out to cause trouble. When neither Harris made a move, she broke the silence. "Maybe we could meet later, at the Copper Queen Hotel. They make a lovely apple pie, if you're up for it," Billie said. They obviously needed help communicating.

"Winn?" Mr. Harris asked.

"Yeah. Sounds good."

"Great," Billie said.

"Great," Mr. Harris said. He took one last look at Winn, and then at the mirror, before continuing down the street.

"That's the longest we've talked in months." Winn stared after his father.

Billie tried not to raise her eyebrows. And she thought the people in her society had trouble communicating. Maybe she'd misjudged Winn's straightforwardness. Maybe it depended on the situation.

"Progress, then," she said.

A puff of mist shot out from between the mirrors.

"We better go." Winn shifted his grip, and they hustled to the energy plant without further interruption. It was a large building close to the mines, with a tall brick smokestack.

"How close do we need to get to the generator?" Billie asked as they climbed the hill. "Because I don't know what we're looking for."

"What are you doing?" Matron said, her voice rising in pitch. There was a flurry of mist shooting out from between the mirrors.

"Since Matron is panicking, we must be getting close enough to disrupt the window's energy."

"Wait, there's my uncle."

They ducked behind a pile of lumber until Uncle Dale and the engineer rounded the corner out of their sight. Then Billie and Winn dashed for the nearest door. Inside, great iron giants filled the room creating a loud and constant whirring sound. Huge spinning wheels, which Billie could only assume were part of the generators her uncle was so interested in.

Winn set the mirror down against the closest one. By this time, the mist had ceased pouring from the mirror, and they couldn't hear Matron over the noise.

"Do you think it's done?" Winn yelled in Billie's ear.

"We have to be sure," she yelled back. Billie couldn't take the mirror to Boston until she knew there was no way Matron could get out until the next window opened.

Winn cut one of the ropes to loosen the mirrors. They both got on their knees to look between the two.

"You'll pay for this!" Matron screamed, causing both of them to jump. "This isn't over." She pounded on the mirror as the remainder of the window grew opaque and the silver coating covered her face like ice freezing over a pond.

"We did it," Billie said. "We're free."

CHAPTER 50

*W*inn adjusted his tie, reminding Billie of their dinner at the Waldorf. Back then they didn't know if they'd ever have a chance at a normal future.

Lou was watching over the mirror in Billie's hotel room while Uncle and Mr. Harris joined Billie and Winn for pie and conversation.

They may be free of the mirror, but the rest of their future was still at stake. Winn needed to repair his relationship with his dad, and Billie had to convince her uncle that her extra baggage was not a magic mirror.

When they met up at the Copper Queen to assure Lou and Fremont that the window had closed, Fremont expressed his regret. "I am sorry I ever brought the mirror here."

Billie and Winn had looked at each other and smiled. "We're not."

Without the mirror, they would have never met. Their story might have been one of walking past each other on the sidewalk by chance one summer, and not knowing what could have been. Had Providence brought them together at a later date, maybe even in Boston, they could have discovered their mutual time spent in

Bisbee and wondered if they'd happened to pass each other on those dusty streets. But they didn't have to imagine. They had met.

"Here he comes." Winn straightened. He smiled and stood, wiping his hands on his trousers. "Hi, Dad. Thanks for coming."

Billie smiled. He'd managed to put more words together this time.

Uncle Dale followed behind and introductions were made. He'd cleaned himself up, shaved his scraggly beard and donned his more characteristic suit and tie. As for herself, Billie had purchased a dark gray skirt and white shirtwaist to show she was leaving deep mourning. Life was moving on in a new direction.

After the pie arrived and the small talk dried up, Winn cleared his throat. "I've thought a lot about my future, and I'd like to pursue an internship with Warren Manning. In Boston." He glanced in Uncle Dale's direction.

"You've straightened your life out?" Mr. Harris said.

Winn nodded. He'd already decided there was no point trying to explain what really happened during all those months but to focus on the future and hope that his dad agreed.

Billie hoped he agreed, too, because if everything continued the way it was going, that future would be her future, too.

"If that's what you want."

Winn nodded. "It is."

"And you could help him, couldn't you, Uncle Dale? Help him find a place to stay and help him get settled...unless you want me to do that?" She batted her eyelashes innocently and took a sip of her tea.

"No, no. I can help him. No need to put you or your mother out."

"Thank you." Mr. Harris rose and shook hands with Uncle Dale. "Winston has always been independent. I'm sure you can point him in the right direction, and he'll be fine."

"Will do."

"I can't see you off tomorrow, Winn. I'll be working." He held out his hand to his son and they shook.

"Yeah, I understand."

"Keep in touch now."

"You can count on it, Pops."

They watched his dad leave, and then Winn said, "That might not seem like much, but for us, it was a big deal."

He looked lighter than Billie had ever seen him. His burden had been lifted, and with his dad's blessing he could start anew.

LOU SAW them off at the station. "You've got a fine niece here," she said to Uncle Dale. "I plan to take her back to Germany with me and show her her roots. Introduce her to the rest of the family."

Uncle Dale looked surprised. "Glad to see our time here was productive. Sorry if my mining adventure was bothersome for you." He handed her an envelope. "I've signed my claim over to you. You can let it lapse or work it, however you want. There's a bit of silver in there, but not enough for my interests."

"Bless my stars," Lou said. "You're not completely heartless after all."

"My intentions have always been honorable." He doffed his hat and boarded the train to join Winn, who, after being tied to one place for so long, was eager to leave.

Lou stared after him for a moment before focusing back on Billie. "I've seen to the mirrors myself," she said. "You'll have to figure out an explanation by the time you reach Boston if your uncle happens to notice you've added some luggage. Maybe Winn can take ownership and help you get them into your house unnoticed, or at the very least unheeded." Lou stopped her instructions to study Billie's face. "What's wrong?"

Billie dabbed her handkerchief at the corner of her eye. "Nothing. I've just grown attached is all."

Lou shuffled her feet. "Girlie, I've got no time for sentimentality. Off with you now before the train leaves you behind."

Billie gave her a quick, tight hug before spinning around and boarding the train. She quickly spotted Winn, hat off and golden hair shining, sitting across from Uncle Dale.

She joined them, settling into the cushioned seat at Winn's side. She couldn't help but think of the last train ride they'd taken together. What a story she had to tell, one that she could never speak of. Even if she could tell Holly, Jane, or Suzanne, they wouldn't believe her.

She glanced at Uncle Dale. His head was down as he poured over business reports. He'd never know how he'd helped with the magic mirror by pointing them to the generator. But that didn't matter. He'd exhausted his search, to his satisfaction, and taken up a new fascination with electric power, and as long as he stayed away from Faro, he'd be okay.

He glanced up. "Thanks for indulging my mining pursuits," he said. "I think I can put that all behind me and go back to a desk job." He cleared his throat. "You're not going to tell your mother, are you?"

Billie laughed. "I think she knows you, Uncle." She tightened her grip on her reticule and the precious bottle of medicine inside. What a new life it would be for Mom.

"Right. And here's something for you. Can't be walking into Boston in those mining work boots of yours." He indicated the box next to him.

"For me?" She dove into the box to find her black and white leather boots with the flower design. She scooped them up. "Oh, how I've missed you."

"I had them cleaned up and resoled for you. To make up for dragging you through the desert."

"I forgive you," Billie said. "Now that it's all over, I'd not change a thing."

"Well, I for one would have liked for my claim to pay off more than it did." He winked conspiratorially at Billie.

Dear Uncle Dale. He'd never know it, but his detour saved his sister.

Finally, Billie's gaze landed on her right hand. It was placed on the seat precariously close to the hand of a certain young man who was leaving Bisbee with his father's blessing to pursue his education in Boston.

While she watched, Winn inched his hand closer to hers until their pinkie fingers touched. With another glance at Uncle Dale, she entwined their fingers. Her uncle may not have struck it rich in Bisbee, but she found everything she hadn't been looking for.

DEAR READER,

Thank you for reading *Snow White's Mirror*. If you are content with this happy ending, then off you go to read another of my fairy tales.

But, if you're the kind of reader who still wonders, "What happens next?" then click over to my website for a download of the Epilogue.

When I told my teen daughter my idea, she cried out, "No! Don't do that." But I couldn't help myself. I thought it would make a delicious continuation. From an author's point of view, anyway. Read it if you dare: *Snow White's Mirror Epilogue* at http://shonnaslayton.com/mirror-epilogue/

HISTORICAL NOTE

Set in 1902, this story takes place near the beginning of the electric age and toward the end of the great mining boomtowns. Bisbee, Arizona is indeed a real place, home of the Copper Queen Mine, one of the richest copper producing mines in the world.

Queen Victoria had died the year before, and as the Victorian age passes into the Edwardian, our main character, Wilhelmina Bergmann, is feeling the change in societal norms and expectations. She begins the story steeped in the traditions of the age, characterized by her adherence to mourning clothes, yet still wearing her favorite pair of boots.

I tried to use as much real-world history as a fairy-tale novel could pack in: the town's incorporation, its Fourth of July celebrations, talk of statehood, and Governor Brodie's visit. I had some fun with a few passing mentions of a little boy named Billy who lives on in Bisbee today as one of the "ghosts" who haunts the Copper Queen Hotel. His drowning as a child was tragic, but I imagined him as a curious, somewhat mischievous boy.

I like to include immigrants in my stories, and this particular tale highlighted German and Finnish characters. The German characters arose out of the Snow White tale itself having originated in Germany, and thus, Billie's family being descendants of the dwarfs. I also wanted to show the multinational nature of early mining in North America, and Finnish miners were one of the European nationalities discriminated against by only being hired for the lesser jobs at the mine. Often, immigrants changed their names to better fit in with English speakers, and so for this novel, I found the Finnish name Haarus was changed to Harris and thought that would work well for Winn. (Speaking of names, Bergmann means "miner" in German.)

Odd fact: camels were brought to America to assist with westward expansion and then later released into the wild. There are several tales of camel sightings in Arizona and one rumor of a train hitting a camel at some unknown time and location.

Bisbee continued to expand in its haphazard way, and with the influence of the City Beautiful Movement of the time, the nearby planned city of Warren was built to relieve overcrowding and improve living conditions for the miners. I can picture young Winn working alongside Warren Manning to create this town named in the landscape architect's honor.

These are just a few of the real-world topics included, and I hope it whets your appetite to dig a little further into this time period.

Resources that were especially helpful in my research include *Bisbee: Queen of the Copper Camps* by Lynn R. Bailey; *Bisbee Daily Review* newspapers from the summer of 1902 (in which you can read the poem, "Fate"); and the Bisbee Museum website and Pinterest page.

ACKNOWLEDGMENTS

Many thanks to the Arizona State Library for their writers-in-residence program which came at the perfect time for researching and drafting this novel. Amy Ledin and Maren Hunt were especially helpful and enthusiastic.

Editors Stacy Abrams and Lydia Sharp for the initial green light and first pass, and so much more. Lisa Knapp, once again, thank you for the final spit-shine and polish.

To my lovely and supportive critique partners Kristi Doyle and Sarah Chanis—what would I do without you? Rebekah Slayton and Andrea Huelsenbeck, this series wouldn't be the same without your encouragement and reader notes.

I feel like I should keep writing in this series if only to see what beautiful cover Jenny Zemanek at Seedlings Design Studio comes up with next. Thanks for another beauty!

A special shout out to Uncle Dale for letting me use his name. (Got to be careful what you suggest to an author!) And thanks to my husband and kids for their endurance—you've survived another book!

Finally, thank you readers for taking the time to go on these fairy tale journeys with me. It's a lot of fun.

ALSO BY SHONNA SLAYTON

Fairy-tale Inheritance Series

Cinderella's Dress

Cinderella's Shoes

Snow White's Mirror

Fairy tales coming soon in

the Fairy-tale Inheritance Series:

Beauty and the Beast

The Little Mermaid

Lost Fairy Tales

The Tower Princess

Historical Women

Liz and Nellie: Nellie Bly and Elisabeth Bisland's Race Around the World
in Eighty Days

With Entangled Teen Publishing

Spindle

Made in the USA
Columbia, SC
04 March 2023

13342787R00193